George Cruikshank, J. Hain (James Hain) Friswell

# Out and About

A Boy's Adventures, Written for Adventurous Boys

George Cruikshank, J. Hain (James Hain) Friswell

**Out and About**
*A Boy's Adventures, Written for Adventurous Boys*

ISBN/EAN: 9783337178215

Printed in Europe, USA, Canada, Australia, Japan

Cover: Foto ©Andreas Hilbeck / pixelio.de

More available books at **www.hansebooks.com**

# OUT AND ABOUT

## A BOY'S ADVENTURES

WRITTEN

FOR ADVENTUROUS BOYS.

BY

## HAIN FRISWELL.

WITH ILLUSTRATIONS BY GEORGE CRUIKSHANK.

LONDON:

GROOMBRIDGE AND SONS, PATERNOSTER ROW
MDCCCLX.

# Dedication.

———

TO

## JOHN MORTIMER, ESQ.,

OF

PIPPINFORD PARK, SUSSEX,

IN REMEMBRANCE

OF A FRIENDSHIP EXTENDED FROM

FATHER TO SON.

# PREFACE.

MEN AND BOY-READERS,—A great German philosopher has said that the future of a nation lies in its young men of nineteen to twenty-five years old. True this is, and altogether as true is it that the destiny of our nation lies in the hearts and heads of her boys of a much younger age, for they, we know, form the coming generation. To these boys we must look to carry on the work which our fathers have founded, and at whose superstructure we have worked and are working.

One great blessing our England hath, and ever had, and that is an abundance of boys—real, genuine boys; not like somebody else's male children (somebody lives over the water) who, are merely little men, little dandies, speculators, philosophers, soldiers, or merchants, as the case may be; no, England's boys are boys. For them this book is written. In them we hope and trust, and in their hearts we would do all that in our power lies to inculcate simplicity, obedience, honesty, truth, and that devotion to duty, to that path which lies immediately before them; which devotion is the stability of this nation and the great glory of Englishmen.

It is no mean thing to write a book for boys; possibly, to write a thoroughly good book for them is one of the most difficult achievements in literature, for the boys, whom we would wish to address are great workers and thinkers too. They are everywhere all over England, these lads; and most of them can tell the sham from the real. In our towns, villages, and our hamlets, or in old farm-houses outlying solitary in fields, in our ships, in our colonies. They are of all sorts as well as sizes. They may be young Raleighs, or young Popes, Cookes, Frobishers, or Defoes, Nelsons, Fergussons or Watts; Shakespeares or Miltons, even Stephensons, Cromwells, or Washingtons. The spirits of these men are not dead, but yet live amongst us; and in the coming years will inspire our boys and make the future of our England.

To help and teach, to amuse, and to silently instil love and faith, boldness of heart, trust, and honesty in such boys, then—to do some little good to every reader—is the aim of this book. Each incident described is true; exaggeration and straining for effect have been kept quite out of our pages, and the dearest wish of the author is that the book may serve the purpose it was written for.

In conclusion, he has to thank those travellers of whose labours he has availed himself in certain portions of his work, and to hope that that which has been written with an honest intent may be received in the same kindly spirit in which his other efforts have been taken.

# CONTENTS.

# CONTENTS.

## CHAPTER VI.



## CHAPTER VII.



## CHAPTER VIII.



## CHAPTER IX.



## CHAPTER X.



## CHAPTER XI.



## CHAPTER XII.



## CHAPTER XIII.

## CHAPTER XIV.



## CHAPTER XV.



## CHAPTER XVI.



## CHAPTER XVII.



## CHAPTER XVIII.



## CHAPTER XIX.



## CHAPTER XX.

## CHAPTER XXI.

## CHAPTER XXIX.



## CHAPTER XXX.



## CHAPTER XXXI.



## CHAPTER XXXII.



## CHAPTER XXXIII.



## CHAPTER XXXIV.



## CHAPTER XXXV.



## CHAPTER XXXVI.

# CONTENTS.

## CHAPTER XXXVII.



## CHAPTER XXXVIII.



## CHAPTER XXXIX.



## CHAPTER XL.



## CHAPTER XLI.



## CHAPTER XLII.

# OUT AND ABOUT.

## CHAPTER I.

### SCHOOL—AN INTERRUPTION.

"Sit on my knee, Ned," said my backer.

I did so. Flushed somewhat, perhaps; face to face for the first time with actual danger, and feeling rather curiously at the interview.

"Hit straight out," he continued, "straight from the shoulder. Don't look at his fists; watch his eye. Recover quickly when you have delivered your blow. Hit as many times in the same place as you can. Be firm on your legs."

He rolled up my shirt sleeves, and made bare an arm no thicker than a rolling pin.

"Not much muscle here," he said, looking on it scientifically; "you must be quick, sudden, sharp, if you want to win."

"But," gasped I, with an immediate revulsion

of feeling, "I don't like it. What if I should knock his eye out?"

"No fear of that, Ned," said my friend. "Only just try it. Little fellows like you can't hurt each other much. You have a purpose before you. You must beat or be beaten."

The words, to use a school phrase, opened my eyes a little. I began to reflect.

I had no time to do so. The keeper of the ring cried "Time." The two backers cried "Time," as they pushed their champions forward; and two boys jumped to their feet, and stood opposite each other.

My name was Edward Paget, that of my opponent was Job Flook.

I was small; Job was large. I was quick, passionate; I believe (but I do not like to speak of my good qualities) that I was generous and physically brave.

Flook had many good qualities, but he was nervous, and physically a coward. Therefore, although his size was much greater, we were equally matched.

I fixed my eyes on his; I saw that they were restless and wandering. Neither of us liked to begin the attack, but a hurried "Now, then!" from Flook's backer made him strike out heavily, so much so as to beat down my guard and to hit me on the face. In a moment my blood was up. I struck straight out from the shoulder with all my force. The blow took effect on the chin of my adversary, and knocked him nearly down. He staggered to the knee of his backer, and there sat rubbing his chin, and looking very rueful, and my backer, radiant with success, patted me on the shoulder, and pronounced the blow a scientific one. "Visit it him," said he, "two or three more times like that, and he will be done."

"I will try," said I.

"Time," cried the keeper of the ring.

"Go it, Paget," chirped a dozen voices.

"Go it, old Flook," said one or two more.

We squared up to each other again, and I had marked Flook's chin for another visitation, when a cry from the boys of "The doctor! the doctor!" put an end to the fray.

In an instant we were all as quiet as church mice. Old Flook sat down with his jacket hurriedly put on, conning an Eutropius (which was the wrong way up), and softly passing his red hand over his still redder chin.

The backers had flown to different desks. One had resumed an old exercise; another seemed busily employed in looking out the quantities of words in a gradus. The time-keeper had clapped his watch in his fob, and had pushed the wet sponge into his jacket pocket. Two or three boys, who did not wish to desert me, stood closely round, whilst I rolled down my shirt sleeves and put on my jacket.

The heavy tread of Dr. Leatherby (his form had been seen by our scouts from the window) was heard on the stair, and presently his dumpy fat figure waddled into the Latin school.

Every boy, I think, liked Dr. Leatherby. I am sure that every one feared him.

He was severe, but not harsh; a disciplinarian, but kindly. He studied the characters of his boys, and he did not expect nor exact so much from the dull as from the clever. Laziness he punished. Dissimulation and want of manliness he detested.

The doctor's round head was carried high; his chin was elevated; his face, generally red up to the roots of his white hair, was rather pale, but there was not the dreaded red spot in his cheek which told of anger. On the contrary, there was a look of pity and compassion in his eye. We used to fancy, we boys, matched as we were against a man's intellect, practised and learned in our ways, that Dr. Leatherby possessed some process of wizardery or mental divination. He appeared to know everything—to guess our most secret thoughts—to plunge to the bottom of our innermost ideas. Prepared as we were, he seemed to have guessed what our business had been. His first words were to ask for me.

"Where is Paget?" said he.

I felt my heart, which had been so stout before my opponent, sink within me. Into my very boots it seemed to fall, and all my bravery I fancied ran out of my fingers' ends.

"Yes, sir, here I am," I cried with as bold a voice as I could summon.

"Paget," said the doctor, in a mild fatherly voice, "I wish to speak to you alone. Come into my study, sir, at once."

Away I walked with the doctor.

The faces of the boys were covered with a blank surprise. Many of them were pale. Simmons, the time-keeper, who knew everything said, "I hate that voice of the doctor, it is as cold as the hiss of a serpent; he will expel him."

"Fudge!" exclaimed Jackson, who always contradicted him, "he will only lecture him, and give him two hundred and fifty lines of Virgil to write out."

"Oh, by jingo!" cried old Flook, jumping up, and showing his Eutropius, "fifty lines of this is hard enough for Paget; if he has all that of Virgil, all I can say is, that I will help him."

"Bravo, old Flook!" shouted one or two of his friends, struck with his generosity.

"Flook," said Jackson, who was the cock of the school, and very authoritative, "Flook is both a fool and a coward. He is afraid of Paget giving him a thrashing."

Most of the boys, who generally adopt ideas which are put before them forcibly, immediately agreed with Jackson. Flook himself looked up boldly, and with some indignation sparkling in his eye.

"Jackson," said he, "you are wrong and you are right. I am not much of a fighter, and I think little Paget would have thrashed me; but I am no coward, and I do not offer to help him because I am afraid of him, but because I think I am more to blame than he to let myself be egged on to fight him. If he gets punished, why should not I be punished too?"

"Had you not better go and tell the doctor all about it, and all about us too?" sneered Jackson, as he took the wet sponge out of his pocket, and chucked it in old Flook's face.

The sneer about Flook's telling the doctor told with the boys. The sponge too was well aimed and successful, and boys as well as men like success. They set up a great shout at poor old Flook, and left him disconsolate, wiping his face, and rubbing his chin, whilst they hurried after the triumphant Jackson.

# CHAPTER II.



"PAGET," said Dr. Leatherby, polishing his glasses, and surveying my face with rather dimmed eyes, "are you courageous, my boy?"

I was puzzled. Why should he ask whether I had courage? Was he about to flog me very, very severely? Was he about to expel me? If so, what would my father say?

These thoughts ran like lightning through my brain. I had prepared myself for a flogging—I now dreaded expulsion. "Doctor," said I, with a hoarse voice, "I am a boy—I can bear a great deal—do not put too much upon me—remember you had a son yourself."

The doctor dropped his eye-glasses, and sat down in the chair. "Heaven pardon you, boy," he said, "for recalling my loss. I was not about to hurt *you*. I was seeking to spare you, and you have wounded me."

A man so harsh and stony as the doctor I had, at that time, I thought, seldom seen. It seemed, then, to me, scarcely less than a miracle, that pity should touch him, as the wondrous rod touched the rock in the wilderness, and made it gush forth. Yes, he was in tears. He had loved that son who had flown from the old home nest, and had gone to America, merely there to die. We all knew that, but to see him weep for him was only reserved for me.

I put my hands on his great rough hand—one laid on his knee, and one shaded his eyes,—and begged his pardon.

"You have some heavy news for me," said I, "but I had been breaking through some school rule, which I thought you had discovered and would punish."

" 'A guilty conscience'—you know the rest, Paget?" said the doctor, with a faint smile.

"Needs no accuser," I answered, completing the sentence. "It does not doctor." I was silent again.

"I will remit the punishment," returned my schoolmaster, "whatever be the rule. But I will again ask you, are you brave—have you presence of mind?" He looked at me as he said this, as if he would look me through.

I waited a moment to collect my thoughts. I ran over what I knew of my father. I had heard from him, and my mother being long since dead he was the only being on earth whom I loved strongly—that he had enemies—that there were

those who wished to rob him of his property—
that there were many wicked men who kept money
from him. I knew that he always was poring
over papers. That he had a law-suit, and that
it kept him poor; and, indeed, that it would be
well for our sakes if he won; and that, if he lost,
it would be very bad indeed. My mind, at once,
called all this up.

"Has he lost his law-suit?" said I, turning pale.
The doctor nodded.

I knew no more of a law-suit than a boy of
eleven years could know, but I knew that some
great evil, in fact, that poverty had come suddenly upon my father, and I burst into tears.

"Poor father," cried I, "how I feel for him;
how hard he has struggled; how bitterly he will
feel this loss; let me go to him, doctor; send me
off this night; he is no longer rich enough to
keep me here; let me be by his side and comfort
him."

"He will feel it no more, Paget," said the schoolmaster solemnly; speaking slowly, and lifting up
his eyes as he did when he read the prayers in
church.

"Oh! but he will," said I, not noticing the
interruption; "bitterly, bitterly he has worked
and prayed, and hoped for this; he will be mad
with disappointment and grief."

"No, my lad," said the doctor, calmly and
quietly, "No. Paget, look me in the face."

I stopped crying, and did as I was told, arrested by the schoolmaster's voice.

"I believe you have courage—more than I have in this matter perhaps. It is well to go through it at once. I will not keep you longer in suspense, nor torment you any more. I told you that your father does not feel this loss. He is past that"—

" He is sick; he is very, very ill." I gasped.

" Nay," continued the doctor, " past that, long past that, too; he will never feel misfortune, or want, or trial more; he is dead."

I felt no more. They told me afterwards that I laughed out as loudly as ever madman did, and then fell to the floor; but fall or not, blow or bruise, crushed limb or crushed form, *I* felt nothing, grief had rendered me senseless, and I had fainted.

# CHAPTER III.

## MRS. TAW'S STORY.

I FELT somewhat cold and weak when I recovered from my stupor, and I was conscious of being in bed. Dr. Barker, the village surgeon, of whom we had a wholesome dread, was sitting by my side. Mrs. Taw, the matron of the school, standing near him with a bason in her hand, and a clean cloth, and some skeins of packthread over her shoulders. The packthread was indeed round her neck. She was never without packthread. She used it to clean our small-tooth combs with, to sew our buttons on, to do a thousand little offices, and she regarded it as her right hand.

Presently, gathering up my ideas, as one so stunned might do, I stirred my left arm, which I found stiff and weak. I felt that it was bandaged also. The truth is, Dr. Barker, never so happy as when he had a lancet in his hand, had bled me.

The curtains were drawn and night had come on, and candles were glittering and twinkling on the table, looking very strange to my poor eyes, as I well remember.

"Can I get up?" said I.

"Oh, ah!" grunted Dr. Barker, "likely thing, Mrs. Taw, patient wants to rise, always the way with young patients, always so hasty."

Rumour said that Dr. Barker's old patients were hasty too, and very glad to get out of his hands, but I had no time to recall any such rumours. My loss came back very freshly and very strongly to me, and I lifted up my voice suddenly, and wept aloud.

"Can't bear this," said old Barker, taking up his cane, and going out of the dormitories quietly; "patient will be all right in the morning, Taw, his head is quite cool and his pulse low, but steady."

Away went old creaking Barker, making a great deal more noise, as some tip-toe people do, than if he had walked boldly out. I continued to cry. Old Mrs. Taw looked at me with some scorn, "Hallo!" she said, "come Paget, be a man."

"But I ain't a man, Mrs. Taw," said I, with a fresh sob.

"No, nor never won't be," returned she, "at such a rate."

The idea that I possibly might *never* grow up to be a man, and that I might almost, at once as it were, die and join my dear, good father, was a relief to me, but at the same time softened me, and made me weep more.

Mrs. Taw stood this scene a long time as hard as a rock, but at last her old eyes began to brighten and redden, and she knelt down and put her arm, cloth, and skeins and all, round my neck and kissed me. "Come," said she, "be a man, then, young one; cheer up, cheer up!"

Mrs. Taw took snuff, Scotch snuff, very dry and very pungent, but if her kisses were not very sweet, her sympathy was.

"Taw, dear, oh, dear old Taw," said I, "what shall I do, what shall I do?"

"What for, my boy, what for?" sniggered and sniffed the snuffy old new-friend that I had made.

"I have lost my father, my dear, dear father," said I, putting my arms round her neck, and throwing the skein of packthread into an alarming state of entanglement.

"No, you haven't," said Taw, with a sob, "he isn't lost, dear, he is only gone before; you have a Father up above."

"But 'tisn't here on earth," cried I, "I shall never see him again."

"Remember what the doctor says in church," whispered Mrs. Taw, patting my head with her rough hand; "you won't be deserted Teddy, any more than I was. I'm an orphan, Master Ted, I am."

"Oh, indeed," said I, gazing at the stiff old creature as she rose, snuffed the candles, and then snuffed her nose. She was so old, angular, and bony, that I didn't in the least pity her.

"Yes," said she, "yes, Master Ted, a real orphan, no father, no mother; but remember it's a secret, you're the first I've told."

And the first boy she had called by the Christian name, I fancied. "Ah," she continued, "it's a long story, if you won't cry I'll tell it you."

"Do, Taw," said I, half interested, and forgetting my own grief.

"Father," said Mrs. Taw, looking at me, "was'nt like your father, but he was quite as good; he was very poor, and used to work at woodcutting. He used to buy bits of land, wood-land as wanted grubbing and clearing, and then would go and cut down the trees, or if they was cut down, would grub up the roots and sell 'em for firewood. Do all he could he could not earn much, because he worked by himself."

"Why did he work by himself?"

"'Cos he was so honest, and wouldn't poach and such like, and so his mates used to cheat and rob him. He fell into a quarrel too one day, and he fit, and the man he fit with died, that was just afore he was married. He was very strong and very brave. Arter that no one would companion him, although the jury said 'twas all right when he was tried for manslaughter, acquitted him, and he wasn't to blame; no more he was, I'll wager," said Taw, looking straight at the candle in a fierce manner.

" Well, if man wouldn't speak to him woman would; my mother, a pretty young thing of a girl, married him, and they took a little hut on the edge of a common and lived very happily till such times as I was born, and soon after poor mother died. Then father *was* melancholy. He brought me up by hand himself. His neighbours came round him, some on 'em helped him, but as they wouldn't have him when she was alive, he wouldn't have much to do with them. When I grew about four years of age he used to take me out into the solemn old woods himself, and I used to bide by him all day, along with an old dog, playing in the warm air, and gathering all sorts of 'nemonies, and blue-bells, and wild flowers that I've forgotten the names on, or, leastways, which I never knew.

" So we lived for a year and a half; that was two summers and a winter, you know. During the winter he used to leave me in charge along of an old woman who kept a school, and I used to be snug at home whilst he was out in the cold.

" It was a warm day, late in the autumn; the leaves had begun to fall early that year, and a week's warm rain had rotted away the stalks, so that although there was little wind, and it was dry enough in the woods where the trees had sheltered it, yet the leaves came pattering down like drops of heavy rain, patter, patter they came in our path; patter, patter on Pincher's back and on my broad straw hat, as my governess, a lady teacher in the dame school, had given me—"

Mrs. Taw stopped suddenly; "Shall I go on with the story, Master Ned?" said she.

"Yes, do," said I, "do, Taw, dear. How old was Pincher?"

"Oh, very old, very old and very cunning; he knew everything a'most, and was very jealous of me at first, but took to me afterwards, and used to walk on the other side of me, father on one and I in the middle, and often looked as if he wanted me to kitch hold of his tail or may be his foreleg, as a prop like."

"Good dog Pincher," said I, "and, stop, Taw—"

"Very good, Master Ned," said she.

"Why do you call me Ned now, and all the other boys by their long names, you know what I mean?"

"Bless you, if I was to call you all by your Chrissum names," she answered, "there be five or six Johns or Jacks, and I don't know how many Toms, so I call 'em all by their surnames, with juniors, and seniors, and minors as the doctor does; it's the best way, Paget."

"So it is, Taw," said I, after reflecting, "now go on, and call me Ned, mind."

" Well, away we walked with Pincher, the dog now and then darting forward and snuffing at a mole which had been caught in the traps, and hung dangling at the side of the path like a manufacturer."

" A malefactor, Taw," said I, " I've seen 'em."

" I see 'em now," said she, musingly, "and old Pincher, too. He would not touch 'em, not he; he knew what they were well enough; if they'd been live rats, now, instid of dead moles, he'd have told a different story, I'll warrant you.

" Well, on we went a good way; nigh miles. Father sometimes carried me, and Pincher carried the dinner in a basket. ' It's the last time,' says father, ' that my little Becky will come out with me this year; its getting too cold for Becky.'

" Pincher turned round and wagged his tail, as much as to say that father was right.

" ' Howsomever,' says father, ' she can go to sleep upon poor old Pincher's back, wrapped up in my coat, cosy and warm, can't you, Becky?'

" ' Yes, father,' said I, for I could speak quite well, and used, indeed, to talk to him a good deal, and he was never tired of talking to me.

" Well, we soon got to our journey's end, and away went father to work, and I to play. When it was twelve o'clock, and I very hungry and pretty nigh tired out, father left off work, put on his jacket, and sat down to dinner, and a very comfortable dinner it was. One or two sportsmen passed us, with their guns, and one threw me a shilling, I well recollect, and father, when he saw it, said it was a lucky day, this last day, and that the money should be put in a bank, which I thought was a pity, fancying he meant it to be the bank of a hedge.

"After dinner father went to work again, leaving me wrapped up in his coat, sleeping with my head resting on old Pincher's nice, warm, clean back.

"I was in the midst of a beautiful sweet dream about angels, when some footsteps woke me, and I saw my father hobbling towards me. He had torn his shirt sleeve off, and had it bound round his leg under his knee. Instead of being white, it was red, blood red, and red with blood. He dropped rather than sat down by me, and I could see that he was deadly pale.

"I jumped up in great fright. 'Oh, father, father,' said I, 'I will run for the doctor.'

"'No, no, my maid,' said he, 'my poor, pretty little maid; dont'ee go, dont'ee leave me, you will lose yourself in the wood.' Old Pincher had jumped up in great haste, and was for bustling away, but my father, with a feeble voice, called him back. 'Stay by her,' he said, 'old dog, stay here, sir.'

"The dog whined and licked his master's hand, and sat quietly by me. He looked uneasily at the ghastly red bandage, and whined again.

" 'Ah! old dog,' said poor father, speaking to him rather than to me, for I was so frightened that I did not dare even to cry, 'it will be soon over with me, I shall soon go.' He put out his wounded leg as he spoke, and the blood gushed out again.

" 'Where, father?' said I in a whisper, looking into his pale face, which grew paler as the day grew darker.

" 'There,' said he, pointing to the sky, 'there, I hope and trust, my little maid. There, to pray for, and watch over you. You see,' he gasped after a pause, 'you will tell the people who ask you, that my axe turned aside at a hard knot, and cut an artery just at the back of my knee. There is no staunching *that* wound, my darling, and I am bleeding to death.'

" 'Oh! father, father,' cried I, putting my little hands to the bandage and dabbing them in his blood, 'don't say that, for Heaven sake. Let me stop it; do, only let me do so, father.'

" 'No use, my maid, no use,' said he, wiping my hands from the stiffening blood on his shirt and waistcoat, 'no use; I die here.' His voice had sunk to a whisper. 'Kiss me, my lass,' said he, 'kiss me.'

" I did kiss him; I can feel that kiss now. A damp moist kiss it was; but his lips clung to mine fondly. 'Now,' said he, with a sigh as he fell backwards, 'I am going to see—to see—to sec—.' I thought he meant the great Ocean, but he did not finish his sentence, and I afterwards reflected, and now I know whom he meant.

"Presently he tried to rise again, and cried hurriedly to me in a weaker voice, say, 'Our Father,' little maid, say 'Our Father, as you do at school.'

"He took my two little hands in his, and placed them to his lips; I felt them moving for some time, and then he fell back, as I supposed, asleep.

"A long time passed. I sat watching, sometimes sobbing, sometimes silent, for fear of waking him; and old Pincher curled himself round me to keep me warmer, and licked the face and lips of my father, who was so fast asleep. He gave every now and then short, sharp, melancholy barks, and howled once or twice, but never once tried to go away.

"At last I fell asleep, nestled against poor father's arm, which seemed to grow more stiff and cold. Everything was cold. The stars twinkled above in the sky, the moon seemed to wander forth past above us, the very leaves of the trees shivered in the cold, and the wind moaned with cold as well.

"Over the distant land fresh and cold breezes came, playing and wandering in my hair, and stirring the locks of my sleeping father; then they would die away and sigh, and rustle in and out the dark shadows of the trees as if some unseen visitors were looking at us from behind them.

"In my sleep I dreamt I was in a land of ice and snow, sleeping on a snow pillow—a pillow of a fallen snow king, such as I had seen the boys of our village make.

"I was awakened roughly.

"A shout of surprise, and an oath, and then a rough hurrying to and fro. Gamekeepers going their rounds in the morning had found the poor woodman dead, and his little girl alone in the world."

"Is that all, Taw?" said I, after a long melancholy pause.

"That's all, mas'r Ned, you see I'm an orphan as well as yourself."

# CHAPTER IV.

## OLD FLOOK'S PHILOSOPHY.

" Dear old Taw," said I to that good woman, when she finished her narrative, " how you must have suffered !"

" Well," she said, " I suppose I did, Mas'r Ted, but I 'spose women *are* born to suffer more than men."

" I 'spose," returned I, after a pause, " that they buried your father in that great big wood."

" Not a bit of it," said she ; " they took him to church and said prayers over him, and the parson called him his brother, and I followed him and many people too, and the good old doctor, who was a good young doctor then, just entered on the school, took me, and brought me up with his servants, and was as kind as an angel to me, and old Pincher died in his service, and was buried under the big Portugal laurel in the doctor's private garden."

I was silent for a long time.  Mrs. Taw was untangling her thread, and I thinking of her story

In pitying her grief, I had quite forgotten my own.

"Do you think your father went to heaven, Mrs. Taw?" said I at last.

"Of course, Paget," she returned, firmly and decisively. "'Twas the very Sunday after that I heard from Dr. Leatherby a splendid sermon, at which I cried away in the corner of a pew till I fell asleep on an old lady's lap. But I seemed to hear the sermon in my sleep: how all men, rich and poor, are equal, and how all the good are rewarded; and that, above all, how the poor are recompensed, even for the pains and troubles they have suffered here. How, after dying in grief and affliction, they came to a place where every sorrow was done away with—every stain washed off, and no pain was ever more suffered.

"When I woke up I dried my eyes, and did not wish my father back again, and as often as I am troubled here I think upon that dream."

"What do you think, Taw," said I, for I had determined to ask her—"What do you think my father and your father do up there?"

"Can't exactly say, Master Ned," she returned; "but the doctor preaches to us about a certain KING, who receives saint and sinner, who made us all, and who especially rejoices over poor sinners who turn to Him at the last; aye, at the very last!"

I mused awhile, quietly thinking of the love

which Mrs. Taw bore her dead father; dead so long, long, ago; and then said, quietly, "Taw, dear, go now: good night."

Mrs. Taw gave me a kiss, and then went to the window and looked out. "Bless me," she said, "they have had prayers; the school is over, and they are coming to bed. Close your eyes, Master Ned; don't say nothing, and they will 'spose you asleep."

Away went Mrs. Taw, and presently up came the boys to the dormitories, as wild as ragged young colts. To do them justice, however, they were kindly silent when they came to my place. Old Flook slept in the same room as I did, and, both by precept and example, silenced the other boys. It was as I lay there, partly pretending to be asleep and partly listening, that I heard what a good, kindly fellow he was. He spoke very highly of me.

"Paget would have beaten me in the long run," said he.

"What a coward, to be sure, to say so," said a boy.

"Do you know what a coward is, Jacks Junior?" said old Flook, quietly, but sternly.

"Why a coward," said Jacks, "is a great, big, strong boy, who lets himself be beaten by a smaller boy."

"That definition," said Flook, who was a very learned boy, and sometimes used longer words than the others, "is only partially true. Perhaps the big boy does not like fighting. But I will give you some definitions which are wholly true."

"No. 1. You are a coward if you fear to tell the truth when you should do so.

"No. 2. You are a coward when you insult the weak.

"No. 3. You are a coward if afraid to do right; if you shrink from defending your opinion, from maintaining what you know to be just and good; and you are especially a coward if you know certain things *of* yourself and dare not own them *to* yourself.

"Now," continued Flook, "I know that I am not cut out for fighting : I am not made for it. I do not want to hurt any boy, and I'm sure I do not want to be hurt. Hence I seldom quarrel, and only was about to fight Paget because some of the big lads persuaded him to give me a blow.

"There now, go to sleep, all of you," said he, quietly jumping into his bed; "be courageous enough to say your prayers, and try to know a little more of yourselves before you accuse others of your own faults."

Old Flook and his friends were soon asleep, and the deep respiration of the boys was heard through the rooms. I lay awake for a long time, thinking of old Flook's sermon, and how true it was, and being very sorry that I should have been ever spurred on to quarrel with him.

I made several good vows and resolutions during

that night—vows which I have but insufficiently kept, and resolutions too weak to restrain me. I have made such again and again ; some I have kept, some broken. But I have found that good resolutions strengthen themselves, that if you keep one, it will enable you to keep another; and that there is no satisfaction so sweet in the world as having strictly kept some noble promise to one-self. At last I fell asleep, and dreamt again the actions of the day, and woke again to find myself an orphan and alone.

# CHAPTER V.

## I GROW MELANCHOLY, AND DESPAIR—OLD FLOOK RAISES MY SPIRITS.

I was of course soon well enough to come again into the school-room, but my loss had a great effect upon me. I grew silent, and did not mix much with my former companions. Schoolboys soon find out a secret. It was whispered about, even before I came again amongst my schoolfellows, that my father had died a bankrupt, and that I was dependent upon the doctor's charity for support.

This was different from other whispers and inuendos circulating in the great world (which are too frequently lies) in a most important item. It was essentially true. The property of my father had disappeared with his expectations. He had broken up and vanished in the great waters of the world, like a ship disappearing in the mid ocean. Few remembered him, and but one mourned him.

True also it was that the doctor had adopted me. He called me into his room, gave me a great deal of the very best and most affectionate advice, and added that, as he had no son, I should be a son to him; that he would educate me and clothe me, and that after he had died that I should have the school. He added, that which Mrs. Taw had told me, that it was my great likeness to his son which first stirred him to love me.

Sometimes the benefits of God seem to be trials, and although my eyes streamed over with gratitude and love, as I thanked the doctor for his kindness, and accepted his offer, still when I sat, as I often then did, on the dark evenings, in the quiet school, musing upon what had happened and what would yet come to pass, I could not feel happy, not only because of my loss, but because of the prospect before me.

To be pent up all day, day after day, for years as a schoolmaster, to see my youth pass away as my boyhood had passed, and my manhood and my age would follow till I dropped into the grave.

This for one, too, who had ardently desired, as what boy has not, to fly away from the old place at home, away, far away, and wander in strange lands where every hour brought a novelty, every advance, even for a mile, something wonderful and rare. The trial was indeed a bitter one, but I met it as became me; I took advice of my own heart, I determined to bend to circumstances, to do the best I could, and to behave as well as I could in the position I was in.

My schoolfellows seemed to grow more shy of me. I was now very often taken into the doctor's parlour. I became, every day, more and more his favorite, and the boys rather avoided me in consequence. Those of honorable minds did so because they did not want to be seen in fellowship with one who they thought was in the doctor's secrets. Those whose thoughts were not elevated imputed to me many base things. Some said I told tales, others would talk openly about fetching and carrying, and, after all, I found that one of the worst things for a boy, if he wishes to be happy with his schoolfellows, is to be in favour with the greater powers.

To be avoided and shunned made me unhappy: the isolation I experienced was dreadful. I sought refuge at last with my old enemy, Flook.

"Flook, my boy," said I, one morning, after our first lessons, and just immediately before breakfast, "Flook, how is it that nobody seems to be familiar with me now?"

"Why," said Flook, "it seems you are going to be our young master, and we don't want to curry favour with you, you know."

I was silent.

"O, then it is true, eh, Ned Paget?" he said.

"Perhaps so," said I.

"Well, and not a bad thing either, for those who like it. It's very honorable to be a school-master, you know, but it's preciously unpleasant."

I gave a sigh.

"My ambition does not lie that way," returned my companion.

"I know it does not," said I. The fact is, Flook's ambition was to be an engineer. How he was to arrive at such a point neither he nor any of us knew. At that period we thought that an engineer was the driver of an engine or something of that sort : we had very confused notions on the subject.

"No," answered Flook, "I mean to be an engineer, and go amongst the Indians and beat them, and blow them up, like they did at Sobraon and Aliwal the other day." Flook had evidently learnt another meaning for engineering. "I should like," he continued, "to build forts, and mount them with cannon."

"Why, Flook, you told me you did not like fighting." I blushed as I said this, for I remembered our quarrel and our interruption.

"Fighting!" continued he. "No, I don't care about it; but it depends upon what you call fighting. I don't care about punching another boy's head, but I would fight for my country like—"

"Like what?"

"Like a Briton," said old Flook, stoutly, in want of a better simile. Perhaps he could not have found a better.

"You're a philosopher, old Flook."

"I try to be so; but, I say, Ned, who would

not strike out for the old land? Who would not try to carry her laws and glorious religion, and her institutions?"

"Her Magna Charta, Flook."

"Her Trial by Jury, Ned," cried he. "Her church and laws."

"And every thing else that's good about her, Flook."

The fact is, we had all been writing a theme in our class upon English freedom, and, as all schoolboys are, and should be, we were fond of our country. We had, too, read in the newspapers which our friends sometimes sent us, the glorious victories in India of Moodkee, Aliwal, Sobraon, and the campaign of the Sutlej. Besides this, as our school was in the Midland counties, and strongly Tory, it happened that we had had a mock election. Flook and I were, therefore, brimful of patriotism.

"Yes," said Flook, after awhile, "I mean to devote my life to India."

"I should like to go with you, old boy," said I. "I don't like stopping here."

"Umph!" said Flook, after a long pause, "yet it is a noble thing to be a schoolmaster; to teach boys to be good and wise, and to grow up to be good and great men. Besides, it seems to me, Paget, that that is your immediate duty; that path lies before you now, take it, and be happy with it. All people can be happy if they choose;

it may be a hard lesson, as the doctor said the other day; but it is wise for us to learn it early in life—to go straight at a thing, and to do the best we can under the circumstances, is the way to be happy."

Flook and I often talked in this way. My father had been dead about three years, and I had been four years in the school, and had learned a great deal; not so much as I might have done; but to do the doctor justice, he had instilled into me a love of knowledge, and had taught me much. Flook, my old friend and companion, had entered on his last half year, and was ready to leave school. I was dull at the prospect of parting—other friends, too, had grown up around me, and were ready to go out into the great world; but alas, I to my regret, was to be left at school.

# CHAPTER VI.



ONE day, when I went into the doctor's study to say some of my more particular tasks—this was shortly after the conversation repeated in the last chapter—I found my kind friend and adopted father poring over a letter. He gave a deep sigh, and folded it up when I came up to him, and heard me my task without saying anything. When done, he smoothed my hair, and said :—

"It seems, Ned, we are to be parted after all."

"Parted, sir!" All his goodness and kindness flashing on my mind at once.

"Yes, parted. Here is a letter from your long-silent uncle claiming your guardianship, and insisting upon your removal to London, even whilst he thanks me for the kindness which he hears I have shown to you."

"He hears! Why, sir, he never came down to see me, he never wrote; why does he appear so suddenly now ?"

The doctor sat still. "My dear boy," said he,

"when you are older, you will find a great number of people who will disappear when you are in trouble, but who, when the storm is over, will find you out. I call them smooth-water sailors."

"I do not like to leave you, sir," said I.

"Nor I to part. Come, tell me, what do you know of this uncle?"

People, I have since found, talk much in the world about the affection which one bears and should bear to our relations. Doubtless, as a rule, this is right. The old proverb is good; but then there are some relations who are positive bars to any advancement in life, who never help you, never honour you, who desert you in misfortune, but who cling to you in prosperity.

My uncle was of these.

I had heard my father talk continually and always sorrowfully for him. When my father was rich, it was he who helped my uncle; when my father was poor, it was my uncle who refused to help him, but who pestered him with advice which he could not take, and wise saws and maxims which did not apply to his case.

I told the doctor this.

"You must, however, go, Paget. He tells me here that your father named him your guardian in his will, and that, if you have been sufficiently taught, he has an opening for you in London."

"Let me see the letter, sir."

It certainly was my uncle's writing—the same phrases, the same manner; the very paper and seal wore the same old characteristic externals of my vacillating uncle, which I so well remembered before.

"Your uncle seems very affectionate towards you, Ned. He must be a good man; he promises well."

"Can a man be good, sir, who does not do good? He used to promise, sir, and never perform. I remember how he behaved to my poor father, and now," said I, "he will part me from my second father." The tears rose in my eyes.

"Never mind, Ned, I am as sorry as you," said the doctor, "and yet it must be done. Duty is a word very often on people's lips, but very, very seldom in their hearts. Where the way is pointed out, whether it be muddy, or dirty, or stony, and full of pitfalls, or whether it be full of green places of delight, of flowers, of sun-shiny meadows and sweet woods, let us take it; a stony lane often leads to a sweet landscape: the scenery about us will open, and a cloudy morning bring a glorious day."

What could I do? I thanked the doctor a thousand times for his kindness, I put my arms round his neck and kissed him, I promised to do my duty.

Doctor Leatherby smiled. "Like a Briton," said he. "Well, 'tis a good phrase, a very good phrase.  I suppose it is because we Britons do do our duty that we have become so great a nation. Well, Ned—here he gave a great sigh—Monday is fixed for your departure to London.  I suppose I must write to your uncle, and tell him that you will come."

"Do, sir, as you think fit; it will be indeed a black Monday for me."

"Black Monday," cried the doctor, with a pleased look; "was it ever that a boy called that Monday black which was to take him *from* a school, not *to* it?"

So the day of my departure was determined on —the day on which I was to be delivered from that life which I once thought tedious, but which now I regretted with all my heart. So it is in life. Look at an object from one point and it is un-pleasant; turn it to the other, and it delights you with its beauty.

# CHAPTER VII.



IT was a very sharp morning on the 6th of October, 18—, when I took my place on the outside of the coach *en route* for town.

I was full of misgivings. One does not easily leave any of those whom one has loved, to go to those we have never seen. Of the character of my uncle I knew little, but I had heard much. He was unstable, irresolute, fond of professing kindly things, but very disinclined to do them. I could not but shudder at the bare idea of living in London with him, for my father had always spoken of his brother with pity, and with an ill-concealed contempt. The full protests which he made, and the braggadocio letters which he sent, served only to show me that my father's opinion was right. Besides this, I had been sticking hard at work, and had half reconciled myself to my fate. I had followed out the principles of the philosopher Flook, and had made such progress that the doctor was delighted, and I satisfied. Self-satisfaction is the sweetest praise, after all.

"Ah, Ned," said the doctor, "I am quite concerned to lose you."

"You have not lost me, sir," said I. "I will return to you when I can; I shall never forget your kindness."

"Tut, tut," returned he, "don't speak of that, Ned, my boy, don't speak of that; but it is a pity that you leave here but half educated. A few more years, say six, would have made you a good classic. Let me see, you have been through Cæsar, and Ovid, and the Georgics of Virgil. Good, very good, for your age. Ah! but think of Livy, my boy, think of Tacitus, and then Herodotus and Homer, when you are but spelling over the Analecta and Xenophon."

The doctor rubbed the back of his head thoughtfully, and his eye glistened as if he had spoken of the greatest treat in life.

"What would I give, Ned," said he, "never to have read Plato, and to go through his banquet for the first time with you!"

"It's all very well, doctor, to talk of banquets, whilst the poor child is starving. Eat away, Paget, do, at that basin of milk—country milk, you know—hot and boiled; you will not get such milk in London," interrupted old Taw.

"Ah!" said the doctor, waking up from his dreamy state. "Here, Ned; here is a pocket-piece for you. Remember, save as much as you can; there is always time for spending." The kind old fellow put a half-sovereign into my hand as he said it. My eyes filled and my heart swelled at the thought of all his kindness.

Old Taw, who was so strong that she could lift at least a hundredweight, bustled into the passage here with my box, and at the top of it a kind of carpet-bag, open at the mouth, and partly filled with straw.

"I can't eat anything, please sir," said I, "I am so—so—" I finished the sentence by letting my head fall into my hand and crying.

"Don'tee, don'tee, Mas'r Ned," cried old Taw. Look at this bag, now; it's my invention. I have known poor little boys come from their winter rides outside coaches so cold that they couldn't feel their poor little feet. Now, to put that all to rights, d'ye see, I have invented a bag, stuffed with straw, wherein they puts their poor little dangling legs, and it saves them wonderfully; you can't think how good it is."

"She's worth a fortune, that woman," said the doctor; "I should never have thought of that— never."

"No, you were talking of Plater's banquets," said Mrs. Taw, quickly. "Beg pardon, sir, but we must hurry—coach up in a minute."

"Egad! so it will be," said the doctor. "Here, Ned, take this glass of sherry; it is good wine, and will warm your little body for a long time. Think of that all your life, and use wine only as a medicine."

" Here's a packet of sandwiches," said Taw, in her turn, cramming them into my hands whilst the glass was yet at my lips. " Not a moment to be lost, you know. Start well. Never be behind time. It is no use running, you know, after a hour that is past; you will never overtake it."

Thus with kindly homely talk, with merriness and sadness, with good advice and calm wisdom, the doctor and his housekeeper entertained me during the few last minutes I was with them. I was inexpressibly touched by their kindness, for I saw both of them felt my loss. It was but a few moments, as I have said, but I remember them now as if they had taken hours.

Presently the horn of the guard was heard at a distance. " Here it is, Ned," said the doctor. Tantarra, tartarra, twang, twang, rung the horn. The gardener came in to carry my box, but Taw took it up like a giantess. " No, thank'ee, Thomas," says she; " I'll carry Ned's box for the last time." My heart sunk within my bosom as she said these words. The coach, however, was at the door. There was no time left for con- sideration or regret.

" Young gent for London?" said the sharp guard, plunging his battered horn into the basket and jumping down to take my box. " Now, Mr.

Paget, please; jump up, sir," he cried.  He had read my name and destination on my box.

"Good bye, Doctor," cried I; "good bye Taw, dear old Taw."  I determined not to be ashamed of anything, and fairly put my arms round the matron's neck and kissed her.  The doctor smiled as he saw it, and in an instant I was mounted on the coach.  The guard blew his horn; old Flook and the boys who had come to see me off, and were engaged in admiring the horses, waved their hands and their caps; the coachman made the thong of his long whip whistle in the air, and away we went.  Away, and away, and away— crunch, crunch, crunch went the stony road under the wheels.  The hedge-rows, trees, and fields spun by me, and seemed to be running a race from us, towards the old place I was leaving. When I looked back, I could scarcely see the old house, through my tears.

# CHAPTER VIII.



DEEP as was my regret, it soon ended. Surrounded by beautiful scenery, with hills rising before me, and sparkling rivers running shining away in the sunshine, with distant outlying farms, with ploughs quietly working their way through the rich loamy soil, bound on each side by hedgerows full of honeysuckle and sweet cuckooflowers, and arched overhead by a bright sky, in which the lark mounted high and sang, poising on its wings for very happiness, the coach, which bore me from such good friends sped onwards, tracing its shadow on the road, now casting it upon a wall, now upon a hedgerow or a heath.

Away we went merrily. I sat next to the guard, and made acquaintance with him. He chatted and talked away, and sometimes played his bugle to amuse me. He said that he had never seen a boy who was leaving school so solemn as I was, and wanted to know why. Was I not going to see my father?

" No," said I; " he is dead."

" Oh," said the guard, " that puts the saddle on another horse."

" I am going to see my uncle," said I.

" A'most as good as your father," returned the guard.

Here a down coach passed us, the coachmen saluted, the passengers all smiled, and the guards blew furious blasts of recognition, the horses even seemed to recognize a kind of rivalry, and went faster.

" Prettily he handles 'is ribbons," cried my companion, in admiration, as he dropped his key bugle into the basket—" you'd think he was born on the box; but he wasn't, master Paget, he wasn't."

" How do you know my name's Paget," said I.

" Didn't I see your name on the box? Lor', bless your hinnocent eyes, if you on'y keep 'em open you'll know an immense deal afore you're my age. There are on'y two kinds o' people in this world, master Edward."

" Indeed," said I, " only two."

" Neer another," returned he—" those who keeps their eyes open, and those who don't." So saying, he climbed on to the roof, to attend to some alteration which he thought necessary in the luggage.

Thus the time passed. It was not very late, for we had started early enough in the morning, when we rattled under Highgate archway, past the figure of Dick Whittington, and so on by the north road into town, past the Angel and the Blue Boy inns at Islington—merry Islington, with its green and its countrified look— and then down into the City, till we came to the Bull and Mouth Inn, the destination of the coach, and the place at which my uncle was to meet me.

All the passengers were thoroughly cold—so cold, indeed, that in these days of railway travelling I do not believe people ever experience the feeling. I well remember that I could not feel the ground when I put my feet to it, although Mrs. Taw, whose care of me was marked with so much kindness, had given me the carpet-bag stuffed with straw, before mentioned, for me to put my legs in. Both the doctor and I had laughed at the idea, but we found it a very good one.

" Welcome back to Lunnon, sir," said the guard. " Now, the very fust thing as I should recommend to your young mind is for you to get the barmaid to give you a wine-glass full o' sound old ale, or a tumbler full o' cold spring water."

" Cold," said I, " why, I am cold enough. I daresay, when I get home, I shall have a nice cup of tea."

" Tea !" returned he contemptuously. " Tea— I haint got no opinion on it myself, and sperrits aint no good for young lads like you. The cold water would have what they calls a counter irritation, and that's good for young fellows ; it would make you as warm as a toast. Luggage, sir, ch." " Now Thomas," said he to a helper who came round, " get this young gentleman's box into the hoffice—Mr. Paget's box. See your huncle, sir ?"

" Why, no," said I, hesitatingly. And, in truth, I did not. There were many people who came to meet their friends, but no one came to meet me. I saw the passengers gather up their luggage and go away. I saw mothers and wives, fathers and friends, greeting. I saw the horses taken from the coach, and go off gleefully down an inclined plane to a huge underground stable, where they told me many, many pairs of horses stood. I saw the coach emptied of passengers and luggage, and wheeled back by four sturdy fellows into the yard, ready to be cleaned on the morrow for its journey. I saw the commercial gentlemen walk into the comfortable bar, and my friend, the guard, trot away, covered with wrappers and great coats, after the coachman, who I, as in duty bound, had " tipped" with a half-crown ; and there I stood in the coach-yard, waiting and alone.

I waited there some time, and no one came. Presently the guard came out again.

" Not," said he, " not come, Master Paget. He must have missed the time. Come and wait in the coffee-room, there's a nice fire there. If he comes he is sure to enquire for you."

The good fellow, whose attention I felt, for I somehow had a presentiment that something was wrong, took me to a handsome room wherein some gentlemen were dining, others talking and reading, and made me sit in a corner by the fire.

"Now," says he, "you're comfortable; now you may wait an hour and you won't hurt. What'll you take? You've only got to shout 'Waiter!' when that gent. in a white neckcloth and pumps comes ·by, and he will get you what you want."

"A cup of tea, if you please," said I, warming myself; "I feel cold all over."

"Oh, don't have tea," said he; he seemed to have taken a great dislike to that beverage. "Have coffee; its much nicer, and ever so much more nobby. Here, William, bring the young gent. some coffee and a hegg."

Yielding to the wishes of my new friend, I ordered the coffee and egg, and, I must say, enjoyed the meal much. The guard, who said he must go home to his missus, bid me good bye in a confidential way, as if we should meet again on the morrow, and promised to leave word in the bar, if a young gent. of the name of Paget was called for, that he was safe and sound in wind and limb in the coffee-room. I bade him good bye with regret.

I soon made my modest meal, and paid for it, and sat by the fire. The time passed quickly: it was soon nine, then ten; and then, fatigued with my journey and the fresh air, I fell asleep. I did not seem to have been asleep ten minutes when the waiter awakened me. I had slept two hours—it was twelve o'clock.

"Will you take a bed, sir? We are about to shut up here."

"All right," said I, rubbing my eyes; "is uncle come."

"Uncle who, sir?" said he. "There hasn't nobody been for you, sir."

I turned pale. "There's some mistake, sir," said I. "My uncle must have been."

"Oh, must he, sir," he answered, without contradicting; "well, I'll go and see." Away he went for a moment, leaving me thoroughly amazed. Presently he came back.

"There hasn't no one been, sir. I 'spose you're the young gent., sir, as was to be called for."

"Yes," said I, "I am."

"Then they've been, and forgot you, sir," said he.

I was stupified. I did not know what to think. Had something happened to my uncle, or had Doctor Leatherby, wishing to get rid of me, sent me thus up to London? My heart sank within me for a moment; but I soon reflected that that could not be. He would never have been so cruel. I tried to remember my uncle's address, but I could not. He had told the doctor in his letter that he had removed to a new house, and that he would be sure and meet me at the coach-office; the doctor, too, had written to him at his place of business, to apprise him of my coming at the very hour appointed.

All this flashed through my brain in a moment. The waiter meanwhile flapped away a little dust with his napkin, and then, with a half-suppressed yawn, again suggested that I should take a bed.

But this I did not agree to. I had an idea that my uncle lived in Portland Street, and I determined to seek him. True, I did not know the number, and I was ignorant of town; but fear, indignation, shame, and other feelings, prevailed upon me, and, buttoning my coat about me, pressing my cap over my eyes, and biting my lower lip, partly with vexation and partly with determination, I bade the waiter good night, told him to keep my luggage till I called for it, and boldly sallied out of the inn into the cold, moonlight streets, whistling a tune as loudly as I could, to prove to all the world that I was not afraid.

# CHAPTER IX.



I MEET WITH A MODERN PROFESSOR, WHO OFFERS
ME A HOME.

As I had no certain knowledge where my uncle
lived, and as it was past midnight when I left the
tavern, it is not to be wondered at that I did not
find his house. There was more than one large
house whereat a party was being given in the
street I went to, and I knocked boldly at the
doors, seeing lights in the windows, and proffered
my questions, but it was all to no purpose. The
footmen and servants seemed to have an idea that
I wanted to steal something, and answered me
curtly, or drove me away. I applied to the
policemen, with the same result, and at last,
wearied and forlorn, I sat down upon the door-
step, hardly knowing what to do.

Here was I, the very first night I arrived in
London, perfectly desolate and without help. I
wished I had taken the waiter's advice, and had
gone to bed at the Bull and Mouth. I did not
know whether they would admit me if I returned.
I was ignorant that in London there are coffee-

houses and inns which are open all night; I therefore buttoned my coat tightly round me, twisted a warm comforter, the gift of Mrs. Taw, round my neck, and sat down to wait till the morning to prosecute my search. I determined to be brave and to be of good cheer.

It was a beautiful night. The harvest moon was shining brightly and purely above the line of lamps, and, as I looked up to her, I thought of the quiet village school, of the doctor, of old Flook, and my other friends, and of good old Mrs. Taw. "It will be light early," said I to myself; "other people have been worse off than I have; I have at least warm clothing; many are without any, or are in rags."

Somehow or another my thoughts reverted to Mrs. Taw's story, and I thought of her, a poor little, helpless girl, sitting by the side of her dead father, in the great, lonely wood.

For her sorrows, I believe, more than my own, my tears began to flow, and I was in the act of looking at the moon through them, and wiping them away, when a passer by, one who had a re- markably unsteady gait, staggered up to me, and, leaning against the door-post, addressed me in a rough, but not unkindly, voice.

"What," cried he, "a soldier, and afeard! Tears! why tears?"

"Please, sir," I answered quickly, "do you know a Mr. Paget in this street?"

"No," said he; then he paused and thought. "My man of mettle," he said, "there's no such dweller in these precincts here."

"Do you live here, sir?" said I.

He pointed vaguely eastward. "There is my domicile, my youthful friend. But I know the names at least of all who live here, and Paget is not one of them. Why Paget, my hero?"

"Please, sir, he's my uncle."

"Uncle, *avunculus*, *patruus*, *puer bonum es?*" he asked in Latin.

"*Bonus*, if you please, sir," said I.

"A good boy, and quick. *Ingenuus puer* as well as *bonus*. How comest thou here, young scholar? Stand up and answer."

I stood up. The stranger was a tall, gray, gentlemanly-looking man. He was shabbily dressed, so shabbily that I could see how worn his clothes were in the moonlight. His nose was hooked, and his eye bright. His hands were without gloves, his hat crushed, and his boots old, and yet he looked a gentleman. His face was full of good humour, but had a carelessly dissipated look; but withal so kindly, that I told him my history, he, the while, steadying himself by leaning on my shoulder.

"Umph," said he, when I had finished. "I am not in a state, Master Paget, to give you good advice, but I can do more. I can give you what your uncle has not given you—a night's lodging. Will you come with me?"

If his gait was unsteady, his looks and his speech were right enough. I answered that I thanked him for his offer, and would accept it.

" 'Tis not in scenes like these or lordly halls that I can pitch my tent—stop, people don't pitch their tents in halls, young scholar—that I dwell, but my roof for the night is yours. Lead on."

" Which way, sir ?" said I.

"I'll show you." He struck out boldly, like a man who distrusted his own legs, but who determined to make them walk straightly, and straightly he walked, and so quickly, that I had to trot by his side to keep pace with him.

We passed soon into Oxford Street, then into St. Giles's, where he said the Corinthians dwelt, which phrase I did not understand. Then we came into Holborn, and went a long way down until we reached Gray's-inn Lane ; down this, for a short distance again, till my companion dived into a network of courts, which were so narrow, squalid, and dark, that they puzzled me. Here my friend took my hand. " Fear nothing," said he ; "I am close upon my domains, young scholar."

The domains, however, were not yet reached. Having emerged from these courts, my new friend turned into Leather Lane, and went to the bottom of it, till, at a little hill which leads from it, he paused, looked around him, and said, "Now we are at home."

At home we were, for passing down some steps which led into a large and rather cleanly court, he led me to a door which stood open, and striking a wax match against the lintel, he lighted me up stairs to a first-floor room, barely, but not uncomfortably furnished, and, in a voice of much good humour, bade me welcome to the apartment of Professor Peter Garle.

There was but one bed in the room; but near the fire, the remains of which burnt brightly, was a comfortable arm-chair, with a thick blanket lying upon it.

"I am an old campaigner," said the professor; "I am fond of this chair. You take the bed, and refresh yourself with Nature's sweet restorer, balmy sleep!"

He would insist on what he said, and so, throwing off my outer garments, I quickly got under the coverlet. The professor sat in his chair and lighted a pipe; and I had not listened five minutes to his regular puffs before I, tired and puzzled with the events of the day, fell into a sound slumber.

# CHAPTER X.



### WHICH CONCERNS MY VERY STRANGE FRIEND.

WHEN I awoke the next morning after dreaming for a long time about school-times and old Flook, who was somehow associated in my dream with my companion of the night before, I found that companion quietly preparing breakfast, and stirring with a long spoon a chocolate pot.

" Well, young scholar," said he, " *somnis, mortis imago,* seems sweet to you. You slept well and soundly."

He stood up before the fire, not without a certain grace in his deportment. He had on an old dressing-gown tied with cords and tassels, slippers on his feet, and on his head a smoking-cap. He walked up and down as I was dressing, talking to me.

" This uncle of yours," said he, " what was he?"

" A solicitor, sir."

" Solicitors do not generally live in Portland Place. Try somewhere else. I have been looking for him this morning."

"Have you been out, sir?" said I, with surprise.

"Oh no," he answered, "only in the 'Directory;' I'll look again." He turned over the leaves with a practised hand. "'Paget, Wm., grocer,' that will not do; 'Paget, John, retail dealer; Paget, Thomas, beer retailer,' none of these will do, young scholar. How are the mighty fallen! here is your great name amongst petty, huxtering tradesmen; no, there are no Pagets here who would serve for your uncle."

I mused as I sat on the bed. What could I do? Had my uncle deceived me? Mr. Peter Garle, my new friend, began to question me. Did I know this uncle well? What was he? Was he very friendly with my father? and many other questions he put to me, the great majority of which I could not answer.

"Young gentleman," said he, sternly, "you are very loose in your information."

"But, sir," said I, "what is a boy to know about relations whom he may not have seen ten times in his life."

"Not much," said the professor, "but try to know all things well. Pay attention, my dear lad, and you don't know how much you will learn. Now, I paid attention to your artless gossip last night, and learn how much I know."

The professor then with astonishing volubility laid bare to me (as I thought) every action of my life. He told me of my father, the doctor, Mrs. Taw, and my schoolfellows, and finally he said that so soon as the post came in he would go and order my luggage to his home, and then set about finding my uncle. "In the mean time I would advise you to write to your friends in the country, and tell them your position. Now, young scholar, *prandium paratum est: prandium*, by the way, is dinner; can you tell me what the Latin for breakfast is?"

I could not.

"Never knew a schoolboy who could; never mind, it will be welcome all the same, I dare say."

Never was such a wonderful old gentleman; all the time he was talking to me he had been washing the tea-cups, laying the tray, stirring the chocolate or cooking the eggs and bacon. He did all nattily and well, and all like a gentleman. He sat down when I was ready, gave me a large portion, and helped himself.

"I can't eat all that," said I.

"Can't you?" said he; "why, when I was your age I could eat anything. *Perge puer*, go on, my boy; age and want of appetite will come soon enough."

We were still at breakfast when the post came in, and the postman who toiled up the stairs to our first floor brought quite a heap of letters to the professor.

The latter was pleased when he saw them. "Fortune has been propitious," said he; "she often is when she sends a new hand to help. If I had not have given you a night's lodging last night I should not have had half these."

"Why, sir, they were written hours before you spoke to me; it could not be through that."

"Never mind," he returned, "I believe in fate, and in fate answering what good one does. My dear child, you see in me an illustration of the force of LUCK; had it not been for that I might have been a magistrate at quarter sessions, and sat and condemned poor people to the treadmill. I might, indeed, have been a minister, a prime minister, I mean. As it is, what am I? I am simply a poor, a very poor, man of letters."

Now, if there was any one in the world whom I had been taught to honour and to love, it was an author. Flook and I had often talked about them, and had wished that we could have boasted a personal acquaintance with old Defoe, or had sat and heard sturdy John Bunyan preach.

"What do you write, sir?" said I, looking up to him with respect.

"Principally," said he, with a twinkling eye, "principally fiction."

"Stories, sir?" said I, questioning him.

"Yes, stories, my boy."

"I should like to read some of your works, sir."

"Perhaps some day you may," he answered, splitting open an envelope, and reading the letter.

"No good there," he muttered as he tossed it aside; "never mind, I will try again. Ha, ha! something here;" he took a post-office order as he spoke, and went on muttering to himself. Seeing him engaged, I looked round the room; it was poorly furnished, but was clean and comfortable. Two long pipes were above the mantel-shelf, and underneath them a very thick book and a 'Court Guide.' The thick book was a directory; both of these were quite new and fresh. I did not see any of the professor's works, and I told him so; he answered laughingly that few authors kept their books at home, and giving me a pen and paper, bade me write to my friends in the country, whilst he arranged matters at home and abroad, "for," said he, "I must go out very shortly."

So with many doubts, fears, and misgivings, and not without a great deal of thankfulness that I had fallen into the hands of so good and kind a friend, I wrote a letter to the doctor, begging to be remembered most kindly to Mrs. Taw and old Flook, and detailing my adventure and position, and earnestly begging the doctor to write to me and to advise me what to do.

# CHAPTER XI.

## HOW TIME PASSED WITH THE PROFESSOR.

I HAD stayed with Professor Peter Garle for more than a week, I had written twice to Doctor Leatherby and had not received an answer, neither had I found my uncle, nor had he called at the inn for me. My situation was full of mystery and trouble, and the constant good humour of my host, his flood of anecdote, his kind ways and curious sayings, amused me, and rendered me less unhappy than I should have been. There were several things about the professor that I could not understand, and many that I did not like. He spent a great deal of his time in writing, but I saw no book or even manuscript of his save these letters. These he despatched with unceasing regularity, and was so much more industrious than his correspondents that he seldom received answers to more than a third of his communications.

His conversation was, as I have said, amusing, but it was full of worldliness—some people call it worldly wisdom. He professed not to believe in good people; he said that all were scheming, plotting, and trying to cheat one another. "One half of mankind," said he, "does not know how the other half lives; shall I tell you why, my boy? Because one half lives *on* the other half. But of course it is of no use trying to make you believe this or understand it. Ah, young scholar, I was once as innocent as you are; soon will come the inevitable hour when your young peepers will be opened, and you will think all people rogues."

"I hope not, sir," said I, "I should be so sorry to do so."

"Poor lad, poor lad," he said, sadly, "and yet 'tis very possible that those who are nearest to you are the greatest. Well, well, dream on; for my part I wish for nothing more than to again enjoy such a dream as yours."

"Then you thought as I do, once?" said I.

"Of course, till a brother rudely woke me up from it, by quietly setting aside my father's will and taking all our property himself. He, sir, is the rich, the honored, the excellent John Garle, of Garlic Hill, rolling in wealth, and saving and amassing money, whilst I am troubled to get my daily bread."

"Well, sir," said I, "but all the world are not as he."

The professor shook his head and smoked his

pipe, giving me plainly to understand that he had not a much better opinion of the rest of mankind.

"But you, sir, how good you are; here you are giving me board and lodging for nothing, till I find my uncle or hear from my friends; and I am sure I don't know when that will be. If I had money enough I would pay my passage again on that coach which brought me from school. What can I do? I am a burthen to you."

"My excellent scholar," replied the sage, "do not look at that box which I caused to be brought here from the Bull and Mouth coach-office, as if you would draw the nails out of the lid. You are a companion to me, you repay me by your talk, you are even of more value to me. Did you not call upon Lady de Quincey to-day, and did you not bring me a packet from her? Have I not sent you on a dozen errands? You go where my old legs would not permit me. Perhaps in a few weeks you will know me more, and prove even more useful than you are. Rest tranquilly assured that you are not a burthen to me."

It was a great pleasure to me to hear my new friend speak thus, for the doctor and old Flook had instilled into me the belief that it was base to be a burthen upon any one.

# CHAPTER XII.



My new friend, the professor, had told me that
he should shortly need my services. He was
right, the time came with the next day. I was
sitting reading a shabby old copy of ' Lord Bacon's
Essays,' which I had purchased at a bookstall
for a few pence, when the professor called to me
and told me that he should want me to visit a
very fashionable lady, in order to obtain an
answer to a letter which he had written to her.

"It is by appointment," said the professor;
" and she wishes to see you."

"To see *me!*" cried I; "what does she know
of me?"

"Very little," said he; "but she wishes to
know something. Will you go at once, if you
please, for great people are punctual? She may
assist you to find your uncle."

"Very good, sir," said I, musing over what he
said; "I will go."

" Will you dress well, particularly well, if you please, Edward?  Let me see, you are in mourning.  That will do; a clean shirt and collar, if you have some in your trunk, and some attention to your hair; yes, that will do.  You will answer all the questions she puts to you, of course, but with discreetness; as much discretion as possible, in fact."

The professor walked up and down nervously. His eyes were twinkling upon me, now on my own, now fixed on my mouth, continually restless, continually on the alert.

" You will tell no secrets of our prison-house. ' *Percontatorem fugito nam garrulus idem est,*' that's in the Latin grammar, is it not?  You do not wish to be known as a blab?"

" I can tell no secrets, sir," said I, puzzled very much, " for in fact I know none."

" Good, very good; the great Talleyrand used to say that the only way to make a man keep a secret was never to trust him with one—good, excellent!  Ah, Talleyrand, you should have been in my profession.  And now, young sir," he continued, giving me the address and some money, " take an omnibus—' away,—from shades of night unto the light of day.'  I myself will convey you to your carriage."

We left the room together, locked up carefully, and were soon in Holborn, whence I took an omnibus to Park Lane.

The professor, in his theatrical way, had quoted some tag or rhyme in a pantomime, about the change of scene I should witness. His verse was right; it was indeed a passage from night to day, to come from a noisome and close court, where wailing children, and noisy, quarrelling women left us no peace, night or day. As I walked into the open town down Park Lane, with its noble, old-fashioned mansions, its trees and flowering shrubs, and the gay people in fine dresses riding and driving up and down, I could not help marking the change between the very rich and the very poor. *These* seemed a different race of beings from *those*. Hunger and dirt had done its worst upon all my neighbours in Leather Lane, from the two-months squalid baby, with its weak and peevish cry, to the old beldame of seventy-five, who, with bent back and palsy-shaken hand, implored charity of those who were nearly as poor and helpless as herself.

Here were people rich, healthy, and beautiful; oh, how sweet and roseate were the cheeks of the ladies; how glossy, and curled, and scented the hair of the children who, under the care of the nursemaid, quite a lady herself, were taking their morning's walk. How beautiful were the horses, how noble and brave the riders. My heart expanded within me, I blessed them all as my fellow creatures, even if I were destitute and lonely and they so rich and grand. But suddenly my forlorn condition came upon me and I bent my head to hide my tears.

At last I reached a grand house, which unlike the others had not a garden in front, but was one of some few which stood back with the pavement up to their doors. I knocked a modest double knock and waited. I waited so long that I was about to repeat my summons, when I heard a voice beneath me crying—

"Hallo! you boy, it's no use knocking; wot d'yer want? Ring the kitchen bell."

"Lady Clanboyle," said I; "I have a note for her."

"Who from, boy?" said the footman, languidly. The magnificent creature was in undress above, but his legs were arrayed in yellow plush and cloth gaiters, he being evidently getting ready to attend the carriage in its morning drive. He came from the area and opened the door for me, and looked down at me with good-natured condescension.

"Who from, did you say, young feller?" said he.

"Professor Peter Garle," said I.

"Oh, Perfessor Garle," said he; "well, if its music we don't think much of that *here*," he answered.

"I believe my lady wished to speak with *me*," said I, mildly.

"Oh, you, eh! why she don't want a page boy, do she?"

It was lucky for the professor that his envelope was thick and secure, for the footman turned it over and over, as if he would have read it through the cover, and then diving into the kitchen appeared with his livery coat half on and half off, and with a silver salver in his hand; depositing the latter thereon he adjusted his coat hurriedly, and with the words, "Now just wait, will yer," left me to my reflections in the passage.

They were soon broken by the same individual coming down stairs with the salver reversed and asking me "to walk up to me leddy." He was much more polite this time, and absolutely called me "sir."

I was shown into a fine drawing-room, the walls of which were covered with a paper richly paneled, and gilt, and the tables, of which there were many, were laden with richly bound books, knick-nackery, and bijouterie. The windows, which opened lengthways, let in the perfume of roses and mignionette, which stood in boxes outside; Venetian blinds warded off the sun, and muslin curtains, trimmed and worked with pink silk, waved backwards and forwards in the summer air.

I looked for an inhabitant to this splendid room and saw none, but a sweet, gentle voice addressed me, and turning to whence it came I saw a little old lady, dressed as plainly as any housekeeper, in black, who begged me to come to her. She sat in an invalid-chair, stuffed and padded, and seemed so small that she was nearly swallowed up in its recesses.

She looked at me earnestly, "You are in mourning," said she—"for whom?"

"For a father, my lady."

"Ah," she said sadly, "a sad loss, a sad loss; I too have lost one as near and dear as any father, nearer and dearer a thousand times."

"Poor lady!" I thought, as I watched her pale, delicate face.

"But I," she continued, "have riches and luxuries; what must the loss be when accompanied by poverty and other trials."

"The person who writes here," she continued, "recommends your case very highly. Tell me how you are situated."

I remembered the professor's recommendation to be discreet, but seeing that I could really do no harm by telling my own story, I did so, without any attempt at pathos or exaggeration. The truth, thought I, will prevail.

"Poor boy, poor boy!" said the lady, when I had finished; "alone in London—how dreadful! What would you have done had it not been for your friend? Here," she said, "I can see the truth in your face, take this; my almoner shall wait on you and see that you do not want. In the mean time I will see whether something permanent cannot be done for you."

She held out to me two guineas, wrapped in a piece of silver paper, and rung a little bell which was on her table, thus intimating to me that the interview was at an end.

I felt somewhat humiliated at taking the money. I did not like to become an object of charity, and I had a great inclination to tell the professor when I reached his rooms that I would try and walk my way back to Huntingdonshire to the kind old doctor again, but when I reached his house I did not have an opportunity of doing so.

The truth was that the professor was, as he termed it, in the hands of the Philistines. How he reached that temporary destination the next chapter will tell the reader.

# CHAPTER XIII.

### HOW I RAN FOR MY LIFE.

THE professor had told me that if I chose I might remain away from our court, to breathe the fresh air of the parks, for some short time, and I was glad to lie in the grass, looking up into the pure sky, far away from the noise and trouble of our court. It was, therefore, nearly four o'clock in the afternoon when I returned. I had bought some biscuits, and made my dinner upon them in the park, but I was hungry enough to look forward with some relish to the comfortable tea which I knew the professor would prepare for me.

When I arrived at the entrance of our court I was, perhaps, not very much astonished to see two policemen there, because, in my short experience, I had found that the presence of the law, embodied in blue coats and pewter buttons, was not unusual there; but I noticed them with an ominous and ill-defined dread.

This feeling amounted to positive terror when I found another of the fraternity at our door;

I had a presentiment that all was not right with my protector. My presentiment was true.

The professor, smiling blandly, as if nothing were the matter, sat at his own table, whilst an officer in plain clothes, one, I believe, of the Mendicity Society, sat opposite to him, with his eye fixed upon him, and another was opening and shutting all the drawers and cupboards in the room.

"I think," said one at last, tapping a bundle of letters which he held in his hand, "that these will be enough for him."

"I think so too. They will do your business, master."

"Very good," returned the professor, jocularly. "I think, gentlemen, that you must be the best judges of the matter. Nevertheless, I do not quite despair; there is the glorious uncertainty of the law."

"No uncertainty here, guv'nor," answered one of his captors. "You're booked, safe as houses."

"As houses!" returned the professor. "A curious expression. Some houses are not safe; thieves break in and steal."

"Better that," said the Mendicity officer, "than go coaxing honest people hout o' their money; a swindling of them."

The professor shrugged his shoulders, as much as to say that the terms were harsh and should not be applied to him, then he took snuff in

a very elegant way, and was in the act of quietly
tapping one or two grains of dust from his nose
when he perceived my scared and terrified face
looking at him from the door."

"Ah!" cried he, "my nephew, gentlemen,
from the country. A fine day in the parks,
Edward, no doubt!"

"Please, sir,—" said I, stammering, for the two
officers and the professor were all looking at me
with open eyes.

"My dear Edward," said the latter, very softly,
and with the words caution, silence, discretion,
written on his speaking countenance as plainly as
ever I saw in any book in my life, "my dear
Edward, I do not want you to stay here to-
night; you had better hurry back home. In
fact, I cannot give you a welcome, as these doors
will be closed. You will take these" (he gave me
two letters, opened, and out of their envelopes),
"which you can read at your leisure. I shall go
away from here in a few minutes in company
with these very pressingly-kind gentlemen—"

The policemen looked at each other and
grinned.

"And shall be absent from home a short time.
You therefore had better get back as quickly as
you can."

He waived me off as he said this, and taking
my proffered hand, squeezed it gently, and left
half a sovereign in my grasp. He then looked

very earnestly and with much meaning at the
door.

"The fact is," said the policeman, sternly, just
as I was about to speak, "the law wants your
uncle, young gentleman, and must have him.  I
aint got nothing again you at present;  so now
just cut."

"Aye, dear Edward," said Peter Garle, nodding
his venerable head, "in the language, delightfully
symbolical, of the officer, you had better 'cut,'
that is, run away, at once."

I needed no second bidding.  I placed the letters in my pocket, and bounded down the stairs
like a frightened animal.  It might have been
that, perceiving my terrified state, the policemen
at the door were willing to humour me, for one of
them, as I passed, made a feint to catch me, but
I avoided him, and away I went.

I had a vague idea that some terrible phantom
—my impersonation of the majesty of the law, was
pursuing me.  My chin, as the Spanish proverb
says, was upon my shoulder, for I looked backwards as I fled, expecting every moment to see
some terrible fellow with a sword, or at least a
policeman's truncheon, drawn and rushing after
me.

So I fled up Back Hill, and along Leather
Lane, between the stalls of the costermongers,
overturning some of them, and being objurgated
accordingly.  Here a crowd of boys, fancying I

was running a race, made way for me and cheered me on, much to my disturbance. I therefore turned down a short street and got into Hatton Garden, where I had a fair field, had not some apprentice or errand boys of the jewellers, who abound there, cried out, at the top of their voices, "Hot beef!" or some vulgar London imitation of "Stop thief!" and, for a short time, joined in chase of me.

I had at school won several matches at running, and fear now gave me wings to my feet. Believing that I was pursued with the terrible cry which the boys set up, and wondering that none of the passengers in any way interfered with me, I again plunged on and on, straining every nerve and sweating at every pore. By the time I had reached the top of Hatton Garden, where it joins Holborn, I had distanced all my pursuers except one, who, with an obstinate determination not to be beaten (which some boys have), still kept up the chase, about a hundred feet behind me. Panting, puffing, and struggling, the mischievous fellow still had the hardihood to call, at intervals, his terrible war-cry, which sounded like "Stop thief!"

I therefore "doubled," turned down Holborn for a few yards, then up the hill again, and away I went as far as Lincoln's Inn Fields, terribly tired and spent, and ready to drop but through my fear. I believe I distanced my pursuer here, for

I did not see him, and had leisure spare enough to tighten a leathern strap which I wore round my waist, and to look around a little before I again started on a slow trot. I turned to the left, towards the West End, ran along the north side of the square, and then, without any definite object, turned down the west side, and retraced my course along the south, arriving, at a slow trot, just in time to see my old enemy wiping his face and looking about him for the object of his chase.

Immediately he saw me he gave a yell of triumph, and away he dashed after me. Without knowing where I went, I dashed down Portugal Street, reached the network of courts about Clare Market, passed through them to the left, and, somehow, reached the Strand. I turned, then eastward, and ran, staggering and panting, till I saw St. Paul's Cathedral, with its gilded cross rise glittering in the sky before me. I ran on towards it, without any defined aim, but somehow thinking that it would be an ark of refuge for me. The mischievous tormentor, the London boy, still panted after me in the distance, I still believing him to be a terrible agent of the police, and he yet, for pure fun and mischief, continuing the pursuit.

I was so tired and wearied with the exertion that he, knowing much better than I the ground and the manner of passing amongst a crowd in London streets, had gained on me so much that, at the bottom of Bridge Street, he nearly touched my shoulder. The terror of being captured gave me new speed and diverted me from my purpose. I turned down Bridge Street, and ran as fast as I could towards the bridge.

The new start I gave distanced my pursuer, who was completely beaten. He stayed and panted, out of breath, somewhere near the great gateway of Bridewell, and I ran on to the bridge. I looked round and found that I was without pursuers; but I, like my rival, was out of breath and exhausted. Seeing, therefore, that no one watched me, I dashed down the steps to the river, and, passing lightly over many boats that lay there, hurried down into the stern-sheets of one, panting with exhaustion, weary with fatigue, footsore with running, and terrified out of my senses. I was glad to get anywhere out of sight and out of pursuit. I therefore covered myself over with a huge roll of tarpaulin, and thus lay perdue in the boat, perspiring at every pore, and with only one fixed purpose in my mind, which was to lie till all pursuit was over, and then to find out some coach-office wherefrom a coach went to the country town where Dr. Leatherby lived, and then, partly by walking and partly with the money I had about me, return to my adopted father, like a lost son.

# CHAPTER XIV.

## I FALL AMONGST VERY STRANGE FELLOWS, AND MEET WITH MR. JOHN BOBUS, A.B.

THE gentle swaying backwards and forwards of the boat on the river, the heat and fatigue I had undergone, sent me quietly to sleep under the old tarpaulin. I lay there in the stern-sheets like a child in the cradle, quietly rocked to rest, and forgetful of all my troubles or my sorrows. Blessed sleep of youth! which yields and comforts all care, and extracts for a time the sharpest sting of fate!

I was shortly awakened. Evening had fallen around me as I lay, and when, shaken by one or two heavy jars, as of men stepping into my place of retreat, I awoke and peeped out of my hiding hole, I saw the sunset gilding the river and purpling the evening clouds above my head. I saw, too, the figure of a huge, brawny fellow, in a tarpaulin hat, who quietly took off his pea-jacket, and rolling it up into a bundle, threw it into the stern-sheets. A tobacco-box and a piece of pigtail tobacco, which were in the pocket, formed a mass hard enough to hit me a shrewd blow on the head, but I dared not cry out, and the sailor did not see me.

Presently he shouted out, in a voice which seemed to split the air, and which was more like a giant's voice than any I had yet heard, " Liberty men—liberty Jacks, ahoy there!" upon which three or four stout fellows came tumbling down, and taking off their jackets, set themselves to row. The first one loosened the boat, and taking a boat-hook, soon pushed her free from the craft amongst which she was lying.

"Well," he said at last, breaking silence, for they all seemed glum and very dull, "we've bin and gone and lost him, or my name arn't Bobus."

" Umph!" grunted the others, with a strong pull at the oars, and sending the boat flying through the tide, which had turned some little time and was then running out.

" What'll Cap'en Seth say—what will he say? He'll cashier the lot on us, he will, and we orter heaved anchor at the full we ort, leastways at turn. As sure as my name's Jack Bobus, he'll do without us."

'Tis all along o' you bein' so tender 'arted," said another; " you might a' bin sure the boy wanted his mother, a tender boy like that'un. No good, no good—a soft handed feller!"

" Soft hands and softer 'art," said old Bobus, with a sigh, and that's why I liked him, poor little Billee.  Whereon another, with a big but musical voice, sang out—

> " Yo ho, poor little Billee !
> Oh, ho, for little Billee !
> There was guzzling Dick,
> And guttling Ned,
> And lazy Jack,
> And handy Ted,
> And likewise was little Billee !"

The four joined in a melancholy howl as they rowed on, and as they shot the bridge their deep voices echoed under it, making the arches ring again, and the people on the top of it look down and wonder.  As it was very dark, I ventured to push aside Bobus's coat and the tarpaulin, and to peep at their upturned faces and manly throats.

" All right, for'ard," said one, when they were silent.

" Right it is," said Bobus.  " What will the cap'en say ?—poor Cap'en Seth !  He'll think as we've drowned Billee."

" The rummest dodge," said another, in a comforting way, " as ever I did heer.  I've heerd o' boys who ran away *to* sea, but nivir o' one who ran away *from* it.  Poor Captain Seth ! he was fond of that lad—a cousin, warn't it ?"

" A niece, I think," said Bobus, reflectingly.

" What! not a woman creetur, surely!" returned the other.

" Maylike," said another, " soft handed and soft hearted, you know, eh! Bobus."

" A little foot Billee had," continued Bobus, " a little foot, and precious 'fraid a getting up the shrouds."

" She *was* a 'oman—a course she was," ejaculated the other three in chorus.

" As rum stories a bin herd before," said Bobus. " There was that young o'man as wint out in the Harry Thusa, with Cap'en Brooke, and as riz to be leftenant o' marines."

" And that one as was shot cos she wouldn't strip her back to bear the cat, and was diskivered to be a 'oman by the surgeon. Billee was a 'oman, and 'as changed his clothes and gone home to see his mother."

The simple seamen seemed agreed in this, and I have no doubt but they would have told Cap'en Seth Smith some similar story, had not the sequel turned out differently. Bobus, who kept continually adjuring his own name, was very much afraid of meeting the captain, for it seems that it was through his intervention alone that little Billy, the cabin-boy, was allowed to go on shore.

So, when they reached the ship, and had shouted out, which they all did, with most powerful voices, " Ship ahoy!" and had attracted the notice of the watch, fastened the boat to the stanchcons, and were ready to mount the side, Master Bobus was the last to leave the boat. He whispered hoarsely to the man above—

"Wot does Cap'en Seth say?"

"Bin a asking arter the boat and the boat's crew a many times. Didn't expect as you would a play'd him sich a trick, an old man-a-war's man too!"

"Ah! I knowed so," returned Bobus, with a groan, "I knowed the cap'en—I knowed as how he trusted Jack Bobus."

"Where's the boy, too, a young monkey? He ort to run up the ladder like a monkey by this time. Wots the matter with him? Does he want to swing up in a chair like a female lady? Send him up, Bobus—send him up."

"Send up wot?" said Jack, fumbling at the oars and boot-hook, and hardly stirring himself.

"Come, look alive! You're just about as orkard as a purser's clerk. Send up the boy, and come yourself."

Bobus evidently dared not answer, but was coming aft, muttering something about his pea-jacket, and fumbling for it in the dark, when I, seeing that it was my last chance, jumped up and cried out, "Here am I, sir!"

"Bless my eyes!" cried old Bobus, nearly falling overboard in surprise. "Why, if it isn't little Billee!"

He made no more ado, but caught me up like a doll in one arm, and running up the rope ladder, carried me on deck to the light at the binnacle, crying in his delight, "I've found her, I've found her! Nearly broke my heart, she did, a young rogue. This 'ere's the lad. Cap'en Seth, Cap'en Seth, I have found the little Billee."

The greater part of the crew rushed forward at the cry of old Bobus, the captain who was being informed by one of the boat's crew of the desertion of the boy ran to me, and I was dropped out of Bobus' arms before the captain and crew of the 'Lively Bessy,' a brig of some hundred and fifty tons burden, fitted out by private enterprise and charity to join in the search, which had long been going on almost without hope, but still with bravery and faith, for Sir John Franklin.

# CHAPTER XV.



I AM INTRODUCED TO THE "LIVELY BESSY," CAPTAIN
SETH SMITH, AND GO TO SEA.—NORTHWARD HO!

THE "Lively Bessy" was a very little ship for
so great a purpose, but the hearts of her captain
and her crew were truly great.   All the crew were
picked men, and men, too, picked from those
who had volunteered for the service.   .

The hull of the "Bessy" was of immense
strength, to stand the pressure of the ice-laden
ocean she was intended to navigate.   She was
indeed double, and could have been described as
a ship within a ship.   An outer sheeting of two-
and-a-half-inch oak was covered with a second
of the same material.   Strips of sheet-iron extended also from the bows to the beam, as a
shield against the cutting action of the ice.   The
very decks were double, and the cracks of the
planking were stuffed with tarred oakum, so that
they were water-tight; between the double decks
also was a layer of tarred felt.   The interior was

lined with a layer of cork, the non-conducting power of which we felt in the northern seas. The winch, capstan, and patent windlass were of the newest and strongest make. Along the length of the ship extra sets of beams, at distances of four feet, ran; these could be shipped or unshipped at pleasure, and to save us from being crushed by the ice; whilst forward, from kelson to deck, was a mass of seven feet of solid timber from the cut-water, so that no mass of ice, however solid, could crush in our bows: for it was the opinion of our captain, and many others, that if the brave and good Sir John had lost his ships, it was through their being crushed by the ice-bergs. Amidships, that is, in the centre of the vessel, was a little hurricane-house, in which was the galley fire which cooked for all hands. A large iron funnel from this circulated the heat around it, and was intended to melt the snow, and so provide us with fresh water to drink. We had, besides, an armourer's forge, ice-anchors, extra cables, whale-boats, harpoons, &c., and warming-stoves for below.

Our crew consisted of the captain, Seth Smith, actually a second lieutenant in the Royal Navy; an acting master and first officer; a midshipman, who was at least twenty-one years of age; a doctor; John Bobus, the boatswain; and thirteen men, and one boy, making a crew of nineteen. I believe that at the time I finished the last chapter about twelve out of the number were looking at me as I stood, half afraid and half ashamed, in the midst of them.

"Why," said one, with a grin, taking hold of my arm, "this here aint our little Billee, cap'en; Bobus has bin and changed him."

"Pass the word for Bobus," said the captain.

Bobus stood forward.

"Now, tell me, what has become of the boy William?"

Bobus looked first at the captain and then at me. "Are you sartin sure, sir," said he, in a desperate case, "are you sartin sure as how t'aint the same."

"The same, stupid," returned the captain, in a fume; "look yourself."

Bobus took a lanthorn from one who held it near, and, peering down into my face, cried, "Well, it aint little Billee, arter all."

"Pish!" said the captain. "And now, youngster, give an account of yourself, will you? How did you come into our boat?"

"Please, sir," said I, touching my cap to him, as I had seen the others do, "if I could speak to you alone, I would tell you. I ran away, sir; but not from home."

"Umph," said Captain Smith; "so did our boy. However, it is almost too late to put you on shore. We can do that at Gravesend, perhaps. Meanwhile, whilst we weigh anchor and start, come down and tell your story."

I did tell my story, and in such a way that the captain became my friend. He asked me whether I would sail with him, and take the place left vacant by the run-a-way boy. I was only too glad to do so, and not only stepped into my predecessor's place, but also, luckily for me, into his very shoes as well, and into his clothes also. Little Billee must have been of my size, for his things fitted me uncommonly well. I had a corner of a cabin, a chest, and a little hammock to myself; and when I had clothed myself in a warm, thick suit of blue broad-cloth, a blue Guernsey, and a sailor's cap, and came on deck, old Bobus came up to me again, with a face marked with surprise and wonder, and cried with astonishment, "Why, arter all, I do believe it is our little Billee!"

I must pass over the beginning of our voyage, for at first I was so poorly that I hardly recollect anything. When I got quite well, and had my "sea-legs," that is, when I could stand on the deck without rolling, and could climb up the shrouds a little, and make myself useful, we were far away from England, and upon the North Sea, steering for Iceland. Northward, ho! was our destination, and the "Lively Bessy," although so heavily built, was an excellent sailer.

Old Bobus grew to be my friend, although he never quite understood how I got so opportunely into the stern sheets of the boat on that eventful night, used to spend many hours with me, teaching me the different names of the parts of the ship and rigging near me. Now, one of old Dr. Leatherby's maxims, and a very good one, too, was that you can never learn too much; that is, you can never acquire too much good knowledge, and almost all knowledge, properly so called, is good. I was so persuaded of the truth of this, that I had determined through life to put it into practice, and I therefore grew an apt scholar under the tuition of old Bobus. Having practised my memory, it became a very good one, and I soon mastered all I wanted to know of the details of the ship.

"Ned," he would say, "if so be as you are not Billee, what am I going to do?"

We were in shore, near one of the northern islands, when he spoke. He had a plummet and a coil of rope in his hands, and presently jumping into the chains he swung it once or twice round his head.

"You are sounding," said I.

"That's right, Ned, now look," and away he threw the lead to a good distance in front of the ship's course.

"Keep your hi on," cried he, as the line, marked at equal distances, run out. Presently the lead touched the bottom, or plumbed, as he called it, and the ship sailing onwards we were quite over the spot where it fell, so that the line when held up was perpendicular. At ten fathoms of line a knot is tied, and it was to just within one fathom of the knot that the lead plumbed. " Sing out, Ned," cried Bobus, " what is it?"

" By the deep nine," I shouted, trying to imitate the deep musical cry of the sailors.

"Good," grunted Bobus, much pleased; " he isn't a lubber, he isn't, we shall make a sailor of him as sure as my name is Jack Bobus."

So we sailed onwards, everything was new around me, I was pleased and happy. I tried to do my duty as my old master had taught me, and in this instance of duty one has only to try to succeed. Bobus was of great use to me; he was as willing to teach as I to learn. I learnt what seamen called sea-going things, blocks, bolts, rove tackle, bobstays, ratlines, futtocks, shrouds, all sorts of names, in short, from the figure-head, and a very pretty one was that of. the " Lively Bessy," to the sternpost, Bobus questioned me and taught me.

My proficiency pleased the captain much; he himself seeing that I took an interest in the ship taught me a good deal too, and the time passed happily enough.

I had almost forgotten to say that in looking into my clothes, which I had left off and packed up when I took to little Billy's legacy, I found the two letters which Professor Garle had put into my hands when I ran away so hurriedly.

They were from Dr. Leatherby and from Mrs. Taw, both of them full of kindness and goodness, begging me to come back to the school and to live with them, "If my uncle had disappointed me," so they said, "they would not."

My eyes filled with tears as I thought of their kindness, and I was very angry with the professor who could so—could so cruelly—have kept them from me, for I saw by the post-mark that they had been written nearly a week before I left London, and immediately on the receipt of mine. Come back to the old school! ah, how distant did it seem to me, with its quiet playground and its old gables! I was on the great ocean of life, no longer a boy, but a man in thought if not in years. I looked forward at the wide sea flecked and dotted with ice, I looked backwards at the sea behind us; I prayed for my friends, but I saw it was too late to go back. I determined to go forward, onward, and upward.

# CHAPTER XVI.



ICE had made its appearance in small masses in the sea for some little time before we made land, but our old sailors saw with a glance that it was only that which had been floated by the gulf stream from the fields of ice far north, for when early in July we reached Iceland and put in at the Port of Reykjavik, in the magnificent Bay of Taxa Fiord, the thermometer stood at sixty-five, and our officers played at chess on deck, and our men went about in their shirt sleeves. The bay is magnificent; from horn to horn its width is fifty miles, and around it noble hills rise in an amphitheatre, topped with snow, and appearing, though many miles distant, close to you, on account of the sharpness of the air.

The captain determined to wait a day or so in this port to get some necessaries for his ship, although the men were not allowed to go on shore. They were, however, permitted to amuse themselves, and various games, boxing and other matches served to beguile the long, long days of the north. Long, indeed, when the sun delayed going to bed till midnight.

One of the sailors, a Londoner, was so proficient in boxing, or, as he called it, the "noble 'art of self-defence," that few could stand up against him, at last, indeed, the majority declined, seeing very little fun in continually parrying his blows, and in getting pretty well punched, without being able to return the compliment. The sailor was not a little proud of his accomplishment and used to laugh at the rest for not coming up "to the scratch."

Bobus, the boatswain, at last told him he could find him his match, and upon one afternoon the doctor, the master, and the seamen, formed a ring to see a little play with the gloves. The Londoner, who was a brawny fellow, put himself into an attitude and was delighting himself by stretching his muscles and walking about like a lion.

"Come, Mr. Bobus," he cried, "come on, where's your champion, sir, 'tisn't the boy, is it?"

"No, 'tisn't the ship boy," said old Bobus, coming forward with a great hulking fellow, a Cornishman, who knew no more of boxing than a girl; "no 'tisn't ship boy, but 'tis a Cornish boy as will play with you."

"Oh, that fellow," said the Londoner, "why he don't know how to handle his fistics."

"No more he doant, yet u'll tak' you," said the Cornishman, fumbling at one glove and then at the other.

The cockney looked very disdainfully at him as he stood opposite him, and scarcely held his guard. Meantime the Cornishman placed himself before his adversary, and suggested that they should begin their "geame."

"Very good," said his antagonist.

Now beginning "the geame," in the Cornishman's idea, was the funniest way that I had ever seen. He first warned his opponent that the only safe way of fighting him consisted in "a watching of his hi," at which the Londoner laughed. "Neaw lad," said the Cornishman, "neaw's the time, watch my hi," and he put himself in a strange attitude, drew himself backwards, almost to the ground, one leg bending close under him, and then springing up as a snake might spring at its prey, he hit, with all his force and the whole impetus of his body, his adversary on the nose. The motion was so quick, the position so strange, and the manœuvre so unexpected that the blow told with a tremendous effect. Luckily the men had boxing-gloves on, or it would, I am afraid, have proved fatal. As it was, the blood spirted from the face of the Londoner and he fell down with great force, and was obliged to be carried below, very much hurt.

"Pilbeam," shouted Bobus, to the Cornishman, "if I was in a king's ship I would give you a round dozen for that blow. If that's how you play, what do you call earnest?"

"I tauld him," returned the other, looking sheepishly, "I tauld him to mind my hi;" and this was the only apology they could get out of him. "Mind your hi," returned Bobus, indignantly; "the fellow wanted taking down, but not knocking down. I thought you knew how to box."

"That's what they call it in our country," said the fellow, sulkily.

"Well, come," returned Bobus, "you shan't march out with all the honours of war, you shan't. Can you play at single stick?"

"Yes," said Pilbeam, "rayther."

"Come, then," said Bobus, "here, bring two rattans forward, and we will show you how they play aboard a man-of-war."

Nothing loth, the Cornishman stood up manfully, and when the two canes were brought, Bobus gave him the choice, and then they set to. The playing was excellent; Bobus wanting to give Pilbeam a punishment, and he being equally ready to guard himself from the blows. At length they were so excited, that they entirely neglected guarding, and merely struck at each other. In this contest Bobus had the best, and at last a smart blow on the wrist which he gave Pilbeam nearly disarmed him, his hand hung down uselessly; his blows were simply the blows of a child. Upon this, greatly to my astonishment Bobus improved the occasion, and taking advantage of his enemy's disabled state, gave him a good sound caning over his back and shoulders.

"There you be," said he, when his adversary grinning spitefully, had lifted up his hand in token of defeat, "I will teach you how to play fair, and to knock a honest fellow down. I'll dust your jacket for you, or my name's not Jack Bobus."

Pilbeam slunk away; his hard carcass covered, I will be bound, with wheals and bruises, and the rest of the crew laughing at him, and applauding Bobus.

The next day we left the harbour, and sailed still more northward. We soon sighted Cape Nord, and passing about 70° N., came in with the outline of the ice track in summer. We had need then of our winter clothing, and that of the cabin boy who had left us, came in very well for me. By the doctor's advice I put on a very thick netted silk and cotton shirt next to my skin, over that a thickly ribbed woollen Guernsey shirt, then a frock which came below my waist, seal skin trowsers, with the skin inside, woollen stockings over my own little thread socks, and boots, with the fur inside, which pulled up over my knees. By the excellent precautions which had been taken, officers and men were alike wrapped up excellently. Over the head we wore first a woollen cap, which came down the nape of the neck and met the collar, and then over that a kind of fur helmet, with, for very severe weather, a mask with two holes in it, to protect the eyes, and a like aperture through for the nostrils and mouth. When we approached the Arctic regions all these appliances were necessary, and even insufficient to keep out the cold.

Strange too, it was, to me, to be in a region where the sun might be said never to set. At eleven o'clock at night we had daylight, and a sun full of brilliancy and glory. Our doctor and captain took scientific observations, and made sketches and drawings of the Aurora Borealis during the winter, which we were obliged to pass there; but the crew were, with Bobus and myself, always busy in clearing away the ice, in working with the ice saw, in hunting bears, or shooting seals. The flesh of these animals we eat, for the scurvy—the scourge of seamen fed upon salt junk—made its appearance amongst the crew, and was only kept down by the fresh meat, which we supplied ourselves with by hunting and shooting.

At about 72° N. and 7 W., we, for the first time, sighted Jan Mayen. We had to thread our way amongst the loose flocs of ice. A *floe* is a large floating patch of ice, as large, I thought, as a small island. When these were of such large dimensions, that the man who went up to the masthead could not see their boundaries, then they were called fields; and, strictly speaking, a *field* is a larger *floe*. Round the edges of these, borne on by the current, and broken up and crumbled with the force of the large field, were smaller masses, which Bobus called *ice brash*. When the ice islands were open enough for us to pass through easily, it was termed *loose, open,* or *drift* ice; and large mountains of ice floating about in the sea, glittering and shining in the sunlight like brilliant glass, were named icebergs. Some of these were as big as cathedrals; some had spires and towers, and caves beneath them, through which the water rushed and ran, and at the slippery sides of which the waves washed and licked, like living tongues of water.

The first sight of Jan Mayen, so named from the Dutch captain who first discovered the island, was grand indeed. It was so cold that one could not hold on to the rigging, and we were surrounded and shut out from every thing by a deep curtain of mist, gray and dark, which hung over us like a pall. Our captain paced the deck anxious and scarcely knowing how far he was from the shore. We were obliged to proceed very cautiously, bumping and grinding against the floating ice, when, just as we least expected it, the curtain of the mist was lifted up, and opened far above our heads, and there, hundreds of feet above us, as if hung in the sky, was the peak of the gigantic mountain covered with crystal glittering snow. Wonder of wonders, beautiful and grand, even in the desert ocean, far away from the track of man, God prepares his landscapes and great pictures full of solemn might, of majesty, and awe.

Our boat shortly afterwards landed on the bleak shore, and in a tin case, bound round a short pole fixed in the earth, we placed a record of our visit, to testify to any ship that might come after us that the " Lively Bessy " and her captain had been thus far upon the search for him who now, alas! never will be found—one of those great captains and discoverers of whom England has produced so many, and who have gone down age after age to penetrate and gauge the wonders of the Arctic regions.

# CHAPTER XVII.



WERE I to chronicle the events of every day, or indeed to write down the story of each week, in this my first voyage, I don't know when I should finish my story. I must tell it, therefore, as briefly as I can.

We soon left Jan Mayen, and sailed northward to prosecute our search. Our men were as anxious as the captain, and under his direction, Bobus had fitted up a cask, which, stuffed with wool and straw, was hoisted up to the masthead, and there fixed. It was called a crow's nest, and there a man, relieved every half hour, stood with his glass in hand, looking out for a sail, for land, or for any present danger.

I had myself mounted one day, watching with Bobus the progress of a fine iceberg which floated down towards us with a slightly rotatory motion. We had not been watching long when a side was presented towards us which we had not before seen.

7

"Look, Bobus," cried I, in amazement, "look there; there is a man!"

"As sure as my name's Jack Bo—!" He did not finish the sentence because he was so surprised, for there, seated on the berg, in a cavity which formed round him like a natural arm-chair, with his head leaning on his hand, and his arm on his knee, was an English sailor. His hair blew wildly about, and his hat was off, and his garments, loose, and covered with hoar frost, blew towards us, so that I thought he beckoned us.

"Yo ho! shipmate. Yo ho!" cried Bobus, franctically. "Yo ho! What cheer?"

The figure never stirred nor answered. The wind blew out the hair and ragged garment as before.

The men were all astir on deck, for they saw the figure, and presently the captain came aloft with his glass and looked at him earnestly.

Slowly the berg bore down upon us, the helm was altered so that the ship wore round and passed the berg at some seventy-feet distance, as nearly as we could with safety to ourselves. Bobus, the most hopeful of us all, continued to shout as our countryman came near.

"An English jib," cried Bobus. "One of Sir John's men, as I make out, Yo ho! shipmet, Yo ho!"

"It's no use shouting, Bobus," cried the captain. "He's been dead for weeks, if not for years. He never will speak more."

THE DEAD MAN'S VOYAGE.

CHAP. 17.

The words had hardly left the captain's mouth than a cold wind blew from the iceberg, and the atmosphere, as it does always near those immense masses of ice, grew colder. The ship wore off from the berg; but, at the same time, as we neared it, the very face of the man was presented to us, and we could see the sunken cheeks, the pale lips, and the eyes. They were open.

"Cap'en Seth Smith," said Bobus, solemnly, "that man's alive."

"As dead as last year, or as Pontius Pilate," returned Captain Seth. "Yo ho! there, on deck; run out a gun, and, when I give the word, fire."

We had a long gun on deck, with which our doctor, a learned man, had been endeavouring to calculate distances by the reverberations and echoes. Under his orders it was quickly charged with powder only, and made ready, and, as the berg floated by, the gunner applied the portfire, and an explosion followed, the smoke of which had no sooner cleared away than we saw the figure rock slightly backwards, and then topple forwards and slide down swiftly the steep sides of the iceberg into the sea. All looked with horror into the deep ocean, but the waves closed over the dead man's head, and he did not rise again to the surface.

"Ah," said the captain, "I knew how it was. He was frozen to death upon that berg."

"How did he get upon it?" said the doctor.

"Heaven only knows. It might have been that the turning of the iceberg overwhelmed his ship, and that he, being upon the mast, jumped off to the berg, only to see his vessel and all hands go down."

Bobus had told me that one of the chief dangers of a vessel, in this northern ocean, laid in the danger of being crushed by a turning berg. They are often prodigiously high; but, whatever their height above the water, they have six times the depth below. That is, when a mountain of ice floats, six sevenths of its bulk are submerged, so that if it be only fifty feet high it is three hundred deep. The temperature of the water also being higher than that of the air, the water being in fact warmer, the ice in the water gradually melts, till, the bottom becoming lighter than the top, it turns over. Of course, if any ship be near it the ship is crushed and borne down.

"No," said the doctor, "he is not the last of the band; he may be one of Sir John's men. He may have come from that mysterious spot where icebergs are formed, and where Sir John has penetrated the Arctic 'OPEN SEA.'"

All started at the words. Each hoped that they might prove true. Every one in the ship had indeed long ago discussed the doctor's theory, that beyond the zone of ice which bound in those frozen regions like an iron wall, was a vast and, probably, a fresh-water ocean, on the banks of which the icebergs were massed together, for we knew that, except at the entrance of immense rivers, no large quantity of fresh water, such as is contained in a berg, could exist.

"Ah," cried old Bobus, turning to the doctor, "I beant a book-larned man, I beant; but what you says, doctor, about that open sea is feasible. About ship, Cap'en Seth; about ship, then, and let us away to find out Sir John."

Cap'en Seth pointed to the iceberg and smiled sadly. "Ah, Bobus," said he, "'tis very easy to talk; but how are we to 'bout ship, and pierce through eternal ice. Why, the great Parry, when he got to latitude 81, abandoned his ship, got upon sledges, and went north; but the drift of the ice carried him further south than he could go, and, taking his bearings after a long journey, he found himself four miles further south than when he started."

"Disappointing enough," said the doctor.

"Aye, aye, but what was he to do? Nature is a great giantess, and conquers the most bold of us."

"But she will be subdued in the long run," continued the doctor. "Who knows but we may some day find out something which will mitigate these perpetual snows and icy cold?"

"Aye, who knows!" said the captain, with a shiver. "Meantime, Bobus, jump into the boat and get aboard the berg. Let us see if that poor Jack Tar hath left any memorial of himself."

We were all willing to be of the party, and I regarded it as a great favour that Bobus took me with him in the boat. The iceberg had floated a little way past us to the stern, but we soon pulled to it. The narrowest part only of it had been towards us, for it had many sides, some broad and some narrow. We easily made out the place where the poor fellow, numbed with cold, had sat down to die, but we could not reach it from that place, for there the ice rose in a perpendicular wall about thirty feet high. We therefore rowed round the berg, which we found to be nearly a mile and a half in circumference. On the opposite side to where we first saw our countrymen irregular steps formed by the ice gave us a foothold, and, some of the stoutest of our party going first, were soon on the berg.

We traversed it as well as we could, but found no traces of our companion, as some had presumed we should, till we came to his resting place; there we found only three things. A pipe, empty indeed, but blackened with smoke; a jack-knife, tied with a lanyard such as sailors use, and an empty meat can, one, indeed, such as had been sent out by Government and by those who fitted out these northern expeditions. We seized these eagerly, and looked roun' for more relics of the poor fellow, but found　　e.

"He aint left no scrap of writing, Ned," said Bobus, "to tell who he was and how he died, or to send his last love to his sweetheart."

"How could he, old spooney?" cried Pilbeam. "He couldn't call for pen an' ink, could he?"

Pilbeam had not forgotten the rattan, and was the only one in our ship who was discontented and illnatured. Bobus looked at him with some contempt, but did not answer.

"Let's scrape away the ice," said one of the sailors. "May be the Jack Tar's left some notion o' who he was." We did so, but found no memorial; the meat can had been carefully wedged in a fissure, and the knife and pipe were laid on the top of it. We were looking forlornly at the place when a gun from the ship gave us the signal to return. When we looked in the direction of the shot we could hardly make our vessel out.

"Let us make haste back, Bobus," said I, "or else we shall undergo the same fate as our poor friend."

"Aye, aye," cried Bobus, and away we scampered over the block to the place where our boat was moored, and where one of our men was in charge. We found the descent much harder than the ascent, and were indeed so long before we all got down into the boat and round the angle of the berg, that the thick mist and fog parted us from our ship. The effect of being alone in the Arctic regions, or at any rate seeming so far away from our companions and hidden from their sight, hardly knowing where we might drift or whether some of the immense masses of loose ice might not overwhelm us, was by no means pleasant.  Under the influence of Bobus, however, none of us despaired, and as the others rowed and he steered according to the directions of a man at the head who looked out for the masses of ice, I was employed in firing off a pistol which I held, so that we should give notice to the ship where we were.

We soon had the relief of hearing them reply, and so pulled straight through the fog to the Lively Bessy.

They were very glad when we got on board, for accidents in those seas are frequent enough, and our good captain was anxious to bring his men home all safe.  "Well," said he, "Bobus, and what trace have you found of our countrymen?"

"None, Cap'en Seth," said Bobus.  "None 'cept these," and he produced the clasp-knife, the tobacco pipe, and the meat can.

"We didn't find no scrap of writin'," said Bobus, in a melancholy tone.

"Eh !" returned the doctor, who had taken the meat can.  "How do you know?  Have you looked here ?"

He unscrewed the lid of the can as he spoke, with a strong wrench, for it had rusted together, and opening it, turned it to the light at the binnacle. There,  sure enough, were letters in rude capitals worked on the inside of the lid with the point of the seaman's knife?

"John Truman<br>
Ship "Sarah"<br>
September 1838.<br>
Left alone on the ice.<br>
May the Lord have mercy!"

"Poor fellow, poor fellow! What ship was that, captain?"

"The ship Sarah," said Captain Seth. "I don't member her name among any of the Arctic searchers. May be she was some whaler driven out far north, and then overwhelmed, as we guessed before."

All this time poor old Bobus was displaying very lively emotion; now clasping his hands, now his forehead. "Give me the box, doctor," said he, "and let me look at his handwritin'. I know summat of that ship."

"Yes," he continued, as he took the tin, "that good ship Sarah was a North Sea whaler, and as good and tight a ship as ever sailed; and this here John Truman—" he struck the box with his great fist as he said it—"was my brother-in-law and married my only sister, whose name likeways was Sarah, long years ago. The good ship and good John never come back, no never, never, and John's parents and wife, who never mistrusted him, thought as how she had foundered in deep water, and no hands had come to land. She, poor girl, lived on a little while and then died, but John's parents live too, and John I seed to-day a sitting with his head upon his hand resting, and thinking of his poor young wife and his friends at home, afore the ice cold came and touched him, and turned him into death."

The good old sailor rubbed the back of his seal-skin glove across his eyes. His companions were silent. "Yes," he continued, "not that I'm sorry for John. I've no doubt he had a hard struggle; but, thank God, he is at peace. Peace and calm rest upon him and with him. If he could rise up from yonder wave he wouldn't see his own true love again, but his spirit knows and loves her now. And if so be as I do get home, I shall tell the old people how John Truman died sitting at his post and waiting quietly for the summons to go aloft."

The old seaman rubbed his moist eyes as he spoke and took off his fur cap and pointed upwards. His gray hair streamed upon the cold night wind by the light of the binnacle, and made him look not unlike John Truman himself. "Give me the articles, cap'en," said he; "I think I may constitoot myself residooary legatee." He smiled faintly when he took them.

"I am not sorry, Cap'en Seth," he said, "that I went on this voyage with you; I kinder thought as I should meet with John, and now I have, and now my mind is at ease."

He looked down to the tin as he spoke and re-read the words on the lid. "All alone in the ice," he said. "Poor fellow, all alone! Well, well, there may be others as are not quite all alone. There may be others as have lost all their boats, but have not lost heart, and are now abandoned on the shores o' that there open sea the doctor speaks of. 'Bout ship, cap'en, 'bout ship, and let us find 'em; steer away for the open Arctic sea!'"

[It is, perhaps, needless to assure the reader that these chapters were written long before Captain M'Clintock's discovery of the remains of the Arctic crews was made public. — H. F.]

# CHAPTER XVIII.



THE sight of the dead man, frozen to death with cold, his sudden disappearance from home, and the little story of his life, gave a new impulse to our wish to find the great captain whose resting-place had so long baffled all attempts at discovery, and we set out afresh, all hoping, like the doctor, to gain the "great unfrozen sea."

For weeks and weeks we bumped about, now steering up one inlet, now up another; now blocked up by the ice, now frozen in ; at one time a huge block of ice was frozen to our stern and we drifted with it at the will of the current, here and there.  Long and melancholy was our voyage. We made little way, and at last the real ills of the Arctic regions came upon us.  Our crew was attacked by scurvy, and we had no fresh meat. We had served out to the men lime-juice and acids, anti-scorbutic medicines and drinks, but we could only ward off the attacks of the scourge.

When I fell ill with it I was oppressed with a deadly lassitude, a weakness accompanied with a loathing of life. I wished only to sleep, to forget everything and quietly to fall into the sea and disappear, as the poor dead mariner had done.

Our doctor fought nobly against the disease, and some bears and white foxes, which were caught by the crew, gave us a little animal food, and served us till we weathered the worst of it. I, amongst the rest, grew well—youth was in my favour—when, worse than all, Captain Seth Smith, the doctor, and the first-lieutenant fell ill.

We were about Lancaster Sound when this disaster came upon us, and we beat about there for some time. At last Bobus and the others came and told the sick captain that we could get no further, and that it would be better to run the ship up one of the ice-openings as far as we could, and then to make her fast and to winter there. There were tears in the poor fellow's eyes, as he told me afterwards of his determination. He had given up all hopes of the open sea.

"We shall be warmer in the snow, Ned," said he; "and when perhaps we get the doctor and the cap'en out of the ship, so as to have a little exercise, they will be better."

"Perhaps so, Bobus; but I wish we could find the open sea. Sir John is very likely there."

"May be, may be," sighed he.

"Cheer up, Bobus," said I; "we may get to

a convenient spot; some of the Esquimaux may visit us, and we may sledge on for miles and miles."

Bobus shook his head, and looked at the black, frowning sky, and pointed to the giant form of a drifting berg.

> " When we sailors go to sea,
> Drearily, oh, drearily !"

he sung out. It was the very faintest ghost of a song that I ever heard him sing. As he sung a gust of wind drove the snow into our faces—a drifting, cutting snow, unlike our more southern snow-storms; snow which, like hot sand, blinded and burnt in its intense cold. I shut my eyes.

" Hallo !" shouted Bobus, " you'll have your ear off, Ned, if you don't look out."

The lower part of my fur cap had got disarranged and the wind had lifted it up, so as to expose one of my ears. In a moment it was frozen. The external cartilage was jaundiced, and of the consistency of tallow; it did not pain me, it was dead. Bobus, however, set it right in a few minutes by catching up a handful of the drift snow and rubbing it violently. Then, with an intense pain, sensation came back, and my ear was recovered. This was the first time I had been so frozen, but others had had their noses, ears, and tongues touched and withered by the frost.

The stern courage of the crew satisfied the captain; he determined, like a bold sailor as he was, not to give up the search whilst he had life. So, in obedience to his wishes, we were driven up an open inlet as far as we could get, the ice saws and the axes of the men set to work, a dock cut in the ice, in which the Lively Bessy righted, the block of ice being cut off her stern, and in which she was frozen up for many weeks.

Oh, the dreariness of that northern winter! I shall never forget it. We dug away the snow near the ship and made ourselves huts. We went excursions over the ice and sat patiently for hours near the breathing holes of seals, to see if when they rose we could strike them, but we were not very successful. We hunted bears, and now and then killed one, and brought the flesh home in triumph to our poor sick captain and doctor.

We made huge fires with some drift wood we had found frozen there, and burnt seal oil and bear's fat upon them, in hopes that some wandering Esquimaux might see the smoke or reflection, and hasten to us in his sledge. In this we were not disappointed. One day Bobus and Pilbeam, who were never very good friends, came running in with such excited faces that we were sure some very good luck had happened to them, that both should feel so pleased. We were not wrong. Pilbeam held up both arms and made signs long before we could hear his voice, and when we could just distinguish the manly tones of Mr. John Bobus, the Arctic wind brought to us these accents —" The Esquimaux! the Esquimaux! the Esquimaux—!!! "

All was then bustle and preparation, for in those far-distant scenes we were ready to welcome the approach of two or three savages, with as great an interest as in England we should have felt for the greatest prince or the kindest old friend. All social distinctions were levelled. The savage was, after all, a man, one of God's creatures, like ourselves; his dirt, his greasy skin, his thievish habits, his ignorance, were all forgotten, and we were ready to welcome him like a brother.

# CHAPTER XIX.



THE captain, who seemed to be recovering, but very slowly, forgot his langour, and the doctor, who was far worse than he, turned round on the couch upon which he was lying, wrapped up in furs and seal skins, when they heard the words of Bobus, repeated by many voices. "Bring them here," said the captain.

The doctor rose languidly and fumbled about for his vocabulary, and staggered to the door of the hut to meet our new visitors.

They were some time before they came, Bobus and his companion having sighted them afar off. But our impatience was not to be of very long duration. A little slightly built sledge in which sat a man and his wife, and to which were attached six dogs, soon glided up to us, and, seeing the signs of the captain, the Esquimaux reined in their dogs and alighted. The animals perceiving that their work was done, sat down in

8

their harness, blinking at us with their small eyes, and eagerly snapping at pieces of the offal of the bears and seals which the men threw them.

Our two new friends, for in those lone regions we called, aye, and we *felt* as we called, every human creature a friend, were very ignorant or very cunning. I do not think they knew much. They drank the rum and accepted the gifts of the captain, but they answered very little to the doctor, and shook their heads when he spoke to them.

" They must understand, doctor, ask them whether they have seen any ships like ours, and where ?"

The doctor did so, and an extra glass of rum served to open the heart of the lady, a little creature scarcely five feet high, with long greasy black hair, bead-like eyes and a face the colour of Russian tallow; she blinked and winked at her lord and master, and nudged him.

" We shall get the secret out of them," said the captain ; " Ned bring me some paper, a chalk pencil, and a map of this place."

I did so at once. " Now, doctor, now ask them again." He took a common little pistol, put a cap on the nipple and exploded it, and gave it to the lady as a present. She touched her forehead with it, smiled, and laid it in the fur-covered lap of her lord. That gentleman smiled.

" Have you seen any ships?" asked the doctor.

The male Esquimaux answered " no," but he made us understand there were others of his nation who had.

" Where?"

The doctor spread the map before us, and the Esquimaux after a long and attentive study seemed to understand it, and with his finger traced a line further north than where we were, to a place, indeed, where no civilised being had yet been and returned.

" By Jingo!" cried the doctor, " it is where I said, the open sea."

" Your theory is madness," muttered the captain, " how can there be an open sea farther north than this, whilst every wave here is blocked with ice, and your gun-barrel, should you touch it with your naked hand, would burn and blister you with cold?"

" Nature is mysterious enough, captain," returned the doctor, " the earth flattened at the poles may have a warmer zone of air there, let us see."

" Ay, *let* us see," returned the captain, bitterly. " We shall never get there, doctor; I feel worn out and disappointed. I shall never find those brave fellows."

" Wait, Captain Smith, wait. Patience and faith go a very long way, a long way, indeed."

The captain sat down, sadly; the male Esqui-

maux taking in his clumsy fingers the chalk pencil, and, without lifting it from the paper, drawing
a rough scheme of the place, and the ship where
she was; and farther on, over the ice, a quantity
of men lying down and with their eyes closed.

"Asleep," asked the doctor in their language.
The Esquimaux smiled and shook his head.

"Not far from here, captain," said the doctor.
"Not very far, that is. We could get there in a
sledge."

"Ask them if we can, and settle with them
how to do so."

This was done, after some haggling by the
doctor, and the Esquimaux agreed to bring, by
the next morning, two sledges and a guide to
convey a party of us to the place. Curiously, the
captain, who was by far the strongest man of the
two, was unable to go with us, but the doctor's
enthusiasm conquered his disease, and, wrapped
up in furs, he was quite ready to accompany us,
when, in accordance with their word, two male
Esquimaux, with two sledges of six dogs each,
came for us next day.

I say next "day," because our instruments
so measured the time in a three months' night.
Light, we had none, but from the Aurora Borealis
and the moon, which gave us a bright twilight.

Wrapped up in furs, the doctor, Bobus, and six
others including myself, seated ourselves in the
dog-sledges, and were drawn rapidly over the

rough ice. We had proceeded almost in one direction about twenty miles, when the Esquimaux ceased beating and encouraging their dogs, and made signs that we had reached our destination.

A bleak bare place it was. Snow and ice all around, and just before us a bare peak towering up many feet into the sky, and covered with perpetual snow. At its base lay, the doctor said, a kind of shore, which however in our Arctic winter was not to be distinguished from the frozen sea beyond it. Beneath this crag was a snow-house, and beyond that a small pillar covered with snow and ice, formed of preserved-meat cans, piled up curiously and carefully.

The house certainly contained some vestiges of being inhabited—a woollen stocking, two gloves which had been, as it were, laid out to dry, and which remained undisturbed, with a stone laid on each palm to keep the glove from being blown away. But beyond these, which undoubtedly were English, there was no sign nor record of the last inhabitants.

"Ah," sighed the doctor, who was full of enthusiasm, "we have come too late to be of any use here. But " and he turned to the Esquimaux, " where are the men asleep?"

Our guides made a sign to them that they quite appreciated and understood the doctor, and bidding us follow them, led us to the rear of the snow hut. There, sure enough, were the men asleep. Twenty little hillocks, side by side, some with a rude cross above them, showed us where the poor fellows lay. The Esquimaux stooping down scraped away the snow; and there, in his blue cloth jacket, looking very little different from the day upon which he had closed his eyes in the eternal sleep, lay one poor Jack tar. The men had lighted a fire in the hut, and the Esquimaux ran and fetched some boiling water and poured it on the face of one of the dead. The mask of ice gave way for an instant, and showed us our own countryman; there, indeed, were the quiet strong English features :

> "There was a hardness in his cheek,
> There was a hardness in his eye,
> As if the man had fixed his face
> In many a solitary place,
> Against the wind and open sky !"

But the hardness was of trial, of trouble, weariness and danger, and the stony look was that of death.

# CHAPTER XX.



WE returned from that bleak shore without
having proceeded towards the discovery of our
lost countrymen one foot. We learnt afterwards
that those dead seamen had once formed part of
the crew of a whaler, that had been forced to take
refuge far up the ice, and whose provisions and
ammunition being gone, had died one by one,
without hope and without help.

From such a fate Heaven preserve all true
mariners !

When we came back we found the captain
worse. He had suffered himself to lose all heart
and hope, and without those a man is worth
little. Hope is the guiding star of us all. Directly we lose that we lose faith in ourselves, and
next in God's good providence. Happily, this
extreme was never the case with Captain Seth
Smith, for a more true-hearted man never existed. He begged, to the last, the doctor to

read prayers to him, and talked with resignation on his approaching death.

"Bury me," he would say, "bury me on the frozen shore, along with those poor fellows there who died as hopelessly as I do."

"No, cap'en, don't say so," old Bobus would murmur; "don't 'ee say so: cheer up, good heart, cheer up; when Christmas has turned we shall be waiting for long days instead o' long nights."

"The long, long nights," muttered the poor captain—"the long, dark, dreary nights, with no change; nothing, except the cracking and swooning of the ice, the tick of the ship clock, the striking of the bell, and with no light, except the flaring lanthorn, and the moon throwing deep shadows all around."

"We shall git back," said Bobus, making haste to be desperately merry, "we shall git back, and talk over these hardships, and make light o' em, as true sailors do."

"Make light of 'em, get back!" cried the captain, striking his hand down on his oaken table, "get back! and whom shall we bring back, eh? Shall we bring old brave Sir John back? shall we bring back his gallant crew? shall we bring help or heart to them who now stand upon the shore of that iceless sea the doctor speaks of, stretching their thin arms to'rd old England, and looking across the water towards the south, where old England lies, from which they fondly hope some help will come?"

Captain Seth's head fell upon his shoulder as he said this, and the tears rose to his poor sick eyes as he raised his thin hand to his face to hide them.

Old Bobus coughed hoarsely to hide his emotion, and turned away.

"Have you ever read the story of Admiral Hosier," said the captain to me, and then he answered his question himself. "The admiral was sent out, as he thought, to take Portobello from the Spaniards; but some state policy, some cunning diplomatic craft, had caused his sealed orders, when he opened them, to condemn him to perpetual inaction. He made an appearance before the town, but did not attack it, and the unhealthy place and the disappointment broke his heart. He and two-thirds of his brave seamen died, and were dropped into the ocean before the town. He was killed, sir," cried the captain, earnestly, "killed by State craft, for the British sailor who is sent to do a thing and fails, never should return alive."

Old Bobus looked up with glistening eyes, and, being entirely in accordance with the captain, muttered "Hear! hear!" probably from some distant idea that it was proper to do so. I hastened to answer.

"Only, sir, when the accomplishment is *pos-*

*sible.* Man cannot do that which is utterly beyond his powers; he cannot fight against the ice, he cannot control the cold, he cannot conquer the works of God!"

The captain burst into tears. "That's it, my boy," said he, "that's it. One cannot conquer snow, frost, and winter, and fields, nay countries, full of ice. They have conquered me. Leave me."

Captain Seth staggered back to his bed. We hastened to send the doctor to him when he came (the doctor was now recovered), but he was long gone beyond *his* power, and he sank quietly to sleep, a few days after he had had that conversation with us, a victim to a deep-rooted and disappointed hope.

We buried Captain Seth Smith upon that bleak shore which the Esquimaux had found for us a long way off our ship, and we put up a handsome cross at his head, and at his feet a slab of oak, upon which we carved his history, the name of his ship, and the service he had died in.

The second officer took the command of the "Lively Bessy," no longer lively now, and the doctor and others tried to cheer us through the winter. It was of little use. The men were disorganised, and we laid one or two more beside the captain before we were released from that lonely shore.

During the whole of this time the character of

the Cornishman, Pilbeam, presented itself in no very amiable light. He was very jealous of Bobus, who was now third officer, and tried to excite discontent and insubordination in the others. Bobus had often to threaten punishment for insubordination, and once to carry his threat into force, upon which Pilbeam vowed vengeance, and swore one or two dreadful oaths.

My dread at this time, I remember, was that this man should set fire to the ship and leave us all to perish, and I had indeed some reason for my fear, for the man had more than once talked of the possibility of a fire happening, and there being no water to quench it, I was so convinced of his evil intentions that I mentioned it to Bobus.

"Bless you," said he, "bless you, Mas'r Ned, he dursn't do it. Don't 'ee see if we suspected him on it we should hang him right out; and if he succeeded he would leave himself to our fate, at least. Oh no, he," and here Bobus gave a look of intense disgust in the direction of the sailor; "he is a cool-blooded fellow and can wait, and will wait I know, till we get nearer home."

Bobus was right.

Time came at last when we were to be relieved from our bondage. I cannot hope to convey to any one the dull, mournful, melancholy which seizes the spirits of those who pass an Arctic winter. There is something so inexpressibly wearying and dull that I do not wonder at many growing ill and dying. It was only by constantly keeping my mind employed, by reading and writing, that I myself kept from despair. As for that wonderful old Bobus, he kept up through mere force of character, being as regular in every duty when fast bound in the ice, as when upon the open sea.

I was out one day trying to shoot a bear, accompanied by one of the men and by Pilbeam. The Cornish seaman never liked me, for he saw that I was too much of a favorite with Bobus. The latter had charged me to be very particular in keeping away from the muzzle of Pilbeam's gun, "'Ces," said he, "he might make a mistake, and if he did there would be an end of my little Billee."

I promised to be very careful in that way, and away we went.

We soon started a very fine bear, whose tracks we had noticed prowling round the remains of a seal we had placed for a bait some hours ago. When she saw us she started off at a shambling gallop, and till then I really had no idea that bears could run so fast. However, we managed over the rough and broken ice to keep up with it, and I did not fire for some time, hoping that the bear would lead us to her cave, for it was my ambition to find a couple of cubs or so, one of which I wanted to tame and to take home.

Mrs. Bruin was, however, fast giving us the slip, but I being lighter than my comrades got on far in advance of them, and then as she turned round a hummock of ice I fired. My ball hit her in the leg, just above the hock, and lamed her; she turned and sprung back towards me with much fury, and I, in my hurry to reload my piece, dropped my ramrod from the fingers of my thick seal skin gloves. The moment comes, thought I, for the death struggle, and I clubbed my gun determined to dash the butt end right in the mouth of the bear. She seemed, however, to have changed her mind as to the attack, for finding that her wound pained her she turned round and bit furiously at her leg, tearing away the fur and extracting the ball, which dropped on the ice, and which I afterwards picked up. Then being more at ease she again made towards me, and quicker than I can speak, for all this seemed but to take a moment, I saw her within a few yards of me. With the strength of despair I thrust forth my gun like a battering ram, full at her mouth, when, at the same time, a ball came whistling past my head, so near that I could hear it, aye, almost feel it through my fur cap, and true as Tell's arrow, entered the eye of the she bear and crashed through her brain. With one great convulsive effort she threw up her paws and fell dead, and Pilbeam's huge, awkward form stood over me, looking at me and my prostrate foe with a somewhat triumphant grin, mingled, I thought, also with considerable disappointment.

" Wal," said he, " Mas'r Ned, I saved your life anyhows there."

" And I thank you for it, Pilbeam," said I ; " the prize belongs to you."

" Oh, never mind that, we shall all eat our lot on it, I dessay," said he ; " only now mind me."

" Yes," said I.

" Are ye all attention ?"

" Yes," I repeated.

" I saved your life, Mas'r Ned," he again said, solemnly ; " mind and remember that some of these days, will you ?"

" I shall never forget it," said I.

" Very good," he said, " and now let us carry along our game."

This was much easier to say than to do. Carrying was out of the question, for the bear was nearly as big as a young bull ; we therefore placed under the bear a kind of light sledge formed of the staves of an old barrel bound together and having staves put sideways, so as to form the sides of the sledge. Having bound our bear firmly upon this, we all three of us harnessed ourselves to it, and trotted away merrily over the ice.

It was getting rather dark, but in those regions there is always a kind of twilight reflection, when Pilbeam, who was pulling with the strength of a giant, and who was our leader, started back with a great cry of horror and alarm.

"Stop!" he cried, "lay by."

"What's the matter?"

"Matter," cried he, "we are within a mile of the ship, and we shall never get to her; lay by, my men, and look there."

We had stopped the sledge and ran to where he pointed, and there, sure enough, right across our path and extending to the right and the left, lay a vast yawning gulf, a crack in the ice, with the black water rushing under it.

"You can see the current now," said Pilbeam; "that's all done since we went out this mornin', and if the ice has begun to move God knows where we may be a driftin' to. I've heerd of men as had drifted south'ard on a bit of ice until it had all gone to pieces, and they had been lost."

"We can jump it," said the other man.

"Try, Jack," returned Pilbeam, sitting down disconsolately at the brink. "By all that's good it moves still."

The yawning chasm did indeed grow wider. Setting the other man to run one way whilst I went in the opposite direction, and Pilbeam sat down watching the gulf stream, we explored the extent of our enemy, the chasm. It was vast, as Pilbeam supposed, and I soon found out that in my direction it ran in a directly opposite direction to the ship.  I therefore turned back and, running swiftly, overtook the other seaman.

"We are lost, lost for ever, Mas'r Ned," cried that poor fellow; "howsomever, I do not care so much for myself as for you.  What shall us do?"

"Hope still; they may send for us from the ship."

"Ah, but things are so sudden in this dreadful climate; an' to think of the old bear, too.  Well, we can live on her for a bit; we must scrape ourselves a snow hut."

"Live, I hope so," said I.  I had scarcely said the word than a gust of wind brought a cloud of sharply pointed snow and fragments of ice into our faces, cutting us like points of pen-knives. "The only way for us to do that is to toss up who cuts open the bear and gets inside it, till the aid comes from the ship.  Such a night as this on the ice will not make a man long lived. Hurrah! there it is at last."

I had looked down as I spoke, and there, surely enough, was some kind of hope for us. The crack in the ice took an angular turn, sudden and sharp, and ran up in the direction of the ship.

"Shipmet, ahoy!" shouted my companion to Pilbeam; come along, and bring along the bear."

Pilbeam heard the words, for the wind lay towards him, and in a minute or so, came joyfully along, pulling the bear-sledge with him.

"I couldn't think of leaving her," said he, "arter all the trouble we have had. What cheer, shipmet?"

"A little," said I. "We may reach home yet."

"No," said he, looking along the ice, and shading his eyes with his hands, "not quite, Mas'r Ned; but it's better than nothing."

Away, therefore, we toiled, following the banks of the chasm, till it brought us within about half a mile of the ship, and then suddenly turned the other way, wider far than before.

"Now for the signal of distress," said I, as I fired my gun; "we must keep this up as long as our ammunition lasts, and let us hope they will hear us."

So we fired off our guns several times, till at last we heard an answer from the ship. We afterwards learnt that the ice had also begun to move round her, and the crew, guessing our situation, placed the smallest boat they had on a sledge, and in a few moments we were relieved from our horrible suspense by seeing a quantity of jolly Jack Tars, fur-clad indeed, and looking as different as possible from the received notion of Jack Tars, running towards us, ready to relieve us from our situation.

I need not say that Bobus was at the head of them. I need not tell the reader how rejoiced he was to find us. He even wrung his old antagonist by the hand, and told him that he was glad to see him safe and sound. Pilbeam grinned a ghastly smile, and said nothing; but one can imagine what he would have given, to have had his old enemy alone upon that dreary track of ice.

"Bahr and all," cried Pilbeam, as they hoisted the huge creature into the boat, "bahr and all. You see, Mas'r Ned, I was a good shot; there is the place where my bullet entered." He pointed, as he spoke, to a huge spot of frozen blood in the eye of the animal. The blood had run somewhat, and had trickled down upon its white skin. Bobus placed his hand underneath the left shoulder of the animal—there was not even a lingering portion of warmth.

"Cold as ice!" he cried; "cold as ice! Ah, Ned, animal warmth don't last long in these regions. It is well as we leaves them. The iceflaws will grow larger and wider, and then we shall sail down one on 'em like a river in a frozen land, and go southward toward merry England."

"So be it," said I; "I long to reach her shore. The voyage has not done what it promised, and has failed; not from want of endeavour, after all, though."

"Failed!" said Pilbeam, as we touched the opposite shore of the ice, "Failed! well, if so be we've failed, others have too. Ho for England, eh! Well, I hopes we shall all reach it,

Mas'r Ned; but there's many a slip 'twixt the cup and the lip."

Bobus and I, talking over matters afterwards, when some of the last portions of our bear were stewing down in the copper, over the galley fire, recalled these words and the look which accompanied them.

"I don't like that 'ere Pilbeam," said he, thoughtfully; "if I was aboard a man-o'-war I would have him tied up to the gratings, and give him a round dozen for his looks. I wish he was rid of the ship."

# CHAPTER XXI.

THE DOCTOR—PILBEAM'S PROPHECY.

UNSUCCESSFUL as had been our voyage, it had yet brought its lessons to me. I was much stronger, and better in health; I had gained in will and determination; I had learned to trust in myself, and I had grown used to command. This was, to me at least, so much clear gain. I doubt whether success teaches self-reliance half so well as misfortune and rebuffs, after all.

I found also that everything I knew was of use to me. Knowledge was indeed power, and I saw that by a quiet, retiring behaviour, I gained a great deal with the crew. They believed, indeed, that I knew much more than I really did, because I never professed to know too much.

Retired also from the world, I had an opportunity of studying men's characters, and of judging them when brought closely under my eye. I found a small world in that ship. The little crew had its distinctions as plainly marked as if the thirty souls that manned her were three millions.

I was very fortunate, also, in meeting with the doctor, who was not only a good and a benevolent, but also a learned, man. He had that best kind of learning, which is humble and quiet; seeking only that which feeds it, and not endeavouring to establish new theories to controvert or overthrow established truths. Doctor Stewart, to say the truth, was crotchety. He had an immense number of original ideas upon most subjects, but those ideas were always full of religion, founding everything upon God's power, and believing that man could do almost anything, but only by God's permission. I wish that all men thought so soundly as Doctor Charles James Stewart, the last descendant, as he declared, of the unfortunate race of kings of that name.

His kindness to the men was continual. He watched them and nursed them as if he were a woman, and although it was with a very bitter pang that, just upon the return of spring, he had to bring back his little ship and scurvy-stricken crew, yet he was as ready to have faced the dangers over again, and to have gone back on the day after he touched old England, as any one could be. He had grown also fond of the vessel, and would talk of her again ploughing the northern ocean, again breasting the ice, again ascending the streams which ran through tracks of frozen land, until she had penetrated into that sea of dreams—the iceless sea.

"Ah," said Pilbeam to me, when one day at Reckavik, on our homeward voyage, I mentioned to him the wishes of the doctor, "Ah! he's a clever man, he is; a main clever fellow, no doubt; but this here ship will never see the frozen ocean agin, mark my words."

There was the same ugly look in the Cornishman's eyes as he said this as I had before observed. His croaking prophecies began to have some effect upon me. I looked at the old vessel somewhat as one would look at a doomed ship, but I did not long indulge this feeling. I was too young to be a friend to foolish and melancholy presentiments, but I well know that I wished heartily to be rid of Pilbeam, as, to say the least, his presence was very undesirable.

# CHAPTER XXII.

A NIGHT ATTACK ON MY FRIEND—I SAVE HIS<br>LIFE.

WE, as I have said, touched at Iceland, took in fresh water and some fresh meat, gave the crew a run on shore, and then set sail homeward. Unsuccessful though we were, our hearts beat with a wild joy at the mere mention of England. It was always called home was that grand land, full of historic interest to me, of home ties and affection to all of us. Old Bobus grew a smart man again, and when on getting into a milder latitude, we left off our furs and winter clothing, and could talk without fear of having our tongues frozen or our noses bitten off by Jack Frost, we enjoyed ourselves as well as our limited means would allow; but, after all, enjoyment lies not so much in the means, as in the occasion and in the feelings.

After leaving Iceland we made for the northern isles of Scotland, intending to run down the German Ocean and enter the port of Hull, the doctor and chief officer having friends there, and being anxious to report themselves at home. The ship was then to make sail for London, wherefrom it was settled between Bobus and myself, that I should set off to visit Doctor Leatherby, and that he should come down and rejoin me there; I being anxious, if the doctor were willing, to devote a few years to a seafaring life. Bobus had grown so fond of me, that he said, his mind being now at ease concerning the loss of his brother-in-law, he should just see that the old couple were all safe at their moorings, and then sail in company with me.

With all these speculations in my head, I was one night on the watch, when I saw a long figure come from the fore part of the vessel where the men lay, and go down the companion aft. Something struck me as very peculiar about this, and I thought I recognised the figure of Pilbeam. I immediately spoke to my mate on the watch to keep a sharp look out, and ran down after the figure.

I was just in time to see a man enter the cabin of Bobus, and to watch the knife gleam in the lamp-light as he cut down the hammock of Bobus, at the head. There was a huge iron-bound chest just beneath the head of the hammock, and it was evidently part of the plan that Bobus should have struck his head against it, and have been stunned by the fall, so that if necessary, the Cornish sailor could spring upon him and finish the work.

But it was not so. Bobus lumbered out of his hammock like a heavy old seaman as he was, but seeing the knife glitter, I had sprung with all my force upon Pilbeam, and caught at his wrist. The attack had driven him down upon one knee, just at the very best point where Bobus could fall, which was upon us both, so that we all three came with some weight upon the cabin floor. The result was, therefore, comic instead of tragic, and my friend's life was saved.

He was up in an instant, fancying that the ship had capsized, or something of that sort, but immediately he perceived us he called out " avast there, shipmet! What are you after?" and making use of a dozen sailor-like objurgations. Pilbeam rose, too, confused and desperate. He more than once endeavoured to throw away the knife, but I held on with both hands to his wrist.

" Wall, Josh Pilbeam, and what do you do in my cabin, at this hour; and what do you do, Ned Paget?" said Bobus.

He had placed his big form at the door, with wonderful quickness, and held in his right hand a pistol, the muzzle of which was towards us both. Pilbeam turned pale, and trembled.

" Please, sir," said I, touching my hat to him, as to my superior officer, " please, sir, I was on watch, and saw this man steal down towards your cabin, with a knife in his hand. I followed him, was just in time to see him cut down your hammock. I sprang upon him, and in preventing your fall—"

" Saved my life, Ned," said he quietly and simply, " and I thankee for it—"

" As for you, shipmet," he continued, looking at Pilbeam with great disdain, " you're about one of the worst lots as ever I eat the Queen's biscuit with ; it will not look very sailor-like, nor very British-like either, when they say as how aboard one of the vessels sent out for the rescue of a brave seaman, one of the crew was so murderous a lubber that he attempted the life of his superior officer, and got shot ; but it will be told so in old England, mark my words. I have caught you with the red hand, as they say in Scotland. All your tackle and gear proclaim you to be pirate, and you shall meet a pirate's fate. Stand aside, Ned Paget, whilst I put a bullet through that traitor, there ; a murderous dog."

Bobus cocked the pistol, and at the sharp click I saw Pilbeam turn pale, and tremble ; his knees smote each other, and dark rings seemed to form round each of his eyes. We were in a high latitude, and the cabin door being open it was not too warm for any of us, but yet the culprit was in a great perspiration, so much so, that great drops of sweat poured off his brow.

" Come," continued Bobus, calmly, " I never

save in battle, when all's fair, 'cos you must look out for yourself, I never sent a man unprepared to his last account. I'll just give you whilst I count two hundred, time to mutter a prayer."

"For Heaven's sake," cried the culprit, falling on his knees, "for Heaven's sake spare me, shipmet."

The only answer he met was the stern one from the lips of Bobus, of "one—two—three—" he had commenced the death count.

Pilbeam wrung his hands, looked at the knife, to see if by any chance there was a possibility of his gaining it and springing on his executioner, but the eye of Bobus followed his, and his foot kicked the weapon, contemptuously, to a farther distance from him.

He had reached fifty.

"Shipmet!" cried the man in a voice of agony, "I sailed two voyages with you before, and never lifted a hand against you. I would n't now 'a done it, but that you beat and cowed me afore the whole crew, and flesh and blood can't stand that."

—"Ninety and one, two, three, four," proceeded the inexorable voice of Bobus. *Mine* refused its office. I would have pleaded for him, with all my power, but could not do it. My tongue seemed glued to the roof of my mouth, and, all the time, the moments were flying so quickly, although each moment in passing seemed an age.

" I'll do anything you wish," cried the wretched man, " if you will only spare my life. I'll be your servant ; I will watch you while you sleep !"

Bobus smiled, grimly, as he heard the words.

—One hundred and one—two—three—" You'd better leave your palaver, shipmet; now's the time for you to remember your prayers, if so be you recollect any from school, are paid attention to the chaplain on Sundays,—four—five—"

" Bobus," cried I, at last, touched by the abject misery of the great fellow who grovelled on the floor, and stretched out his hands, blindly, as if to grasp the feet of his executioner, " Bobus ! did I do you any service just now, in coming into the cabin ?"

" You saved my life, boy," he returned quickly, and but for a moment interrupting the count.

" Then as a return give me his. Give him up to justice in England, if you like, let him be confined till he gets ashore, and then let the laws deal with him. Do not take his life with your own hands. I am witness of the justice of it, but what will the world say, what will your conscience say, if you refuse him mercy ?"

" Aye," groaned the wretch, " what will the law in England say for taking a man's life?— spare me !"

" There be queer things done at sea," said Bobus, giving up his count, " but the superior officer, if he finds a man prowling about his cabin, may shoot him like a dog. Aye, and does do so. But you, you have gained your point, lad. You have saved mine, take his, but ware hawk, ware hawk; if ever you come to grief through that foolish quality of mercy, remember Jack Bobus."

"Get up, man, go to your berth, and I'll dispose of you in the mornin'. Take this barker, Paget," said he, "and see this fellow safely stowed, and then come back to me." He gave me his pistol.

When I returned I found the stern old sailor on his knees, thanking God for his deliverance and praying for me. He would have done the same, he said, if he had only that moment cleared the corpse of that villain out of the cabin, where it should have laid had it not been for me. He gave me a thousand grateful thanks for watching over him, and with a perfectly solemn and serious way, which he believed, I fancy, legal, declared that henceforward, so long as I wished it, we should sail together, that he had no relations for whom he particularly cared, and that if I would consent, I should become his son and heir.

I thanked him a hundred times, and accepted the filial office with much pleasure, so far as I could; for in good truth I had grown attached to a seafaring life, and loved old Bobus like an uncle, if not like a father.

"And now, Ned," said he, "let's turn in and go to sleep. All's right on deck you say. Aye,

aye, all's right on deck, but it won't be all right in ship till that villain is out, and so ware hawk, ware hawk."

Repeating this very solemnly, he left me to go upon deck and muse upon the strange scene I had just witnessed.

# CHAPTER XXIII.



WE were on a smooth sea, and had a prosperous wind, and in our slow sailing vessel expected to reach England in a week. The men did not know the extent of Pilbeam's guilt, for had they done so, they would, I think, have there and then taken vengeance upon him; he was confined down in a spare berth formed out of an old corner when they made the store-room, and being actually below the wave edge of the vessel it was not a very pleasant place, but Bobus had, of course, reported the attack upon himself to the chief officer, and he, willing to look upon the matter as a drunken offence, not as an attempt at murder, yet would not listen to any suggestion of a mitigated punishment whilst Pilbeam was in the ship. The rest of the crew, who certainly had no love for their comrade, were by no means unwilling to get rid of him, and in a week he was hardly spoken of, save when his rations were taken to him in his place of durance.

A week passed over our heads, and we had sailed by Faroe and the Shetland Isles, glided by the Orkneys, and dropped down into the North Sea. I was walking the deck with Bobus, when he called my attention to the way in which the gulls flew about our prow and stern. The sea birds were so close to the water, that the still and quiet sea gave back a momentary reflection of their white wings, a reflection which looked all the brighter as the sky above was dark and lowering.

"I tell ye what, Ned," said Bobus, "if I could get you and me out of this vessel I would. I wouldn't sail in it another four-and-twenty hours. We oughter have shot that villain and chucked him overboard, but because we didn't a storm has followed the ship, and she will have it to night."

He looked aloft, and gave orders that even the little sail which we then carried should be taken in. "Make everything taut above," he said, "we shall have it to night, look there!"

The lazy clouds, which seemed to mass themselves so firmly behind us, to pack themselves one upon another like the drift hummocks we had passed through, assumed, in the rays of the setting sun a deep red, angry tint, and bulged out at us their swollen cheeks, as if they were so many furious enemies.

"I never see the likes of that, and many a

time I *have* seen it," ejaculated my companion, "but I know we shall have it sooner or later, it may be this moment."

"But this stout old ship," said I to Bobus, "will stand anything and ride through any storm. She is half solid, you know."

"Aye, aye, lad; the young ones will teach the old ones, will they? I tell you, Ned, that if she were as solid as this block of timber, as solid as can be, she would not live even in smooth water, if so be she is, as I suspects she is, a *doomed ship*.

The face of the old sailor was so very serious as he said this that, although I looked up with a smile, I found no response. "I do not believe in doomed ships, Bobus," said I.

"Nor I," said the doctor, catching my words, and coming upon us suddenly. "I don't believe in doomed ships. In fact, I have not made up my mind about luck yet, but all sailors believe in it. What is luck? None of us know exactly, and yet——"

He paused as if puzzled.

"Some catch the fish and some don't," returned Bobus, in continuation. "You are a learned man, doctor; I am a poor sailor. You give *reasons*, I answer with *facts*. You may charter two North-sea whalers, each good ships, manned with good men, commanded by good captains. They shall both leave the port at the same time, and yet, on their return, after a voyage to the same waters, and staying out the same time, one will have two thousand tons of oil and five whales, and the other shall have captured only a few seals. How do you account for that? Reckon up the log as cleverly as you can, doctor, you can't always account for the reckoning."

"True, quite true," answered the doctor; " but yet, Paget, you remember that true and beautiful passage of Shakespeare you read in my cabin last night :

> 'The fault, dear Brutus, is not in the stars,
> But in *ourselves*, that we are thus and thus.'

"Ah !" retorted Bobus, shaking his head wisely, " that is all very well, but whosoever wrote that had never sailed in a doomed ship. I have."

As he said the words " doomed ship," the thunder broke out in a sudden clap, not like one hears on land, but sharper and louder by far. It was followed by a succession of reports, like a continuous discharge of artillery; and as we looked to the waters in our wake we saw them, at a short distance, boiling and surging, the billows lashed into a sudden foam, and seemingly coming with full rush after us. It was indeed so. In a moment the storm was upon us. The Lively Bessy was struck suddenly, and gave a great pitch forward and a roll with a tremble all over, and then started away before the storm, borne along by the tempest as a frightened horse might start away with its rider.

"By the way," said the doctor, who was holding fast by the shrouds as the storm of hail, rain, sea-water, and wind, swept by us, "you seem as if you would have a material proof of your theory." His cap had been carried away, and his long grizzled hair was floating in the wind. "It seems as if we were going to have a rough night of it; I had rather be in that northern, iceless sea, than here. I will just go down to my cabin."

"Aye, aye, sir," said the other, all alive with excitement. "The ship stands it well. She may roll and toss for hours, but so long as we keep her off the rocks we are safe. Keep on deck, Paget, and just see what a storm is. Never mind a drenching. Sea-water never harmed any man yet."

The doctor had gone to his cabin. Our second in command, now since Captain Seth's death our captain, rushed on deck, and seeing all right above, nodded approvingly to Bobus, buttoned his coat, pulled down his cap over his eyes, and prepared for the worst. He had a battered speaking-trumpet in his hand, and walked about anxiously. Now and then he looked at his watch, and, following his example, I did so at mine. It was but four in the afternoon, or, as we should say, five bells, yet the doctor had talked about a stormy night. It was, in fact, as black as night, and the Lively Bessy was driving under bare poles before the storm, pitching and rolling, but as safe in the wide ocean as she could be.

The excitement of the storm had done Bobus good. He walked up and down with his speaking-trumpet, watching the actions of the chief in command, and ready to give aid at the slightest gesture. But we were safe. Lashed into fury by the wind, tormented also as it were by their own motion, the billows ran, as it seemed to us, mountains high; now toppling over us with huge crests of foam, broken into a thousand jagged forms, in which one might imagine that he saw angry faces, threatening arms, and upraised hands ready to strike him; suddenly, however, spent with their own fury, the waves would subside and fall down, breaking over our deck, or sometimes disappearing under our lee and lifting up our boat some feet nearer heaven. Then, again, we were cast down into a deep trough, and on each side and all around us angry waves were imminent, threatening, and vast, but in a moment up we mounted, to still keep our course and to drive before the wind.

The noise was terrific. The ship, dry and withered by the Arctic winter, groaned, creaked, and complained at the rough usage. All the hands were on deck, told out into parties ready to do their duty. We were all afraid of our spars and masts, for both those and the running rigging were sapped and dried by the intense frosts, thus rendered rotten and weak. The old ship, which we had all grown to regard as a living creature, behaved well, and Bobus was congratulating himself on our safety, when a fiercer blast than hitherto snapped the foremast by the board, as if it had been no stronger than a deal ruler. All hands sprang forward, and with hatchets and axes freed the mast from its cordage and gear, and let it go overboard into the boiling ocean.

The excitement past, our first officer and Bobus smiled pleasantly, and congratulated themselves that it was no worse; but the latter having gone aft, came back with his face full of alarm, and told the officer that we had sprung a leak, for that the ship rode heavily, and that she would scarcely answer her rudder.

"A leak," cried the lieutenant; "why how can that be? She is as taut a vessel as ever sailed, and pretty nearly solid wood in front, waist and stern; she was built for ice and rough weather."

"I know," cried Bobus, with a puzzled air, "but ——" here he paused for a moment, and then suddenly shouted "Pilbeam!" The truth flashed at once upon all of us. Whilst we were busy on deck, Pilbeam, to revenge himself upon us, had managed somehow to scuttle the Lively Bessy.

We rushed at once below. Our suppositions were true enough; the water was pouring in, and gradually rising higher and higher. There was no hope for us; the pumps and gear were out of order; our boats, injured by the ice, were not of much use.

"Don't let the villain escape," cried the lieutenant, aghast. "He has brought us to death; before we die let us give him his due."

"Leave that to me," cried Bobus, sternly, wrenching the lock and bolts from the cabin door in which the Cornishman was confined. A rush of water upon us when the door opened, a gurgling noise, and a heavy mass falling, was the answer. The wretch, dreading discovery and punishment, had managed to plug every aperture in his cabin, so that the water had filled it like a tank before the rest of the ship, and had suffocated him. The half-naked dead body, borne out by the water, fell at the lieutenant's feet. The light which we held up flickered and fell upon his ghastly face. His teeth were tightly clenched, his eyes open and running with moisture, his long lank hair floating over his face. "He is beyond our vengeance," said the lieutenant; "we have no war with the dead, we must look to ourselves now."

We went on deck orderly and calm. The Lively Bessy sailed but heavily now, and was quite waterlogged. We calculated that in about an hour's time she would go down; we knew we were in the German Ocean, we were not quite sure as to our right bearings. Still, when morning came, we looked to find many vessels passing us who would help us.

So the men were told off in watches, the boats got out and made ready, the lieutenant taking one, the doctor, whose great care seemed to be to save his scientific notes and calculations, being put at the head of the second, and Bobus and the midshipman going in the third. We kept as long as we could to the wreck, in hopes that the storm would subside, which it did in a great degree, but the swing and turmoil of the waves still continued.

Bobus, who was as kind and as thoughtful towards me as if I had been his son instead of a stranger, insisted upon taking with us the step of the foremast and some loose spars, which he towed after the boat, putting me in my old place, the stern-sheets. It was lucky that he took these precautions, for very soon after our boat, which was the second, the lieutenant being the last to leave the ship, was launched, a huge wave, breaking not far from her stern, fell over her and filled her, and she went down like a piece of lead. Some of the men regained the sinking vessel; I caught hold of the rope which towed the spars, and cutting it with my jack-knife, which was fastened by a lanyard round my waist, prevented its being borne down, and then getting astride of the mast, shouted out "Bobus!" with all my might.

I felt no fear and no dread, but I then felt that I was struggling with death. A few more moments I might be choked with salt water, borne along fathoms deep by the undercurrent. I said my prayers, and taking some cordage bound myself on the mast and shouted out again "Bobus!"

"Aye, aye, lad!" said a gruff voice near me, and a flash of lightning showed me my old friend emerging from the water like a Newfoundland dog after a dive. "Why," said he, "you are quite a seaman, Ned; all taut on deck there, eh, lad?"

"Aye, aye," I answered, "come on."

"No," he said, "no, lad, I'll be on to these spars," and taking a rope and holding on to the centre of one, he managed to interweave a rope with them so that he bound them together like a small raft. Then flinging himself into the centre, he proved, to my great delight, they would bear him.

"This is a great deal better than a boat, Ned," said he; "we want an oar or two just to paddle along. When the lightning comes we shall see one. You must lash yours to mine; we cannot part company."

"Here's an oar," cried I, as one washed by the waves struck my leg and gave me a shrewdly heavy blow.

"All right," cried he. "Look there!"

This cry was occasioned by a flash of lightning

which showed us the Lively Bessy settling in the water, and the crew, with their pale determined faces, pushing off in the last boat. The lieutenant was the last to leave, and as the vessel went down he stood up in the boat, and with the crew raised a parting cheer. The wind blew the melancholy farewell to us, for our lighter craft had been borne on ahead, and old Bobus cried out "True to the last! that lieutenant's a good officer. One cheer more, Ned." And placing his hand to his cheek, he gave a last cheer to his comrades. I joined as loudly as I could, and when our shouts had died away, we saw, with a sudden lurch, pitch and reel, the Lively Bessy settle in her watery grave.

# CHAPTER XXIV.



I REMEMBER beating about for hours on that dreadful night. I thought morning would *never* come. My feet, immersed in the cold water, seemed frozen and benumbed; my hands, face, and body, continually soaked and drenched with sea-water, shivered with the cold. Bobus, who was a little in advance of me with his raft, was stronger and more able to bear the cold than I, and once swam to me, took me off the spars, so as to take my feet out of the water; placed me on his raft, putting in my mouth as he did so a flask of brandy and water, a draught from which warmed and revived me.

To him I owed my life, for shortly after this, although I strove against the feeling as much as I possibly could, a drowsy sense of numbness, un-accompanied by pain and equally without dread, came over me, and I fell forward on the mast, and floated senseless on the waves. Light just dawned when I did so, and luckily, in placing me for the last time upon the spars (since the raft would not bear us both), Bobus had lashed me tightly to my safeguard in such a manner that my head was lifted above water.

When I came to my senses I found everything around me new and strange—so new, so strange, so pleasant, that I could not but fancy myself still occupied in·some delicious dream.

White dimity curtains, fringed with pink, alone reminded me by their whiteness of the fields of snow to which I had so long been accustomed. The bed in which I lay no longer confined my limbs and restrained my movements like the little hammock on board the Lively Bessy. Instead of blanket and coarse huckaback, sheets of the finest and whitest linen ; instead of a little cupboard, for it was not much more, confining me on every side, a room papered with neatness and taste, and smelling in that honest, hearty, fresh way in which country bedrooms have smelt from time immemorial. Through a chink at the bottom of the bed I saw that the window was open, that the sun was shining outside, and could feel the gentle air which stole in at the casement, and then, fainting with the burden of scents which it bore, died away with a gentle murmur.

To me this was paradise. I thought of the

lone seaboy on the mast, the ever trembling, never ceasing waves, the dreadful death which I had escaped, and the many causes of gratitude which I had towards that good Creator by whose will alone I was saved. Tears swam in my eyes and rolled down my cheeks, wetting my pillow with drops of gratitude and joy.

Presently I heard voices. I had almost dreamed in my waking moments, and these seemed to awaken me with a strange shock on my memory. "And so, doctor," said one, "knowing the interest you took in him and the love you bore him, we thought it best to communicate with you, and to let you know where he was."

"My dear boy," another voice spoke in return, "your perceptions were always kind, and therefore in the right direction. I thank you for your forethought, my dear Flook."

"Flook ! I know that name; part of an anchor, eh ?"

Thus my mind, dreamily to itself, being too much flurried and disturbed to be very accurate or searching.

"Was there no one else saved with him?" continued the elder voice.

"But one; a strange sort of sea-bird, but an admirable fellow. He had been so knocked about by the waves, so starved and half-drowned in his sea-voyage and his wreck, that when he had seen this boy into a place of safety he went off into a three days' delirium, crying out nothing but such Arctic phrases and sailor speeches as his brain had of late affected, and being very very anxious, in the lull of his paroxysms, to save little Billee, who was about, he said, to be murdered by one Pilbeam. Since he has come too he has told me more of the ill-fated vessel, and has described the crew and officers. He has been to London, and has reported himself at the Admiralty, and will be down here again to-night to visit this boy, whom he has vowed never to part company with as long as his timbers hold together."

"Then I must take him home with me," said the doctor, laughing, "and make him marry Mrs. Taw, eh, Flook?"

This idea pleased the latter, who laughed so that I had to cry out "Doctor!" twice before he heard me.

They both ran to me. The dear old doctor put his arms round my neck and kissed me on the forehead, Flook shook my hands, trembled himself, and called for the nurse, whereon some one ran up stairs, and I, half in laughter, half in tears, feeling very flighty and lightheaded, thanked them all. "Where am I, sir?" said I, to the doctor; "at school?"

"No, at Great Yarmouth, where a portion of your ship was driven in after the wreck, with you on the top of it, lashed firmly, but senseless. Bobus came in afterwards, nearly killed by being bumped against a rock; but he is now safe and sound."

"Thank God," said I, fervently.

"And, as for you, Ned," said Flook, "you have had brain-fever and that sort of thing, and I, living here, as you know, barely recognised you when brought down to the beach, and have had you nursed through it, and have sent for the doctor, and—hallo! here's your nurse; thank her."

He pushed forward, as he spoke, a young lady about my own age, but so calm, wise-looking, so pretty, well-dressed, so neat and sedate, and, withal, so well-grown and tall, that I thought her ever so much my superior and better, as indeed she was.

"She is my eldest sister," continued Flook; " and, being wise and notable, our house-keeper."

I had not been in company with a lady since I had parted with Mrs. Taw. The few I saw during the time I was with the professor I could not call acquaintances; and this young lady was so different, and so beautiful, that I shut my eyes at the sight, and muttered *" O! Dea certe."*

"He has not forgotten his Latin," cried the doctor.

"What did he say?" said the young lady, offering me some cooling drink.

" Why, that you were a goddess, or an angel,

as we should say now," said Flook, with a smile. "What do you think of the compliment, Lucy?"

"I think that he meant it," she answered, quietly, putting her cool hand upon my heated forehead.

I could have kissed that soft hand, only I dared not, and presently my schoolfellow, taking upon himself the part of a physician, ordered all out of the room save himself and the doctor, and urged upon me the wisdom of going to sleep.

"You are past all danger, Ned," said he. "Sleep, and refresh yourself; grow strong, and get up; you are past all danger now. You will live to do great things yet."

I did fall asleep, not without silently giving way to my almost unutterable feeling of thankfulness. I awoke, the next morning, a new creature, and, day after day, mended rapidly. Old Bobus was delighted when he saw me, and prophecied that I should soon be "out of dock," and be all taut and right. He told me that he had heard some rumours of the two boats and their crews having been picked up by a German vessel, and was in great hopes that all, except Pilbeam, had been saved.

The family of my old schoolfellow I found excelling in kindness. They were five in all—two sons and one daughter, of whom Flook was the eldest, and the father, an admirable gentleman, who perfectly knew how to govern and regulate his family, and, at the same time, to be kind, and, indeed, full of jollity and merriment. Bobus was constituted an out-door lodger, and would come to breakfast in time to join in daily prayers, and, when necessary, to take me out. He was never satisfied with praising the family, one of his reasons for admiration being that they were governed as well as on board a man-of-war. "All order, all punctuality," said he. "Dinner for servants at seven bells, for family at nine bells. Get up early, go to bed early, never in a hurry; captain always on the look-out for squalls—that's the family for me."

He more than once referred me to Miss Lucy, as one who, when I settled in life, and determined to do "short duty," I might take as a good partner. "She," he said, "was well built, and, morally speaking, had every timber sound. Moreover, she would answer her helm, as the present commander could testify, and, in fact, she was as neat and pretty a craft as any one would wish to sail with over life's ocean."

Lucy's tenderness and care, her solicitude and gentleness, the anxiety which her clear and pretty blue eyes expressed if I felt a little more poorly than before, certainly had a great effect upon me. Pity is akin to love, and I loved her as a brother might a fond, good sister. I had not been brought up with girls, and the feelings I entertained for one of the opposite sex were distant and respectful.

The rough speeches of Bobus made me first sensible of a passion different from any which had ever been present in my bosom before, but I kept my own counsel and said nothing. I was a poor friendless boy, without money, almost without prospects, and until I had achieved something in life I could not think of letting an affection root itself.

When I had grown stronger, I found every one rejoiced, and grew so fond of me, that upon the proposal of the doctor to take me away into the country, back to the old school, which was, he said, to be my home, all looked sorrowful and sad. "Let him stay here a little while, doctor," said my schoolfellow's father.

"You forget, sir, that Mrs. Taw and one or two kind friends are burning to see him."

"She will find him vastly improved, no doubt," answered Mr. Flook; "taller and stronger, my son says, by a great deal. He is quite a hero too. A boy who before he is twenty has gone through the perils and dangers of an Arctic voyage, is indeed some one. He will be the admiration of your little village. How well his friend and companion Bobus speaks of him."

As he said these words, as if called into our presence by the mention of his name, who should enter but Bobus, with a large, long letter in his hand, upon which was printed, "*On Her Majesty's Service.*" "Good news! Mas'r Ned," he cried, "good news! The commander's safe and sound, so is the doctor, and so are all the crew of the Lively Bessy but two."

"Hurrah!" I cried, jumping up, and waving my handkerchief. "Hurrah!" cried the doctor, and Mr. Flook joined also in the sailor's cheer.

Bobus continued, "You are allowed a twelve-months' leave of absence—"

"Absence! I don't belong to any ship," I interrupted, with the greatest surprise.

"And in consideration of your conduct, as reported both by the doctor and the lieutenant, you are to take rank as midshipman in her Majesty's service."

"Bravo!" cried old Flook, who came in time to hear the last. "Why, Ned's an officer at last."

"He'll live long on his midshipman's half-pay, won't he?" said Flook.

"I do not know what to tell Mrs. Taw and your school-friends, Paget," said the doctor somewhat sorrowfully. "I had hoped that you would have consented to spend the rest of your life with me. I now find that I must grieve for my adopted child as for all the rest."

"Tell ye what it is, old gentleman," said Bobus to the doctor. "No doubt you're a good man; indeed, the best of men. Many's the time that Ned has told me all about you in the long watches in the Arctic clime. Many a time, when the very breath as it came from our lips froze, have our hearts beat warm for those at home. Bless you, I seem to know you all as I looks round. You are familiar to me—all the ship's crew."

Miss Lucy smiled at the expression, and putting out her hand wished me joy at my promotion.

"I know how good you are; but avast there! lay by! You are not going to spoil this boy of mine. He must go out and about. He has'nt seen half the world yet; he began at the wrong end, and saw the worst part first. Well, then, what must he do? Why, go aboard ship, to be sure. England wants sailors, such sailors as will make good and great men. Besides that, my shipmates, when once a man has been aboard ship, England arn't half big enough for him; he wants to stretch himself a bit, and so does Mas'r Ned; and in whatever ship he sails in, I'll sail too.

To make a long story short, it was agreed that I should start at once for the old school, and spend a few days there; that Mr. Flook should go up to London and try to find out my uncle, and the reason for his mysterious disappearance; and that then, having written and thanked my late commander and the doctor, I should study during my long leave of absence, so as to fit myself for my future profession. The doctor did not fail to give me a long lesson upon the utility of the schoolmaster, who, he said, should be looked upon with great honour in every country, quite as much, indeed, as a naval or military officer. It might be, he said, even more, because a sailor or soldier only defended the goods of the citizens, but a schoolmaster had care of their children's minds and souls. To all of this I assented, but answered that, although I honoured, as I was bound to do, by the ties of gratitude and love, schoolmasters in general, and especially one, yet I did not feel that I was adapted for the profession, while, as several who knew me said, that I would make a good sailor, and that I had now an opportunity. However, I declared that I placed myself in the doctor's hands, and would let him choose for me.

The doctor was delighted at what he called my generous obedience, and praised, perhaps more highly than it deserved, that readiness which I showed to give up a cherished project at his bidding. "It is not easy," he said, "for a man, who knows what the failures of this world are, to put aside anything he has set his heart upon; how much more difficult is it for a boy, whose impressions are so much more vivid, whose hopes are a thousand times brighter, whose feelings are more acute, never having been dulled or blunted by the world."

I had, moreover, the sweet approval of Miss Lucy and her father. Lucy was full of romantic ideas as to teaching. She was ready to make all the boys good and all the lessons easy. She would have no punishment, she would govern all the boys by persuasion, gentleness, and an appeal to their feelings and their sense of honour. To which the doctor replied that, from experience, he could state that some boys had no feelings, and were only to be appealed to by their "seat of honour," at which both the old gentlemen laughed immoderately, and Lucy and I looked abashed. She was not daunted, however, and advised me to settle down as a schoolmaster in a pretty village, and to do my duty there as elsewhere.

To this harangue my schoolfellow old Flook and my friend Bobus replied, that I was not suited to be a schoolmaster. That it was as noble to teach men in a ship to do their duty as to teach boys; in fact, said the philosopher, " it appears to me, with deference to father and the doctor, that it does not so much matter what a man does in life, as how he does it. If honour and glory were to be apportioned by the wise and good as they are in the world, true honour and glory would be at an end. The man who, in a humble station, never made himself heard beyond his home, but who did his duty there, taught his children well, and set an example to his wife, would be overlooked or not heard of; whilst he who, in a moment of excitement, perilled his life to lead one troop of men to destroy another troop, would be, as he is, trumpeted all over the world, laden with stars and ribbons, called a lord, and be mentioned after his death as a hero. Whereas," said old Flook, in conclusion, "it is harder to do the first than the second."

"Precisely, Herbert," said the doctor. "You have given us the benefit of an excellent argument in our favour; your discourse might have made a theme on that passage of Horace—

"Quæ virtus et quanta," &c.

"What and how great the virtue and the art
To live on little with a cheerful heart."

"If so be as I may speak," said Bobus, striking in, "about this here, Mas'r Ned, I should say this. Lay by there and sound the depths! Don't sail in a hurry! What call have you to take away a young sailor from her Majesty's service? Sometimes boys know what to do with themselves better than their born and natural parents. Look at the chart for that. S'pose you had a made your great inventor, Master Watt, a greengrocer, or had a turned Master Nelson into a parson, eh! D'ye think we should a had steam, or have beaten the French at Trafal-GAR. Lay by, then! Look at the log! Don't run out many knots afore you sound agin, or you'll be on the rocks, or my name arnt Jack Bobus." After this oracular wisdom, the boatswain slapped his thigh, put his tarpaulin hat on his head, and walked out into the garden. My friends had nothing to say against it. As Bobus afterwards said, one broadside had demolished the whole fleet, the question was settled, and my course in life determined on.

# CHAPTER XXV.



## WE DETERMINE TO TRAVEL ON THE OCEAN OF LAND—NEW YORK.

On this portion of my adventures I feel that I should be as brief as possible. To the regret of my kind friends, who were sorry to part with us even for so short a time, my schoolfellow, old Flook, as I still called him affectionately, and I set forward one fine day from Yarmouth to our old midland school village, and when there spent a great many happy days at the school. Two years had made a vast difference. Little boys had grown to big ones, and big ones had gone away; we found few who knew and remembered us.

Old Taw was delighted. She never cared much for Flook, but she loved me with all the warmth she had. She was never tired of admiring my growth and the alteration in me. She declared I was quite a man, and when I told her how kind all had been to me, she said that nobody could help it. " Don't you like a straightforward, honest person, when you meet him, Ned, eh?" she asked, "and don't you think they will like you?" Bless you, they must. Good people find good friends."

"Not always," said Flook, trying to combat her honest faith.

"More shame to those who say it," she answered; "aye, and more than this, God helps the fatherless, and many a lonely lad thrives more than those who have rich friends and many to help them."

"Bravo, Taw!' ' cried Flook, clapping his great hands, and opening his great eyes. "Here's a health to you, Taw; you're a trump."

Here the doctor came in to the little study, his face beaming with delight. He held a paper in his hand. "Do you know," he cried, " Paget, what has become of your friend, the professor, eh? I mean that person who wrote so many letters, and sometimes received money in the answers? He was a mere begging-letter writer, of course, and 'tis lucky you were separated from him."

"No," I answered, "I have scarcely thought of him. I have even given up all thoughts of my uncle."

"He was your uncle," answered the doctor. "Nay, do not be ashamed," I blushed deeply. "Learn this—no spot or stain can attach to any one but through his own faults and actions. Peter Garle was an assumed name. Under it he has expiated his swindling crimes, and has come out of prison with some determination to be respectable. He sent me a letter but the day before yesterday, declaring his sorrow, deploring your loss — for of course he knows nothing of your adventures, and adding, that he has been engaged as a surgeon on board an emigrant ship, that he intends getting into practice in Victoria, and hopes henceforward to live a worthy and honest life."

"I hope he will," said I. "He had passed as a surgeon, and was clever—so I have heard my father say."

"How is it that you did not know him, Paget?" asked Flook.

"I had not seen him for seven years, and I never suspected that I should meet him as I did. He must have tracked me from the inn; our meeting was surely not accidental."

"Of course not; how could it be? He wanted you, by your innocence, your looks, and age, to aid him in his peculiar method of getting a livelihood. A year's imprisonment and his subsequent hard life has taught him the value of honesty, which, by the way, some men do not learn till late in life. Well, he is off to Australia; do not disturb him; I will write him word of your welfare should I, as he promises, hear from him again."

I was glad to dismiss so painful a subject from

my mind, and during the whole time that I stayed with the doctor, which was three weeks, did not allude to it. We were then recalled to Yarmouth, to celebrate my friend's twenty-first birthday, and during the gaieties on that occasion I had the opportunity of dancing more than once with pretty Miss Lucy, whom I found more engaging than ever.

It had been arranged that after Flook's coming of age he should travel. Now, his whole idea and impulse had been to be an engineer and to go out to India, but his health not being strong, and his father having a competent fortune, that was overruled, and after due deliberation it was agreed that we should go to another of old Flook's early loves—America. He wanted to see the prairies, that ocean of land which he declared must be more wonderful than the ocean of water. Bobus, who had not yet got his ship, and who was, in fact, waiting for me, to my great delight and little surprise declared that he too would join us.

So it was determined upon. Doctor Leatherby furnished me with money, Flook was amply provided, berths were taken in one of the Cunard line of steamers, and after a voyage of twenty-one days —I say nothing of leave-taking—we three found ourselves in the chief city of the Great Republic —New York.

# CHAPTER XXVI.



HE who determines to write his adventures must take care to leave out certain portions of his life, or he will tire his readers. Most men live a life of incident; indeed, the most quiet amongst us has had his hair-breadth scapes, his troubles, and his trials, which would, if properly set forth, fill a volume. There are two kinds of life—the thinking and the acting—and he who lives the busiest does not always live the best, nor is that portion of our lives which is fullest of adventure always the wisest or the most profitable.

I write this because I must make a jump in the relation of my own adventures in one or two portions of my life—at this present portion and at another when the reader will doubtlessly find it out.

He will therefore kindly suppose that I and my schoolfellow stayed some weeks with Doctor Leatherby, who every day taught us something, and endeavoured to instil some honorable and worthy principle. If I loved him before, when I left him, a friendless boy, for London, I loved him now with ten times more ardour. I perceived his value, for I had sense enough to know that one wiser and older than yourself, who constantly sets truth before you, who cheers you on in the pursuit of knowledge, and who strengthens you in the practice of virtue, is indeed above and beyond all price. Such to me was my dear old friend, Dr. Leatherby.

To travel had been a long-cherished idea of my friend Flook. In our school-days he wished to become an Indian engineer, but his friends, and especially his father, had begged him to lay aside that idea. He had done so obediently, but his desire to travel was not conquered, and he had obtained leave and licence to go to another land of wonders—that land of vast expanse, of wondrous space, of gigantic rivers, and endless prairies.

In obedience to this wish, behold us in New York, for we must omit a sorrowful parting with friends at home, with Dr. Leatherby, Miss Lucy, and poor old Mrs. Taw. As for Bobus, he had determined to accompany us, and to drop for a time the character of the sailor in that of the "long-shore" traveller.

New York has been described so often that we need not repeat anything here. To us it was a city of contradictions. It was English and not English, yet it was not foreign; strange it was, strange in the glaring colours of its houses, in its vast hotels, in its "blocks" of streets, in its fanciful, energetic, curious inhabitants, in its manners and customs. Presuming cities to have terms of natural life, I should say that this city was much younger than ours at home, and had strange freaks and whimsies, and was altogether more demonstrative and presuming, as is the manner of youth. This was especially seen in sign-boards, advertisements, and shop-fronts, and occasionally overran the whole of a house, and appeared at its sides.

We made one or two acquaintances during our stay at a gigantic hotel, which boasted of the population of an English hamlet, and then, under the auspices of one free and friendly young gentleman, who said he could see we were a couple of freshly-caught young Britishers, we began our travels in the States, one of our special objects being to observe how slavery worked. Our young friend advised us very plainly not to give our opinions too freely upon anything in the States, because, he said, they were mighty jealous of any stranger, and were determined to defend their peculiar institutions to the last.

He pronounced this with the greatest good humour, emphasizing every third word, and especially the last in every sentence, and with a peculiar twang, which it is impossible to give in print.

"Ah!" grunted Bobus, looking at him with some disdain, "we are not to pass the signal, eh! and to go through this voyage in dumb show." •

"Wal," answered the New Yorker, "I calc'late it's better, stranger. You've bin in the sea-faring line, and know the valy of a pilot in a strange sea. Now, I'm that pilot, and you obey orders."

"Oh!" said Bobus, cutting a bit of pigtail, and putting it in his mouth.

"Pass a bit here, stranger," said our friend. He took a huge plug, and chewed it with all the zest of an old sailor. Bobus cast up his eyes in wonder.

Our friend was not more than nineteen; he looked about sixteen. He was small, sharp-visaged, and wiry; in looks, as I said, a mere boy, in every action a cool, calm, calculating man. His talk was of dollars and cents, he had a good knowledge of the money-market, and was quite ready to speculate. He was not refined or gentlemanly in his manners, still less was he vulgar. He was a complete man of the world, and yet, as Bobus said, a child. The wonder was, not that he was so, but that he formed no exception to the general rule. There were dozens of his class, size, shape, and figure, travelling, talking, buying, and selling, giving opinions on religion, trade, morality, and politics, everywhere.

"The Yankees," said Bobus, " are a wonderful people!" He looked at our friend as he said it, and remained happily dumb with wonder.

"Wal," said the young fellow, " we air, sir; but we air not all Yankees. They air only 'Yankees' in New Hamp*shear*, Vermont, Massachusetts, Connec*ti*cut, and Maine. In O*h*io they air ' Buckeyes;' in Ar*kan*sas, ' Yahoos ;' in Indiana, ' Hosiers ;' in Carolina, ' Nullyfiers ;' in Ken*tuck*, 'Comerakers ;' in Illinois, 'Suckers ;' in Michigan, ' Wolverines ;' and in New York, 'Cockneys.' But you Britishers are so main ignorant that you call us all Yankees."

Our young friend, being from Vermont, was a Yankee, and was proud of it; he was very attentive to us, and not having any particular object at present, attached himself to us and to our governor, as he called Bobus, and determined to travel with us.

"I will open your eyes a little, I will. I calc'late that they *do* keep you down so in the old country; that they won't let you out without him." He pointed to old Bobus as he said this, and again intimated that he was our "governor," that is, sent to take care of us.

We both smiled, and chatted with our young friend, and, English-like, let him into our confidence, and told him what our object was. I will say this, that immediately he found we had trusted him, and given him our confidence, he was delighted to be our friend, and served us truly. He was about, he said, to set out to Charleston, South Carolina, a reg'lar slave-nest, as he said. Thence he would proceed to Independence, and thence, joining a trader's caravan, would buy a few lots, charter a wagon, and proceed across the prairies to Santa Fé. He thought that we could not do better than join him.

We thought so too, and in a few days our vessel, with a heavy head-wind setting at our bows, tacked into Charleston Harbour. Entering it, we passed Fort Sumpter, then just commenced, which was to be mounted with fifty pieces of cannon, "able," said our young friend, "to lift any British ship out of the water if she wanted to come to Charleston agin." We also passed another fortress, called Fort Johnson, nearer the town, and strongly defended with artillery, and soon after moored abreast of the pier.

# CHAPTER XXVII.



A SLAVE SALE AT CHARLESTOWN—OLD FLOOK PUR-
CHASES A NIGGER.

THERE was a look about the capital city of
North Carolina which put Bobus very much in
mind of Portsmouth, and which caused the old
sailor to stroll about King Street in a free and
easy way. Our young friend again warned us to
say nothing about slavery, as here all were violent
partisans in its favour, and the majority carried
the new repeating pistols, which we now term
revolvers, as well as bowie knives, and were very
apt to use them suddenly.

Bobus and Flook, out of respect to our friend,
agreed to be silent, and I, desirous of continuing
our journey, and perfectly hopeless of doing any
good by interference, did not wish to irritate any
one by reference to the " peculiar institution."

Having refreshed ourselves at our hotel we
rambled through the streets of the city, finding
its inhabitants very pale and sickly in appearance,
and many of them in mourning, which showed

that the place was not very healthy to the Anglo-Saxon race. The black population was, however, healthy and merry enough, and clothed in the gayest of colours.

We had not walked a very long way before Bobus was, as he termed it, " brought up sudden " before a door upon which hung a printed bill. He was so intent upon it that we ran to see what it was. The document advertised the inhabitants of Charleston, and the United States generally, that Messrs. Franklyn and Washington were, on that very day at noon, to offer, for public competition, several very likely lots of slaves, both male and female. The " Conditions of Sale " were attached, by which we were further made aware that the highest bidder was to be the purchaser, and that if any dispute arose as to two bidders, the " lot " was to be put up again, and the usual " conditions of sale " were to be submitted to.

We were looking at the bill when the rumbling of a cart, accompanied with a rough request to " stand aside," caused us to turn round. A small clumsily-built cart, full of black children, perfectly naked, and tumbled together like calves, drew up at the gates of the building, which opened to admit them. Four black women, naked to the waist, followed them. We could not but be struck with the similarity between these poor creatures and the cows and calves which one saw proceeding to market in England, nor can I ever fully describe the appalling sensation of dread, terror, and helplessness which came over me as the cart rolled into the yard. We entered also.

We found the slaves chattering and talking together in a "barrack," as they called it; a wooden outhouse or barn, as much resembling a cattle-shed as need be. Too much so, indeed, for English eyes; but we were so much convinced that, in this instance, a still tongue makes a wise head, that we were, very naturally, silent.

A stoutly-built and florid individual, a northerner, I believe, who looked very much like an English cattle-driver—I cannot help referring to cattle in everything—stood by with a thin cane in hand, tapping his highlow boot, and glancing round every moment as if he were in want of customers, and was watching the faces of those who came in, and judging thence the probability of their desiring to be purchasers of a "likely lot" of "ebony"—such was the term applied to our black fellow men.

As we entered the barrack the auctioneer, a thin, cadaverous individual, stood upon a sort of raised platform, and, by striking his hammer, gave notice that the sale was about to commence.

Lot 1 was a negress, with or without her infant of four months. "She had," said the auctioneer, "good milk, was very healthy, and was kind and tender to children. She had neither vices nor defects; could sew, wash, starch, and cook, and all in perfection. The motive for selling her was simply because she had been disobedient to her mistress."

A fine negress stood up, as he described her, with a flashing indignant eye, but with now and then a plaintive and a piteous smile upon her face, when she saw any one approach whose face she thought good and gentle, and whom she might have desired as a purchaser. There was a smart bidding for this negress, and the auctioneer used his eloquence considerably in descanting on her virtues. She was at last "knocked down" for, I forget how many dollars.

Then came other lots, the women and children were sold first. I was so sickened that I turned away from the human traffic. Flook, with a lowering brow, and Bobus, with a frown on his face, and with the end of his rattan stuffed into his mouth, as if to prevent himself from speaking, listened quietly.

Next came other lots. The males were more noisy; and some, who had been sold once or twice before, would now and then interrupt the auctioneer, and have their say in the bargain which so nearly concerned themselves. Thus, the auctioneer put up a "lot," named Joe. "This, gentlemen," said he, "is a prime lot, an excellent field hand."

A hard-featured, cruel-eyed man had been

looking at the teeth and testing the museles of Joe, and the latter did not like the looks of his probable master.

"A prime lot, gentlemen," cried the auctioneer.

"Ain't a prime lot," said Joe; "I'm a werry unlikely nigger: don't no one buy me."

"A sound, industrious, capital field hand, gentlemen," continued the seller.

"Don't know nuffin. Ain't a sound, fust-rate field hand. Don't know how to plant rice, I don't," continued Joe.

"Why, what's the matter with you, Joe?" said one, catching hold of Joe's muscular leg.

"Bad rheumatis can't be cured by Massa Parr's pills," whimpered Joe; "ain't fit to do no work."

"Why does he say so?" asked I of our friend.

"'Cos he knows if any one gives a good price for him he will expect more work out of him than a low-priced nigger, d'ye see? If any one gives 600 dollars for him, he will expect less work than from one who cost him 800 or 1000 dollars."

So the sale went on. We became at last quite interested in this curious dialogue.

"Here's a capital lively boy, gentlemen," said the auctioneer, when Joe had been "knocked down."

"Aint a capital lively boy. Am berry lazy, and broke my foot last fall."

" Quite without vice, and a prime lot for your money."

" Plenty of wice, berry sulky, and isn't a prime lot for no one's money," rejoined the young negro.

The boy was, however, sold; and presently a very old decrepit negro, with white head and shaking limbs, stood up on the little stage. He had to be lifted up, and when on the platform shook and shivered in a pitiable way.

Murmurs of pity for the negro, and anger against the auctioneer, arose from the crowd.

" It's a shame to sell him," said one.

" It's like selling your grandfather."

" Poor old Ebony, how weak he is!"

" He ought to be kept on the estate."

" He's not worth his keep."

" Look at his gray hairs."

" What am I to do, gentlemen? Here am I to sell this lot. If they put one here like this I can only do my duty."

" He should be set free," whispered Flook. " I'll buy him."

Our Yankee friend stared at him.

" Do buy me, gentlemen," said the old fellow. " My name's Massa Stumph. Am berry 'fectionate old nigger." His voice was certainly low and weak, and he fixed his eyes upon us with a look of entreaty.

" He is a very faithful servant," said the seller.

" He was for many years on the estate of Mr. Stumph, the deceased gentleman for whose executors I now appear. He calls himself 'Old Stump.' What will you bid, gentlemen?"

" He is not worth his keep," said one, drawing away.

" You will have to nurse him," said another.

" Make a bidding, gentlemen. Shall we say five dollars?"

No one answered, and the auctioneer spoke again; and then old Flook, who had for a moment consulted me, cried, "Five dollars." The auctioneer, who was glad enough to end the sale, let his hammer fall, and old Flook and I were, for the first time in our lives, possessed of a slave.

No sooner had the hammer fallen than, to our intense surprise, an immense change took place in our slave. He jumped at once to the ground, and ran up to Flook, crying, " I'm yours, massa, Old Stump your lawful nigger! Sarve you well, massa; ain't so old as I look; beat many a young nigger yet." He bared his muscular arm as he said this, and made the muscle of it swell out like a cricket-ball. The whole company burst out into a roar of laughter; our friend paid the five dollars, and we went out of the sale-room, followed by old Stump, and hardly knowing what to do with our new purchase.

Our first care was to buy him a decent cotton suit, and to give him some dinner. After he had

had that, and was washed, he looked at least ten years younger. He waited on us at our hotel with the grace and activity of a London waiter, and was full of smiles and grins at the idea of having cheated the auctioneer.

"Old Stump," he said, "berry much pleased at cheating white rascal. Like white gentl'n, Stump do. Sarbe white gentl'n, he will. Cheat wretched auctioneer."

· "That will do, Stump," said our young friend, putting an end to his talk. "Go down stairs with the other niggers; be ready for us to-morrow. Can you drive?"

"Yes, massa," said Stump.

"Ah, very good: now, cut it; slope; make tracks, old man." By which language our friend meant that Stump should disappear, which he did.

"What will you do with him?" said he to us. "He will be useful as far as Santa Fé and back; but what then?"

"I will set him free in Canada, and buy him some land," said Flook.

"Oh, ha!" returned the Yankee, with a whistle; "and now let us talk of going on to Independence and to Santa Fé. Westward, ho! across the prairies, and the nigger shall drive our wagon."

"Agreed," said we all; and then, tired with the voyage, we sought our room.

We spent a few days in travelling about North Carolina, visited the rice plantations, and saw various phases and scenes of slavery—scenes which did not prejudice me very much in its favour. But we saw one thing, namely, that God does temper the wind to the shorn lamb, and that He as surely mitigates the cruelty of one class of society towards another. Unhappy the slaves were not. If laughter, good condition, sleek appearance, plenty of food, and few cares could make people happy, the black people we saw were so. But the material success of evil, or its prosperous duration, cannot make it good, nor will evil produce good. We saw the bright side of slavery and its dark side also. We heard of murders and whippings, scourgings, torturings, and horrible revenges; we saw cruelty and ignorance, dense stupidity and enormous vice; we found God's gospel denied to the poor, and, in a Christian land, the chief blessing of Christianity denied.

"Come," said I, one morning, "let us again be ' out and about.' I am tired of this land of mourning and darkness. We can do no good, let us away from them."

"By all means," said Flook, stretching his arms, and yawning as if awakened from an unpleasant dream.

"If we don't," said Bobus, "I shall ship myself aboard a ship and go home to the little island, the best place in the world."

" Except the great United States, stranger," added our friend. " Wal,' I calc'late I've pretty nigh used up North Car'lina. 'Spose we make our way to Independence."

" Ah! we're all independent enuff," interrupted Bobus.

" 'Tis a town o'that name, stranger," said our young friend, " whence they start on the great Santa Fé journey."

" Then I'm for going," said I.

" And I," cried Flook.

" Wal, we'll tak' our places in the cy'ars;" by which last word our friend meant the railway carriages; a small railway running in the northwest direction towards our destination. The other part of the journey we were to undertake on horseback. Elated as he was at the prospect of being again far away from slavery, we took old Stump and our friend with us to buy rifles, and some other necessaries, and must now leave the reader till we meet again at Independence.

# CHAPTER XXVIII.



BEHOLD us, then, at last, in the far west of that great Republic whose home is in the setting sun. We had left Bobus behind at Richmond, but he was only to make some purchases and join us in the new and beautiful city of Independence. Our wagons, which we had purchased at Pittsburg, were large vehicles, built lightly and possessing much room, so that they could be laden with the miscellaneous property which the traders sought to dispose of at Santa Fé. Twelve mules drew the larger wagons, and eight or ten the smaller. Some few had oxen, whose feet were shod in a peculiar manner, to tread well upon the slippery prairie grass. Some of the oxen had their feet tied up in a bag of raw buffalo hide, which lasted well when the weather was dry; wet weather rotted them through. We, ourselves, had a light chaise with four wheels and a head covering, drawn by one horse. We also had three horses to ride, and for a change often took the saddle off one, and put him into the harness. By careful grooming and attention, we managed to keep our animals in very good condition, whilst others grew thin, lost flesh, and some died on the road, which was itself pretty well marked out by the skeletons of animals that had perished in previous journeys, and the bones of buffaloes that had been slain for the repast of the travellers. To manage our chaise, we had brought with us the old nigger, Stump, whom Flook had purchased as before related. Stump, himself, was, as he phrased it, " a good niggar, Sar! berry good niggar," but only with those whom he loved and respected. I am bound to say that with others he was very refractory, but to us he was always good, and took especial care of our Dearborn wagon, or since he would persist that the Yankee who sold it us cheated, as Flook called it, our dear-bought wagon. On the 21st of May, on a beautiful morning, the little party met at a place called Council Grove, thence to commence our journey over the ocean of land. One or two valetudinarians, " swells" of the Upper Ten Thousand from New York, accompanied us, for a journey across the prairies is frequently recommended as a restorative of health, the fine free bracing air, the change of scene, the hard, yet wholesome living, all conducing to this result. One of these, a young gentleman rejoicing in the name of Lafayette Peabody, attached himself to the

Britishers as they called us.  Before we reached Council Grove, which is about one hundred and fifty miles from Independence, we overtook a caravan of thirty more wagons, which had set out from another town, and which, with our twelve, made an imposing array of forty-two, which were formed in three lines abreast, and about fourteen feet from each other.  Our light wagon and about ten horsemen led the van, beyond these four or five horsemen, with rifles, made an advanced guard.  Two small and light cannons, six pounders, mounted upon carriages, were in the centre of the caravan, and a body of armed merchants, travellers, loafers, or valetudinarians who had joined the expedition brought up the rear; a party of four, mounted on very fleet horses, and with rifles ready for a moment's notice, formed the rear-guard of the company.

We were altogether a company of nearly one hundred members.  This company was formed into watches, commanded by eight lieutenants.  An experienced prairie traveller and merchant was entrusted with the command of the whole, and eight serjeants of the watch took upon themselves the onerous duty of seeing that all took their turn, and that none slept at their posts, so as to let us be surprised by Indians.  The dresses of our company were as various as their nations and persons.  The backwoodsman exhibited his leathern hunting-shirt, the wagoner, a flannel jacket, dyed red or blue, with flannel sleeves. The New Yorker had a fustian jacket with a multitude of pockets, the Englishman his blue worsted jersey over-all, with a belt round him, containing a multitude of pockets, and through which belt also he stuck his pistols. Our party was as variously armed. Colt's revolvers and repeating guns figured by the side of double-barrelled fowling-pieces, old rifles, flint-guns, and even the bell-mouthed blunderbuss, which the prairie men called " the scatter-gun," but which was proved to be useful in night attacks and surprises. Bowie-knives, axes, clasp-knives, and picturesque daggers hung about the clothes of our various friends, and made us look more like a predatory band of fillibusters than a peaceful party assembled solely for the purposes of trade. The axes were soon brought into requisition at Council Grove, all the fit timber we could see we cut for spare axle-trees and other wagon mending purposes, in case of accidents happening where we could not get timber nor aid.

When all was ready, for at Council Grove we waited for others, and the place is indeed a point of debarkation, the port on the land-ocean from which one sets sail, the captain, on the 30th of May, gave the word " Catch up," the preliminary order before starting. To " catch up " is simply the order to the teamsters to put to, and each was anxious to show his superior quickness or agility.

Old Stump had our horses in readiness, Bobus being seated in the wagon and not exactly caring to get on deck, as he called it, across a horse. The others were all bustle and hurry. The oxen were the first caught. The mules showed their natural obstinacy, and one or two of them, placing their fore feet on the ground, as if they had grown there, refused to stir. On the other hand, the oxen were willing enough, but every now and then would frighten each other by the jingle of their harness, or the rattle of the yoke, and start off on a stampede across the prairie, the teamsters running after them and the horsemen galloping ahead to turn them round.

Harnessed and in motion we soon were, and our caravan started with good hopes and prospects. Bobus had himself embarked some money in the venture, being determined to trade with the Santa Fe-ans.

Our route lay through a vast ocean of land, an uninterrupted prairie for about five hundred miles, broken only by fringes of timber edging the streams, or scattered clumps of trees miles and miles apart, and of very small extent. Each of us were on the look out for adventure, Stump being terribly afraid of the "Injuns," as he called them, and for the first few miles continually looking to the priming of his scatter-gun, to see that it was ready for the foe.

We had not proceeded ten miles on our way,

before our captain, who, with others, had ridden on ahead of us, blew his horn and called a halt. The teamsters stopped their wagons regularly, and within certain distances, whilst the horsemen rode to the front, those in the wagons looking to their rifles. When we came up we found the chiefs debating. The advanced guard had seen right in our track a pole stuck in the ground, upon which was the notice, " The Pawnees are out, beware !"

It had rather alarmed our foremost men, and there are always plenty of croakers in a camp. The older hands and stouter men, amongst whom was Bobus, however, pointed out that the grass had grown up round the pole, and that the card-board on which the notice was written, with a burnt stick, had been drenched and soaked with rain. Now, we had not had rain for ten days. Therefore, urged Bobus and the captain, the notice must have been at least ten days old, if not more.

" Them critturs hangs about a long time, stranger," said a cute Yankee, in a leathern jacket, and whose belt bristled with revolvers and bowie knives.

" You know better than I, sir," said Flook; " but the notice is an old one."

" It's as well to be cautious," said the captain, as he ordered the small cannon to be brought in front; " and we may as well be prepared."

"Ready it is, sir," said Bobus, "as they say board ship. I'll march with the cannon, I can use them if wanted."

The captain conferred apart, and then gave the word to advance, and the smacking of whips and the creaking of the wagons was soon heard again.

"Mas'r Flook, Mas'r Paget," cried old Stump to us, as he drove up our light wagon to our side; "do git on tother side the waggin, do, there's dear jantlemin, out o' the way of the Engins."

"Which engines?" said Flook.

"Them Pawnees is dreffle," continued Stump; "scalp ebery one, live or dead; scalp father, mother, and little piccaniny."

Flook did not pay much attention to our black friend, and we rode forward, and after two or three miles of slow progression we heard another cry. This time, although Stump was ready to declare that the "Engins" really had come upon us, it was really a cry of "Game, game ahead;" and there, a long way off, we saw a gathering of black bodies half buried in the long grass.

"Them's buffalo! buffalo!" cried the Yankee, all eagerness, putting spurs to his mustang, a fleet, beautiful creature. The word ran like an electric spark from one end to another of our line, and all who could ride pressed forward to the chase.

Flook and I were soon in the front rank, thanks

to the goodness of our horses. The teamsters of
one or two wagons left their cattle to take care of
themselves, and joined in the chase afoot. The
caravan was almost deserted, and Stump was
left in an agony of terror lest the Pawnees should
in reality come down. The Mexicans put their
lances in rest and rode straight at the herd, which
all at once alarmed, put their tails up in the air,
and galloped with a thundering heavy noise away,
scattering themselves on all sides.

The fleetest of us were soon in the midst of the
game, and a few sharp cracks of the rifles told us
that destruction had begun. But many shots
must have gone for nothing, for we soon halted
to count our spoils, and only five buffaloes lay on
the grass dying or dead. The dying were soon
dispatched ; the dead dragged to a circle, and
the captain gave word that the wagons should
be brought up, a halt was sounded, and our tents
pitched for the night, every one of the travellers,
who each had a prairie appetite, being ready and
willing to join in the feast, and taste the prairie
luxury of buffalo flesh.

Some skinned the beeves, and cut them up in
joints, strips, and slices; others kindled fires and
got ready the cooking apparatus, a frying pan, a
sheet iron kettle and coffee pot, and the never-
failing butcher's knife. All was bustle and anima-
tion, and it was determined that we should make
a short day's travel, and encamp for the night.

Now came the duties of the lieutenants. Spaces were measured out and assigned to each wagon, the mules and cattle were hoppled, that is, their front legs were tied so that they should not roam away, the wagons arranged in a circle, and the watchers chosen, and the feasting began.

This feasting put me very much in mind of what we used to read in Homer, under Doctor Leatherby's guidance, of the feasts of the Grecian heroes who besieged Troy. The immense slices of buffalo beef, which, I confess, was very nice, which we saw disappear beneath the knives of our travellers struck us with amazement, and I confess we did our share towards making the meat scarce. We did not leave much behind us, several of our company cutting huge strips of raw meat off the animals, rubbing them with salt on the outside, and hanging them on the wagons to dry.

"Isn't this prime?" said Flook, taking his third slice; "by Jove, I am eating like a Grecian hero."

"Just what I was thinking of," said I.

"Yes," said Flook, taking a long pull at his coffee tin which held about a pint; "but I'm thinking of—" here he paused.

"What?" I asked.

"Why, I'm thinking that supposing there had been a poet on the other side, the Trojan side, you know, whether we should not have heard a very different account of the matter, eh! Ah, it is not all true that we read in history. I wonder what the Indians here think of us."

" Tink, you berry nice young gen'l'um to scalp," said Stump, catching old of a rib-bone, and picking it with his white shining teeth.

" Catch'em at it," said Flook. " No, I suppose that if we look at things in one way, we shall find that the uppermost side is the best. Look round us now, look at these vast prairies and think what good must be when they are waving with yellow corn, or maize, enough to feed half the teeming population of Europe. Now the Indians would never think of cultivating the soil. They want to make hunting grounds of it, and look you, it is plain that the soil of God's earth belongs to his creature, man, for the purpose of cultivation and reproduction. He must prove his right to it by hard work."

" Engine," said Stump, speaking oracularly, " much like niggar, not berry fond o' work."

" You speak like a book, Mas'r Flook," said Bobus. " A little more coffee with your pipe, eh ?"

So the evening was spent, and the night wore on ; round the watch-fires, the travellers were gathering in groups after their feast, telling each other tales of trade, travel and adventure, the timid half-frightening others by long stories of cruelties and murders, and as cruel reprisals practised on the Comanches, Pawnees, Arrapahos, Loups and Eutaw Indians, whilst above them the calm majestic moon shone out in the clear heavens, and the stars surrounded her with their sparkling glory.

"Don't listen to those stories," said I to Flook, " let us turn in under our tent ; we have not to watch to-night, let us pray for safety in danger to One who watches all."

We did so, and soon we were lulled to sleep by the monotonous tread of the sentinels walking slowly round the camp, interrupted by nothing, save the sharp cry of the prairie bird, or the distant howl of the wild dog, as he bayed the moon.

# CHAPTER XXIX.



WE were awakened the next morning by a popping of pistols, a cracking of whips, and shouting of teamsters, which made us jump up in great haste.  Our party had discovered a perfect nest of rattlesnakes, and the sun and warm dew of the morning had caused them to crawl every where. They were not very large, nor very dangerous, and were, indeed, soon despatched; the great fear of our people being lest any should escape amongst the stock to bite the animals, for we had a perfect relay of mules, mustangs and colts, which had become attached to the caravan, in a very short time, and which followed it with an imperfect docility, occasionally fighting amongst themselves, and more than once being disturbed by a stray wild colt, which having lost its dam, came bolting amongst the stock, as amongst its own herd.

The rattle-snakes were all killed, and old Stump who, we had reason to believe, had shown no particular valour, came into our quarters, dragging the very largest snake, amongst some hundreds, which he had tied by the neck with a piece of raw hide cut from the buffaloes.

" Hallo, Stump, what are you going to do with that snake?" cried Flook and Bobus, in a breath.

" Will you eat him, like you did the buffalo?" I asked.

" No, Mas'r Ned," said Stump, with a grin which exhibited the whole of his white teeth. "No, dough de niggars do eat snake, snake chop not bad; but we no eat snake, make physic ob him."

" He's at some blessed Obi work," said Bobus, " I knew he would be."

" How will you make physic of him, Stump?"

" White genl'um," returned the negro, holding up a thick black finger, of about the circumference of one of Doctor Leatherby's rulers, " don't know chery thing—dis is what *dis* child,"—meaning himself, " will do—him will bissect de 'cad, take out de brain, and when am bit by rattlesnake, rub dat and some of 'im fat on de wound. Den am well ten minnit." He cut a caper after this, as if to show how the wounded man would jump after his revival.

" Come along, you old nigger, you, and make the coffee, we shall have to ' catch up' presently," said Flook. " Hang that villainous snake at the back of the dear-born. It's a good idea, Ned, we will take the fellow's skin home to the doctor, eh?"

This we immediately agreed upon, and Bobus, thinking he should like a skin for a tobacco-pouch, procured one as well. Then we had breakfast, with a little more buffalo, which Stump had secreted for us. We had scarcely finished eating when, "catch up" resounded from all parts of our camp, the teamsters hurried to their work, the whips smacked, horns blew, pistols were fired, and away we were *en route* again.

This day, nothing particular happened. We did not even sight a buffalo, although our friends continually rode in advance, hoping to do so. In the evening, we pitched our tent opposite the celebrated "*Caches*" of which an American border friend, who came to our tent to have a chat, and who peremptorily ordered old Stump to a distance, because he would not sit with a nigger, gave us the account which follows.

"The word *cache*," said he, "comes from *cacher*, to conceal, a French word—"

"What," interrupted Bobus, "have the Parleywoos been over here, then?"

"Aye, that they have," said the American, who had French blood in him, "don't you Britishers know that Canada belonged to them."

"Sartainly," returned Bobus, quickly, "it did, until we beat 'em out."

"Well," continued the narrator, "the French

traders used frequently to find themselves beset with Indians, who were a deal bolder and more full of fight than they are now. When these were on their track, the traders built in the prairie a place of concealment, by hollowing out the ground in the shape of a jug; this was lined with grass and dry sticks to protect its contents, the goods which were put in it, the turf was then replaced, and in a short time grew again, or fires lit a top, or cattle penned, which removed all traces of the cache to those who did not know the precise spot. Then the traders fled, and returned when the danger was over."

" Sometimes they must have forgotten the place," said I.

" No doubt; and sometimes they were cut off by their enemies. They used these caches not only in going, but in returning, and the earth which they removed they threw into the river, hence the caches are generally found by banks of streams. In these they sometimes placed. their gold, the result of a life of industry or fraud, and as some never returned, we have now amongst us 'cute Yankee gold finders, who spend half their lives in seeking these old caches, in hopes of suddenly jumping into fortune at once. Wal', I calculates, here comes one his self."

As he said this a tall, gaunt figure, with a wild aspect, a hooked nose, and long hair, which from underneath a steeple-crowned hat floated over his tanned and sun-blackened face, came towards the camp. He had a long, brown rifle slung at his back, and a tall stick, some eight feet high, shod for four feet at least with bright steel, in his right hand. As he came towards us he glared round, and held up his left hand with the palm towards us, as if to enlist us in his favour.

"Aye, aye," cried the Yankee, "we know all that; come on, old hoss, we shan't put a piece of lead through you."

The gold finder came to us.

"What luck, old man, what luck?" enquired the Yankee.

"Luck!" cried the gold finder, raising his withered arm, his coat, torn and worn, fluttering in strips of leather in the wind; "luck! not much, not much since the Sioux shot my wife."

"What, lost your squaw, eh! how's that, old hoss, eh?"

The gold finder shook his head, and did not answer.

"Wal'," continued the pert American, "that's not much loss to you, you can go on with your gold finding, or rather gold seeking, eh? You can move quicker than ever without a squaw, and pick up about double as much of what you love so well."

The eye of the old wanderer lighted up with a glance of deep resentment. "Love it so well," cried he, "and do not you love it well, young man, do not all of your people love it and seek it, in cheating others, in robbing your own flesh and blood; in false swearing and lying, in huckstering and bartering, in buying human flesh? that is how you Americans go gold seeking; but I, with this (here he lifted high his iron staff), merely go wandering over the face of the earth, killing no more than serves for my food, eating the fruits of the trees, or the wild roots that are strewn about; and seeking for what dead men have left, that with it I may purchase some small security for my worn out life. My life is more honest than yours."

"Bravo, Leather-stockings," cried old Flook, who listened with great interest; "now come, and sit down here, and tell us some of your adventures. Here is a can of coffee, and here is some white bread. That will tempt you, I am sure."

With a grim smile, half of triumph and half of satisfaction, the old, leather-clad fellow sat down stiffly, and took the bread, the buffalo flesh, and well filled can.

"Do you know," continued Flook, "that I am not sure that you are quite right with our friend here; you hit him hard about huckstering, cheating, and buying and selling human flesh. Those means are not the fair way of getting gold. But, look you, a trader who stores and distributes goods, who sends them into far countries, and who lives upon the enhanced price which such distribution must bring him, is an honest and a useful man ; very useful indeed. He brings his labour and judgment to the common store, he works, and others profit by his work ; but a gold seeker creates nothing, does nothing ; he brings more gold into the market, and men value that ; but you cannot eat that nor drink it, nor wear it. That's what I call political economy."

" Hey !" said our New York friend ; " the Britisher talks 'tarnation cute. If he were one of us he might be in the White House in a few years."

"Thankee, rather be in my own, in merry England," said Flook ; " I say, Leather-stockings, have you ever come upon a cache ?"

" Have I ?" returned the wanderer, indignantly pointing to the holes, by the river side, of caches which had been opened and explored. " Rather, my young friend. I have found gold, and vestments, and skins, and furs ; precious stones, and metals, old bottles full of rare liquid, and merchandise which had been buried a hundred years, and which was of no more value than the bones of its owner. Look here." He drew from his breast a Roman Catholic missal, bound in brown leather, and with ornamental silver corners and clasps. I took it, and, with Flook, examined it. Inside the cover was written, in faded ink, the name of " *Père Hennepin, A°· S*ˢ*· 1671." In smaller and more hastily written letters were the words, in English, " Leffte under the Earthe with merchandise and armes, 1680. To escape oure enemies we burie our chattels beneathe the sodd. Lord prevente us with thy care !"

"Well, and what do you make of that?" said the gold finder.

"It belonged, I suppose, to one of the Jesuit Fathers, who came here in the early missions. Some of them for the sake of religion, some, I fear, only to make money for their order," returned Flook.

"Some were martyred, cruelly put to death with frightful torments, roasted alive, or, with small iron pins driven under each nail, on toe or finger, left to perish in misery. No! belie not the religion of those men; they were the good, the faithful, and the bold, who left the cunning of the priests, and the chicanery of so-called religion, to those in town, and came here to spread the good tidings of the Cross."

The old man crossed himself reverently as he said this, and, having finished his meal, rose.

"Will you not travel further with us?" said I, "You can tell us more about your adventures, and you may possibly find other treasures on the banks of the streams we cross."

"No," cried he, lifting up his iron-pointed rod, and looking taller and more gaunt than before. "No, I have a purpose before me, which I must fulfil."

"Gold finding, stranger, I guess," lisped the Yankee.

"No," cried he, in a voice of thunder; "No, revenge!  I go amongst those Sioux warriors to slay the slayer of my wife.  I found her dead body, and I know that he who killed her, if he lives, wears her scalp hung to his belt, or waving in his wigwam.  I know those dear locks well, and he who wears them, if I meet him, dies!  That is, at present, all the gold I seek."

Without a word more, he stalked away southward.  The setting sun, the red rim of which was just seen above the land-ocean, into which it seemed sinking, threw his long shadow across the waving prairie-grass, and made him seem more gaunt, more fantastic, more wild and weird than before.

"I calkilate," said the Yankee, "that he's half senile, that stranger."

"He means what he says," answered Bobus.

"And all about his squaw, eh?  Wal', some people do kind o' feel the loss.  I shall take a pipe, and turn in.  Good night, you Britishers."  And our guest left us for his tent.

# CHAPTER XXX.



WE had not proceeded many miles the next
morning before we discovered water. The spur of
a river ran across our path, and, as we had drunk
but pond water lately, we were all very ready to
reach it.

Away, therefore, we started; and it also happened that, having been on a short supply, and
being tired also from a long pull, our cattle were
just as eager as ourselves. Hence the mischief.
We had nearly all of us quenched our thirst,
when one of the hindmost wagons came thundering down the bank, drawn by oxen, so thirsty
and eager that the drivers could not stop them,
and the wagon was turned over into the water.
There was a great row, of course; everybody was
anxious to give directions, and few to follow them,
which is a great source of trouble; but Bobus,
Flook, and myself jumped into the stream, de-

termined to show that the "Britishers" could lend a hand in distress. We had soon very many helping hands, and in a short time about an acre of ground was covered with cotton goods, cloths, stuffs, and other merchandise, spread out to dry. Misfortunes never come alone. The bustle of this had hardly ceased, when we heard the most dreaded cry of all—"The Indians! The Indians!"

We were completely taken by surprise. Many of our travellers were very careless, and the cries of "Where's my powder!" "I've spilt my caps!" "My lock is unshipped!" "Who has any bullets?" &c., were innumerable. Captain Johnston, the gentleman who had been elected to command the caravan, found few to obey his orders. A dozen voices, besides those of his lieutenants, offered advice. "Fire at 'em, captain; hit the beggars; look how they grin. Now's your time." But far above this row was heard the calm voice of our leader—his firmness saved our little band.

"The first man who fires, before I give the word, I will shoot," cried he, pointing his revolver along the irregular line.

"Bravo, cap'en," rejoined Bobus; "nothing like discipline. I'll shoot the second."

"First twenty form in line," continued the captain. Old Stump with his blunderbuss, Flook, Bobus, and myself, stood at the head of this; and a first line being formed, a second and third soon gathered in order, whilst the wagons, with wheels locked in wheels, were formed into a circle, the two cannons brought in front, and our drum and fife put to the left of our party.

We had too many volunteer artillerymen; but the captain ordered them back, and called Bobus to take the command of the larger piece, which was loaded with canister. In very little time the Anglo-Saxon element of duty and combination began to show itself. The Indians were upon us, but we were ready to receive them. They galloped up with a great show, all of the warriors being mounted on horses or mustangs. When they came near they hoisted a flag—simply a coloured handkerchief. This took away much of our uneasiness, and the party turning out to comprise only about eighty Sioux Indians, we were quite assured. Our communications we carried on by signs; and as the chief, with much pretension, lighted and smoked a long calumet, or pipe of peace, we were very nearly at our ease. Still we kept guard.

From signs, however, we learned something which did not please us. They conveyed to us the news that there was a very large party of Blackfeet and Comanches very near us. The number of these new enemies were, as far as we could gather, immense. What was to be done?

A council of war was held; a noisy one it was.

Here I must note the evil effects of insubordination and want of government. Our captain had been elected by the whole body, but none seemed willing to obey him; he was an experienced traveller, having been over the prairies five times, and a brave, calm, firm man, and yet our camp was split into various divisions. The example of Bobus, the old man-of-war's-man, of ourselves, and still more the threats and determined looks of the latter, gave weight to the authority of the leader, and we agreed at last to double the watch, and to assume something like military order in our march.

It was lucky that we did so. The first party of Indians soon departed, but on the morning of the 26th of June on descending into the valley of the Amazon and hastening to reach the river, which the scarcity of water, and want of rain, had made us long to approach, we found drawn up before us a great body of savages. These, too, were only the vanguard. One of the foremost gave a shriek or whoop, and then from the opposite ridges, troop upon troop came pouring.

We were soon face to face with about two thousand of the tribes which the small body of the Sioux had told us of, and from which they themselves had fled. Two lines of our men formed as before with loaded rifles, and with strict orders to reserve their fire; behind these the two cannons were posted. The wagons were quickly formed, and the more cautious and timid of our men took their stand in that circle, with protruding rifles, ready to sell their lives as dearly as they could. We had agreed on certain signals, and the presence of great danger made our company obedient and willing.

The chief line of the Indians, amongst whom were several horsemen with the lasso, stood in array fronting us, and their faces seemed to me to wear every determination of attack. Their eyes were lit up with a strong passionate desire, and they knew well enough that in our wagons was merchandise which would make them comparatively rich.

"Well Flook," said I, as we stood face to face with the foe, "how do you feel?"

"How do you?" returned Flook, "I am as cool as a cucumber. How's old Stump, there?"

"Berry nicely massa," said the nigger, looking to the pan of his scatter-gun; "don't fear red man, no black man does; fear white man, red man berry 'ferior hanimal, black man no fear him."

"Aye," said Flook, "but there's such a lot of these 'ferior animals, d'ye see."

"Neber mind, kill many wid my gun, shoot 'em like de chicken."

By 'chicken' old Bobus understood the prairie grouse, of which in his time he had no doubt bagged a few. I was not so certain but that our red friends might bag us.

"Hold your fire! here they come," cried the captain, "be firm and wait my words."  The Indians made certainly a demonstration of attack, and some of the fiery backwoodsmen in our ranks were nearly letting fly at them with their rusty rifles, rusty indeed, but pieces which never missed aim.  The captain, however, who stood at our head, waved his hand to stay us, and at the same time shouted, "Open lines, forward with the artillery!" and our two little pieces, loaded nearly to the muzzle with grape and canister, were run out in front about ten paces; Bobus, as chief artilleryman, and a dozen stalwart fellows with rifles and ready port-fires behind them.  "Steady, my men!" cried Bobus, levelling the cannon at the serried mass of Indians, "now we have them! Ready, cap'en, when you are."

Luckily the captain had no reason to give the word.  The Indians knew very well the nature of the cannon, encounters with several caravans who carried them taught them this.  They had in fact never been successful in attacking so large a force as we mustered, although, as the United States' Government knew to their cost, they slew small bands like those of Captains Smith and Sublette, and solitary travellers.  When they saw our cannon they started back in great alarm, their warriors and fighting men breaking into small knots, and evidently taking counsel as to their proceedings. Presently they opened their lines, and two or three chiefs, headed by a principal chief who was dressed in coarse red cloth ornamented with porcupine quills and the fur of the badger, came forward, looking perfectly composed, and serenely smoking the pipe of peace!

"Aha! ha, ha!" laughed an old backwoodsman next to me, as he lowered his rifle, "They wont fight now, and dang me," said he, pointing to a long train of people coming over the hill, "there are the squaws and papooses."

His sight was better than ours, for in a few minutes we saw that he was right, and that the women and children were coming over the hill. By that time the captain had taken one or two whiffs of the pipe, and made signals to the chief to cause his men to retire. This they did, and our people, forming a front and rear guard, again moved on, whilst the greater portion of the Indians went back to their camp.

The chief and other heads of the tribes, however, hovered about us, accompanied with two or three hundred warriors, and in a short time invited our captain to a "big talk," in which, to make matters short, the Indians gave us to understand that they expected a present for letting us pass them.

This method of levying "black mail" was disagreeable, but the wiser men of our party over-ruled the more adventurous, and one or two 'lots' were made up and given to the Indians, with which they retired.

But after one trouble came another; our caravan was surrounded by the squaws and papooses, who came so evidently for the triple purpose of begging, borrowing, and stealing, that our guards sent them, sternly, to the right about, and though we were annoyed for a day or two, we were at last allowed to continue our journey in peace.

# CHAPTER XXXI.

## THE PRAIRIE WOLF—THE WATER SCRAPE.

THE prairie journey had done wonders with old Flook and myself. We were stronger, bolder, and more active. We had grown so used to the saddle that we passed whole days in it, we grew attached to our horses, and by constantly grooming them and feeding them, had made them so fond of us that they would trot to us at our call, and even when the mules and other cattle were seized with that extraordinary fit of terror, called the stampede, in which all gallop off together, each terrifying the other, and are frequently lost for ever to the owners, our horses came towards us, trembling, and frightened, indeed, but passive enough to be caught and reassured.

In our wagons we had also taken the precaution to bring some oats and a little " timothy,"* tame

* Called so by the Americans, to distinguish it from the wild prairie grass.

or cultivated hay, a very little of which mixed with the grass of the prairie sweetened it, cured it of its roughness, gave it flavour, and, consequently, kept our horses in condition long after those of our friends in the caravan looked very deplorable, indeed, and were unable to do their work well.

We found, in fact, that paying attention and showing kindness to an animal was never thrown away, and more than once we owed our lives to the very animals we had tended. I had a little dog, which we brought from Charleston, a little ugly fellow, upon whom, when in that city, everybody looked with some degree of dislike : he was of a miserable temper, and snapped at everybody, in short, so ill-grained a cur, that every one seemed to think it an especial duty to tease and worry him, as *he* thought it a duty to bark and howl. I was puzzled at the dog's ill-nature, and strove to find a cause for it, believing that dogs, when well treated, are almost always good tempered. I, therefore, petted, played with, and fed it, much to the surprise of old Flook, who could not think what I could see in the brute. At last, however, ' Growler,' as he was called, abandoned his ill-temper, at least to me, and would, when tired, run by the side of my horse, and beg prettily to be taken up at my saddle-bow.

We were camping out, one night, not long after we met with the Indians, and after a long ride, I had fallen asleep. We, were, I remember, very hungry too, for we had not eaten meat for a day or so, having not fallen in with any buffalo. I was dreaming of our pleasant fields in England, and the woods and walks about the old school, when I was awoke by a terrible growling and a noise of two bodies rolling over and over in our tent. Both Flook and myself jumped up, and in the grey light of the morning we saw two dogs fighting, as we thought, one was our friend Growler, the other I tried to seize by the throat to pull him off my dog, who was getting the worst of it, when I found to my horror that it was a she wolf.

Flook had jumped up with a huge stick in his hand, but I cried out, " take care, it is a wolf, Flook."

" Here, I have my revolver," he cried, cocking that weapon and firing, but without effect. In the meantime, my hand had fallen upon a thin rapier blade, which had I bought at New York, and wore in a cane; quick as thought, I had drawn it and passed it through the heart of the wolf, pinning her to the ground. She was dead in an instant and without a struggle; and we dragged out poor Growler from under her body. In saving our lives, poor Growler had lost his own. He was bitten dreadfully, one of his ears torn off; his muzzle mangled, and worse than all, his loins were bitten through. He knew, I think, that he was dying, and tried to wag his poor tail, and licked our hands with his bleeding tongue, as he lay on the ground. The wolf had, no doubt, crept into our tent, and would very likely have sprung at our throats, had it not been attacked by poor, faithful Growler. The dog died, as we squeezed into his mouth some water, to quench his last thirst. His eyes brightened up and flashed out affection at the last, and the dying howl he gave, as he turned to us, for the last time, seemed expressive of his love.

"Poor fellow," said Flook, softly, as he lifted up the dog's head and let it drop again : "and yet I never liked the dog ; how affectionate and brave the poor fellow was."

Our Yankee friend, who had come into our tent, hearing the pistol, and the noise, took his continual pipe out of his mouth, and sentimentalised, à la Byron. "Ya'as," said he, "I calculates dogs are good'uns. A darned sight 'cuter and better nor men, and as for 'fection, why, may I never, if I wouldn't rather trust the love of a dog, than that of a man. Wal', I calculate you'll skin that 'ere carcase, for sake of the dog. Good mornin' !"

"That there young feller ought to go to school again," said Bobus : "I should like to put him under Doctor Leatherby's care, or on board a good English ship, with a tight captain and a stiff first lieutenant. They'd teach him something as he never knowed before. Love a dog better than man! He must be a dog to say it."

" To believe it, rather," said Flook, " most of these young men speak for effect, and you must not believe what they say. He thinks it fine, as a distinguished poet thought it fine, to pretend to love a dog rather than man. But now, who is going to help me skin the wolf?"

Both Bobus and myself volunteered, and after Stump had made our coffee, we took the two dead animals and gave one honourable burial, putting a pole up over his grave, and enclosing in a box a description of himself, and the manner of his death. We then fastened the hind legs of the grey prairie wolf to the tail of our wagon, and although I had never skinned any animals, save mice and moles, at school, we managed to take its coat off, capitally. We then threw away the body, thoroughly washed the skin, and hung it up, rubbed with salt, to the cover of our dearborn, in which situation, the air of the prairies being remarkably pure, it became half-tanned leather before we reached Santa Fé, at which city I got it thoroughly dressed.

Our next adventure was to get into a " water serape," which, in the language of the Americans, expressed one of the most horrible positions of the prairie traveller. It bears this name because there is no water to be found, and both travellers and cattle are fainting for want of it. Solitary travellers, exhausted and weak, often perish miserably in this way, but with us there was not so much danger.

The Indian difficulty, and our hurry to press through it, had made us forget to fill our barrels and cans at the stream in which our wagon was overturned, and it was in the midst of a sultry day that thirst came upon us with all its horrors.

Horrible it was, a burning, sickening, drying feeling. A mawkish longing, worse and more debilitating than that of hunger, took possession of us. The mules fell. The cattle thrust out their tongues, the teamsters staggered along almost speechless. The great, gruff voices of men which could have been heard at the distance of half a mile, sank and dwindled to a whisper. Then it was that I felt that moisture was as necessary as the tongue for speech, the tongue unaided by the exhausted glands refused to do its duty, or stammered and hesitated in its work.

Still we staggered on. Some mounted the highest wagon, and with their glasses swept the country round. Others galloped ahead in hopeless search of places pointed out, merely to come back exhausted, burning with a feverish heat and irritated at the loss of time. The captain had one or two of our oxen killed, and each of us sucked a portion of the blood, or chewed the moist and raw flesh. Some scraped at the prairie roots and bit at the dry grass; a great majority, insisting that we were lost, gave themselves up to despair; indeed, had we remained much longer in our dilemma, I am afraid that more than one would have sank under it, had not old Stump, who bore the trial better than any, come in with the joyful news of help and hope. He had found at about a mile to the southward a little pond, dried up, indeed, but with the remains of moisture, in which he thought by digging we might find some relief.

The majority of our party hurried to the place indicated, and by hard labour and patience managed to get a little water, but the process was painfully slow, and the men were ready to quarrel with each other for priority at the well. Others, too impatient to wait their turn, rode off in other directions. Some laughed bitterly at our little muddy supply, some knelt down and prayed, more earnestly and heartily than those rough natures had done for days and years—for rain. Slightly relieved by the few drops which trickled into the well we had formed, with our cattle too exhausted to move, we laid down and waited, scarcely knowing what to do. The cloudless sky was still above us, and the declining sun darted his slanting rays upon us, blinding us with the glare. From the prairie rose a thin mephitic vapour, and winds began to blow over the ocean of land; the barometer fell, and the more experienced of our companions predicted a coming storm. Then out of the west a slight and dark cloud, a vapour almost, at first arose, next it grew more intense in its blackness, though it was no bigger than a man's hand. It changed rapidly, and overspread full half the sky.

"It's comin', I tell ye; give glory to whom it is due; it's comin'; I prayed for it," gasped and whispered one old man, as we sat and watched it.

"It will be a prairie storm," said the captain; "form the wagons, and place the cattle in the circle; hopple the mules, and stake out your grounds, quick!" With a new energy, and a new hope our little band set to work, and shortly got all right, stretching strong sheeting and tarpauling, over the wagons, fixing the tents with extra ropes. Those who had left us, warned by the blackness of the sky, retraced their steps, and hardly were we all safe when the storm began.

A flash of light and one sudden clap of thunder, so loud, so terrific as to appal the stoutest there, followed by a series of discharges like platoon firing, and multiplied a hundred fold by reverberations, opened the storm. The earth shook under us, and the black sky, shaken as it were into rain, poured down a cataract of water, which moistening our parched skins gave us immediate relief.

"We're saved, we're saved!" cried he who

prayed, stretching out his hands to catch the water.

"I calc'late," said the Yankee, "that you Britishers never saw the likes o' this. When we rain in America we *do* rain, just a trifle."

We were safe under the cover of our dearborn, looking at the storm. The cattle huddled together with their backs to it, licked the wet grass with delight, and with an exquisite sense of relief.

"Look at that 'ere nigger," cried Bobus, after drinking a handful of rain water.

Stump had stood the thirst better than all of us, but his delight at the rain was intense. He was lying on his back, enjoying the shower-bath to his heart's content, and kicking about as if he were swimming.

"Oh, golly, Mas'r Ned, isn't him berry good, berry much refresh poor old niggar, 'fought he was a goin to be dried up like a bit of buffalo flesh, but dis child is all safe in dis bootiful storm."

# CHAPTER XXXII.



OUR trouble for want of water was nearly the last which we encountered on our journey across the prairies. The next morning, after the storm, the whole face of nature seemed changed and refreshed, the birds sang, the sun shone, and all looked hopeful and joyful.

A poor mule singled out in the midst of the cattle, and struck dead by the lightning, formed the only exception. Our misfortunes were soon forgotten, and our trials seemed to have vanished, the teamsters hastened to 'catch up'; the captain gave the word 'forward,' and away we once more started on our long journey, a journey now nearly at its end.

It was early in July when we arrived at the 'Upper Spring,' a clear crystal fountain breaking through the rocky banks of a ravine which declines towards the Cinvarron, about four miles to the

15

north. We halted there, and the next morning being the well-known fourth of July, all the Americans of our party celebrated the anniversary of their Independence, and the commencement of the Union. Guns were fired, whips cracked, the artillery discharged, and the fife and drum brought into continual request. The jubilee was perfect, all the more so because we now found that we were within two hundred miles of Santa Fé, and our hopes were at their highest.

There were men in our camp called " runners," a sort of *avant couriers* which always accompany a caravan, who started at once for Santa Fé, being pretty well safe from all danger, and having the double object of making good terms with the custom-house officers, and advertising the merchants of our arrival. This being done, they purposed starting again to meet us, with various articles and fresh provisions, which they knew we wanted. The " runners " started in the night, so as to avoid any enemies who might be lurking round our camp.

The next day our march being resumed, we halted at a huge mound, from the summit of which we could trace the track of our caravans, and see our rear-guard slowly toiling on with their tired cattle and wagons, and beyond which the eye wandered over the flat prairies, till it lost all vision in the distance.

From this eminence we saw the prairie on fire.

The hot sun had again dried the grass, and had sucked every moisture from it, and the tobacco from the pipe of one of our stragglers served to light it. Luckily the wind set from us, not towards us, and we were enabled to view with safety, the great body of flame and smoke as it roared and raced onwards. Every now and then we could see with our glasses wild deer and other animals, frightened and driven before the flame, bound away into the distance, seeking and often in vain, safety in flight. Reason had we to be thankful that we had escaped the trial and danger ; the blackened smoking prairie where the fire had passed, showed dreadful and hideous in the glistening sunlight, charred mounds of earth, stumps of old trees, dead snakes and reptiles, lay here and there when we galloped over the place.

In two days from this we were met by a horseman who came from Santa Fé, into the prairies, buffalo hunting. The Mexicans called him a *cibolero*, and he was dressed in leathern trousers and jacket, the former made wide in the legs, and with a row of silver buttons down the side of the leg. A broad hat, a *sombrero*, covered his head. At his back hung a *carcage* or quiver, in which were bow and arrows. A long rifle swung at the other shoulder, and on the pomel of his saddle, nattily coiled up, was his *lasso*. A sharply pointed lance, from the top of which depended a tassel of party-coloured stuffs, silk and worsted, hung in its rest, and was kept upright by a loop of leather around his arm.

Our front rank of horsemen rode at once to meet him, and he, equally rejoiced at the sight of our faces, rode forward. "What news from Santa Fé?" we cried. "What chance for trade? How are goods?" He returned these questions, almost before answering, by asking what we had brought, and what news we had from the States.

From him we learned the sad fate of the caravan which had preceded ours by about a month. Having lost their track they had strayed northward, and their captain had been slain, with many of his men, by a band of Indians. The remnant had escaped, but fared badly; their cattle had died, and they were obliged to abandon half their wagons in the prairie. Some had, distrusting others, set forward to find out another track, and never having reached Santa Fé were supposed to have perished by hunger or thirst!

"Who were the Indians who slew them?" cried the old woodsmen, gripping hard their rifles, and exhibiting a decided determination to avenge their comrades, should they catch the black-skins. "What tribe were they of?"

"Of two," returned the *cibolero* lighting his pipe; "they were Comanches and Gros Ventres, but they are far beyond your vengeance now, *Amigos Americanos*. There will come a time, no doubt, when we shall exterminate those *diablos*."

"Or civilise them," suggested I. My American friends burst into a loud laugh. "An Indian," said they, "cannot live in a civilised state any how. You must be content with him as he is, or kill him."

Our cibolero brought from a little encampment where he had settled, prairie beef, jerked and hung, soft bread, and other delicacies for our travellers, and having dealt with as many as he could, proposed to those who were well mounted to show the way to Santa Fé.

Eager to get there at all hazards, many embraced the offer, and we were of the number. Leaving old Stump to take care of our dear-born, and staunch old Bobus to guard our goods, I and Flook and several others who were well mounted, pushed forward for Santa Fé.

The road, as we advanced, became more and more strewn with broken wagons and goods. Those travellers who had exhausted their teams, and their own patience, or whose animals and provisions were quite spent, had been compelled to leave behind them many hundreds of dollars' worth of goods. Travellers hurrying on across the rocky mountains by way of the prairies to California, emigrants to Utah, traders to Santa Fé, had each and all been forced to abandon their merchandise. In the general land-wreck the heaviest articles had been thrown overboard first.

Big sea-chests, chests of drawers, old arm chairs, brought across the Atlantic perhaps, and the relics of humble English homes lay scattered here and there. Caddies, looking-glasses, fenders, and old guns, saddles, and harness, tables, desks broken open and rifled of their contents, feather-beds, sacking, pictures and old mirrors, which lay up, glittering like silver in the open sky, clocks, cabinets, boxes of tools, old swords, books, pillows, clothes, and various other household goods, marked the track as we went along. Here and there was a broken down wagon, with the skeletons of the exhausted mules which had died in their harness. Now and then we came upon a dead saddle-horse. Eager to escape desolation and death in the wilderness the traveller had ridden his horse till the animal could go no further, had dismounted and hurried on on foot, often without, so I heard, even having the mercy to shoot the poor animal which had served him so faithfully.

"Ah, *amigos mios*," said the *cibolero*, twisting some of his light tobacco in a light husk called the *hoja*, and forming a *cigarito*, "ah, but the life of a man is dear; to save *that* he will abandon anything. Look at this track. We are now one hundred miles from *Santa Fé de San Francisco*, and you will find every mile of the way strewn in this manner. I knew a *ranchero*, a peasant, who made money by going out with a span of mules and bringing into Santa Fé the property thus scattered about by the *Americanos.*"

"What's that?" said Flook, looking ahead and shading his eyes with his hand.

"Ha!" cried the Mexican, throwing away the cigarita and taking his lasso from his shoulder; "a fine young buffalo; look, senhors," and away he galloped like the wind. His horse, up to his work, and understanding the chase, pressed forwards as eagerly as his master. The reins hung loosely on his neck, the huge Mexican spurs were not needed, his rider pressing his knees into the saddle, and leaning forward. The *cibolero* rode near to the buffalo before it perceived him, for it was grazing quietly. It raised its horned head for a moment, the lasso was flung out, and after describing two or three circles in the air fell with unerring aim around the neck of its prey. The hunter gave a peculiar cry, and the horse started away from the game, leaning from it when the cord drew tight, and adding its weight to the strength of its master.

The struggle was not of long duration. Choked by the noose, the buffalo calf gave two or three leaps and plunges, and fell exhausted to the ground. The *cibolero* pulled the noose tighter and tighter for a few moments, and then dismounting ran to his prey and gave him the *coup de grace* with his hunting-knife.

We galloped to our friend and found that he had already begun to skin his prey, and, having camped, we lit a fire, produced our coffee pot, and broiling some steak ate a capital meal upon the prairies, then stretching our blankets under us, having first tethered our horses, we wrapped ourselves warmly up and went to sleep.

In two days after this we sighted Santa Fé, much to our delight. The town is not much to look at, the houses flat, very much like heaps of bricks, inasmuch as, when entering the town, we thought that we had come only upon the suburbs of the town.

Here we met our runners, who were ready to go out again to meet the wagons, having arranged with the custom-house officers and the different merchants of the place. We found that we should have an excellent market, and our *cibolero* took us to some friends who offered us money for our dear-born wagon upon the report of our friend.

It was six days after our arrival that our caravan came in sight. The inhabitants of Santa Fé were quite as glad to see them as the teamsters were to reach the wished-for city. The latter had put on their Sunday clothes, washed their faces and oiled their hair, and put the best face both upon themselves and their wagons and teams. As they drove into the town they made the air resound by cracking their whips, shouting, firing pistols, and making other noises. The inhabitants made quite a gala night of it, the custom-house officers took charge of the goods, and our long long journey was at an end.

Although separated for so short a time, our joy in again meeting with Bobus and old Stump was great, and the feeling was mutual. Our black servant, for Flook and I had long ago made him a present of himself, had grown very much attached to us, and had been really valuable; how he chaffered and bartered, and the manner in which he sold all our goods at a handsome profit, deserves a chapter to itself had we space in the book for half of our adventures. Stump had also distinguished himself, and had saved, or partly saved the live of Jack Bobus.

The manner of it was this. On the very evening upon which we left them, the caravan had encamped near a beautiful ravine, amongst the rocks and caves of which one or two of the adventurous hunters hoped to find a " grizzly Bahr," or old grizzly, as they called the North American bear, often met with in those regions and places.

As the cattle needed rest, and there was a plentiful supply of grass and water, the captain determined to stay there for a day, and Jack Bobus, tired of the restraint of the wagon, determined to lie out and bask in the sun. He was fast asleep on some dry grass, in a little nook, near the ravine, when the hunters started a great grizzly she-bear and cub; the latter fell a victim at once, and the mother flying from the hunters, and full of rage and fury, took refuge in the very nook where Bobus lay. It was on the edge of the ravine, and the old sailor was awakened to find his path blocked by a bear, with glaring eyes, and hunted into fury. There was no escape—at his back was a precipice, before him the bear, and Jack Bobus was as near death, perhaps, as ever the stout old fellow had been in his life. He was unarmed, save by his jack-knife, which he wore with a lanyard round his waist. This he opened, and rushed on the bear, determined to plunge it in its heart.

Stump, eager to signalise himself, with his old scatter-gun had hurried to the scene, and knowing where Bobus was, was horrified. But the brave old nigger rushed on to save his friend, one of the backwoodsmen, armed with a " five-shooter" pistol, a revolver, ran also with him. They found Bobus in the very grasp of the bear, the pistol was discharged in its ear, the muzzle of the blunderbuss thrust into its mouth, both exploded together, and Bobus was saved, scarcely knowing to which to attribute his life; to the bravery, the alertness, and steadiness of Stump and his old, rusty scatter-gun, which for once went off at the right time, and in the right place, or to the pistol of the backwoodsman. Stump, however, took all the credit to himself and his wonderful gun, and the skin of the " grizzly," the head perforated with many balls, hung as a trophy to the tail-board of our wagon.

" He is a brave old nigger, anyhow," said Bobus, " and if he comes to England with us, he shall enter the Queen's service, and I will get him a berth aboard ship; he shall be rated as cook, or my name's not Jack Bobus."

# CHAPTER XXXIII.

THE JOURNEY ACROSS THE ROCKY MOUNTAINS—
THE GOLD DIGGERS—WE SET SAIL FOR FIJI.

WE found that acting upon the advice of our American friend, and aided by Stump, we had made a very fair venture with our merchandise. It had paid all our expenses to Santa Fé, and we had somewhat to spare. We sold our wagon, but kept our horses, purchasing one for Bobus, and a mule for our black friend.

We stayed at Santa Fé some time to rest, but were not very favorably impressed with the people. Below the middle height, well made, athletic, and full of passion, the Mexicans are cowardly, yet desperate, revengeful, indolent and proud. They are proud of their Spanish blood, which is yet so mixed with the Indian, and with that of other nations, that in the small town of Santa Fé one finds almost all complexions, skins and nations. They are considerably less than half-civilised, these people, full of blind superstitions, following any one who chooses to lead them, for the time, and then deserting him, for the next one who promises anything.

The women have beautiful figures, dance lightly and well, but are vain, and if offended are terrible in their revenge. The people are hospitable, for it costs them little to give, they are glad to entertain a stranger, for the entertainment is their only amusement. They hate the Americans, for they have too often felt the power of the States, but they love and welcome the English, and the fact of our nationality introduced us to many houses.

I had sojourned there a month, when leaning against a wall, listening to the eternal twang, twanging of the guitar, and watching a *fandango*, when our young American friend came up, and calc'lated that he was tired of this sort of thing, and meant to start in a day or two, by way of the great salt lake city to California, and from St. Francisco he should take a sea voyage round the Horn, and then, when he landed at New York, he should calc'late that he had seen the world.

Flook had just joined us, and began philosophising about the manners and customs of the people, when our young American, with a yawn, said, " that the people might be darned, for his part, he intended to make to St. Francisco, and that he would take a peep at the diggers."

To which proposition Flook readily assented.

Bobus and old Stump were, we found, quite as ready to go as we were, and we all set about our preparations in good earnest.

"Across those rocky mountains," said the American, "arn't much of a joke. However, I will take a guide, and we must trust to luck."

Luck was, however, against us. Our voyage this time was full of difficulty and danger, our guide was drowned in passing a branch of the river Colorado. Our cattle died, we were obliged to abandon one wagon, and, at last, reached the diggins in a miserable plight. Old Stump was nearly worn to the skin, and the city, in which we rested, was not the most delightful in the world. I often recalled the words of the old woodsman, about gold, when I listened to the quarrels, blasphemy, and utter want of peace in that crowded city. All were there upon one common mission. All actuated by one common low passion, the love of suddenly growing rich. That one low passion had levelled all. Jealousy of each other's success, disappointment at their own "luck," utter disregard of anything, but a good haul, distinguished the place. The struggle for gold, which preach as we will, and write as we will, goes on all over the world, was here brought into a small circle. The vices of the community were subjected to a magnifying focus, as a drop of water is, when placed under a microscope, and our common humanity was far from gaining by the process. Sudden wealth, acquired too often, we thought, by the vulgar and the low, brought out the pride, the cruelty, or the lust of the possessor in horrible relief. Murders were of frequent occurrence, suicides arising from disappointed hopes, acting upon weak minds perhaps as frequent. I sickened at the contact of these men, and begged Flook to depart.

"By Jingo, Paget," said that philosopher, "you are right. It is well to watch the diggers and the washers of gold; it is well to mark the various kinds of men—the proud gentleman shouldering the escaped thief; the strong navvy, who knows his muscles are of more value here than any amount of brain; but it is sickening, positively sickening. When we find an opportunity we will go."

The opportunity soon offered. An English vessel, sailing about those places on a trading expedition, and soon about to return to Europe, round the Horn, put into San Francisco to take on board some necessaries, and, eager to escape, we four, Bobus, Stump, my schoolfellow and myself, took our passage on board her. We were rejoiced to find that, having some idea of gaining further knowledge of the plants indigenous to Polynesia, a *savant* had made an agreement with the skipper that he should bend somewhat from his course, and visit the islands of Fiji.

# CHAPTER XXXIV.



IT was early in December that we sighted the first of an outlying group of islands, the whole range of which has been called the "Fidji," or "Feejee," group. The captain of our bark had, with a very blame-worthy improvidence, allowed us to run short of water, and it was necessary for us to put into one of the numerous bays we saw to escape a second "water scrape;" but, this time, not on land, but at sea.

Bobus, who had been inactive and silent enough when on land, showed to great advantage when at sea, and spoke with bitterness and contempt of our skipper. He would not call him captain; that honorable distinction he always reserved at sea to him who alone ought to bear it—a captain in the service of the Crown.

As we drew near the islands a sight of beauty broke upon us. We were near the Polynesian group. We were in a sea of islands. Everywhere before us the ocean was studded with beautiful islands, some only islets, others worthy of being the seat of a king. Rare foliage, a brilliant atmosphere, soft breezes, and a calm sea, united to make a scene full of beauty. Coral-reefs, lying a mile or so from each coast, served as natural break-waters, and, in the centre of each land, mountain forms, purple in the sun's light, rose into the calm heavens.

We were soon observed from the shore of the principal island, to which we bent our course, Thikomba, which lies about 16¼° north and 178° east from Greenwhich. As we passed into the bay, proas and canoes were seen on each side, and, as we came near, swimmers, both male and female, swam out to receive us, and, with strange shouts, clamoured round our vessel.

"Don't trust 'em, skipper," said Bobus; "Don't do it, if you value your ship and cargo. I know them. False they are, and treacherous. They are cannibals, like all the rest of this group, and they would not object to eat a white man any more than one of their own kith and kin. I remember them well."

"Have you ever seen them do so?" said one of the crew.

"Have I? I should think so. I remember, years ago, when I was in a South-Sea whaler, a hunting about for sparmacitty whales, that on our passage home we touched at one of these islands. A precious nice lot they were. Our boat's crew, armed with muskets, was too strong for them, so they invited us to a kind of talkee talkee; for when they fear the white man they are civil to him. Now, what do you think we had for dinner?"

"Pigs," said one.

"Fowls," suggested another.

"Turtle-soup," cried a third, remembering that some of the islands are called the "Turtle Isles."

"All very good guesses," said Bobus; "but not all right. Fowls we had, and pigs; we did not see any turtle; but we saw the wretches eat the legs, arms, tongues, and hearts of a lot of young girls they had slaughtered for the purpose."

"Their enemies, of course," said I, recovering from the sickening sensation which the story gave me.

"Well, I don't know. Not always. I have known a chief slay his own wife, and call in some of his friends to help him eat her. Savages they are, lustful, full of pride, hatred, malice, deceit. 'Tis all very well to talk about people being good, and excellent, and all that, when in a state of nature. The state of nature that I have seen is very bad nature, and wants civilising; a little discipline like, something which will make them think and act like men, not brutes."

"They are fine men," said Flook, looking through his glass at a party of them gathered on the shore in menacing attitudes, evidently taking council against us.

I looked through the glass, and there I saw about a hundred savages collected. They were, indeed, fine men. Thin in the haunches, wide and muscular in the chests, with splendidly developed muscles, shoulders and arms fit for a Hercules, the men seemed ready and able to slay the whole crew of the ship, should we dare to land; and yet we dared not do otherwise, our want of water was so pressing.

" Wal', Britisher, shall we give them a salute?" said the captain.

" No; the best thing you can do is to man the boat and put into shore. Stay, I will go with her. Get ready the long gun and run her forward; and, if you see any danger, load her ready with grape and fire her. And, I say, fire her over our heads, you lubbers, d'ye hear ?"

" Aye, aye," said the sailors, with a grin.

" Now, who is for shore ?" cried Bobus, as the boat was lowered.

" I, for one," cried I, leaping into the fore part of the boat.

" And I," said Flook, following my example. Old Stump tumbled in after us. " Him gwoin'," he said, " to see his brudder black-a-men, dat him was." He took good care, however, to bring with him his old scatter-gun, charged to the muzzle, which, ever since the adventure of the " grizzly," he took care to carry with him, loaded with as much as she could carry. " She do her dooty," said he, with much pleasure, looking at the pan of the gun. " Prime gun, berry, dat, much good dat gun 'bis."

He laid it down beside him, and took up one of the oars; three other volunteers soon leapt into the boat, and Bobus steered, whilst I stood up in the fore part of the boat, ready to communicate with the inhabitants.

" Do you know a word of their lingo, Bobus?" said I.

" Not a word, Mas'r Ned," said he, touching his hat to me, as his superior officer. " You must make signs."

I did make signs. I stretched my open hand towards them, and touched my forehead and my mouth. They still preserved, however, their menacing front. Some of them capered and danced, others brandished their clubs; others let off muskets, firing in the air; but more with the idea of showing us that they possessed fire-arms than anything else.

WE LAND AT FIJI.

CHAP. 34.

" Years haven't made them better; they did just this, when Captain Cook was amongst them," said Bobus. "The missionaries make them better, but slowly, slowly enough."

" Ship your oars, men," I cried, as we neared the shore.

The men, after a vigorous, final pull, obeyed, and the keel of the boat grated on the fine sand of the bay.

" Leap out, lads," cried I, still holding my hand up, and setting the example.

The stalwart fellows, each with a musket in his hand, did so, and formed upon the beach. The natives had drawn back a little, and regarded us with some little awe. Giving my gun to Bobus, and advancing towards them, with my hand still held up, I proved to them, by being without arms, that I did not seek any thing by force. They waited till I came to them. I made signs, as if thirsty; the savages at once understood me, and made one of their people fetch an earthen vessel of water, from which they poured me out about half a pint, in a cocoa-nut shell. Refreshing as the draught was, I merely put my lips to it, and made signs that it was for the ship, and not for myself, that I needed it. Upon this being understood, a number of them ran back, for the purpose, I presumed, of calling their chief.

I was tired of making signs, which they either would not, or could not understand, when with a sounding of conch-shells, and a monotonous music blown through the nose into a kind of flute, announced the approach of the monarch. Sundry guards ran two and two before him, shouting and hallooing, brandishing their clubs, and darting their spears, to show how mighty a man he was. Not terrified in the least, by this exhibition, we stood still, awaiting the approach of his majesty.

The chiefs around the king, were fine men. They stood at least six feet high, some of them, perhaps, exceeding that standard. They were clothed round the middle with a cincture of woven grass, which fell nearly to their knees. Their heads were covered with a mass of black hair, very bushy, and dressed with a peculiar art, so that it seemed to extend much beyond the head itself. Some had their hair frizzed out, like a barrister's wig, others had two rows of white hair over their forehead, others, feathers and bunches of hair like crests. Their hair and whiskers and moustaches, their faces painted in patches and stripes, their sinewy active forms, broad chests, light steps and glittering eyes, gave them a terrible appearance, but our men stood firm, although we were not ten to one hundred.

The chief, contrary to the usual custom of these islands, was by no means, the finest man amongst them. There was also this difference, that whereas these men, in common with the whole Papuan race, were black, and presented a purplish hue in the sun; some call them " purple men" on that account; his majesty had a dark brown skin, not even so dark as a Malayan, and presenting a decidedly European aspect.

His face was painted, but the bare part was that of a white, and his hair frizzed out and covered with a black powder, still gave indications of a deep glowing red. The same might be said of his beard and whiskers.

His gait was not majestic. That of the other chiefs was, indeed, so. Their faces, when not distended with the horrid grin of war, were grave, and even majestic; his had a merry look, even in its ferocity, and his eye twinkled with a savage fun. Nay, when he gave orders, I fancy I could distinguish a more cultivated pronunciation than that of those around him, more flexibility, as it were, of lip and tongue. I have referred to his majesty's walk, it was not active nor majestic, but rather resembled the roll and swagger of a British sailor, when he endeavours to be very important and impressive.

Standing a little in advance of my men, with Bobus to my right, and Flook on the left of me, I was wondering at the aspect of the chief, as well as actively watching the movements of the savages, when the monarch spoke out with that peculiar accent, which when once heard, is never forgotten. I fancied that he demanded our business. I replied, by going through a series of signs expressive of drinking, of being thirsty, and of the ship herself being thirsty, and much in want of water.

Another phrase in Fijian, followed my pantomime.

Bobus, in the mean time, seemed struck with wonder. He slapped his forehead, his thigh, his knee; he twitched up his breeches, stuck his cap over his forehead, and scratched his head; at length, all doubts seemed to have given way, and with a voice of thunder, he shouted out, looking the chief full in the face—

" What cheer, messmate! ship ahoy!"

The savages looked round in astonishment. The chief was puzzled, a broad grin spread over his face, for a minute, a twinkle lighted up his eye; then, by an immense effort, he spoke in the Fijian language, pointing first to the ship, and then to us.

Bobus was not to be shaken. He cut a rapid caper forward, by performing a step from the sailor's hornpipe.

" What," cried he, " d'ye think that Jack Bobus is like a lubber, sailing on the wrong tack? D'ye think that when I sights a ship I've once sailed in company with, I don't know the cut of her jib? What cheer, ahoy, messmate! I know ye, notwithstanding your kingship and your fine war paint. You and I have eaten the king's biscuit, my hearty, and if you arn't my old friend, Paddy Quain, a native of Cork, old fellow, you may rate me as a land-lubber, and stop my grog. Here's my hand, my hearty," he continued, advancing right to the king, "and you know it carries its heart in it. ' *Crom a boo. Erin go bragh.*' What cheer, ahoy, Paddy Quain ?"

The heart of the king was not proof against such an appeal. His face expanded to a grin. He forgot his dignity, dropped his club, and putting his two hands on his knees, cried out, as he looked at Bobus—

" What cheer, ahoy, messmate! Ship in distress, run up your signal, and Paddy Quain will lend you a hand."

So saying, he extended his hand, browned with exposure, paint and dust, and hardened with work, to Jack Bobus, and gave him a grip which I, for one, did not envy.

# CHAPTER XXXV.



Tui Nayau, alias Paddy Quain, was acknowledged king or chief of the Island of Thikomba, and to do him justice, gave us welcome in a regal way. He signalled to the ship, caused his people to get water ready for the casks when brought on shore, and endeavoured by all means, to prove to us the love in which he held us. Paddy was a curious animal. Where other men would have failed, men of better temperament and finer mould, he succeeded. His rough nature was suited to the savages with whom he had to deal, and he had moreover a very fair share of diplomatic skill and tact. Thus he kept the petty chiefs under him at a respectful distance, calmed their jealousies, acted upon their fears, and repressed their discontents. The people under him loved him as much as they feared him. Everything that the island contained was his, or at his command. He had but to express a wish, and it was executed, and to give Paddy Quain credit, although his wishes were by no means small, yet they were never cruel. In this he was very different from his predecessor.

His story was this. Sailing some fifteen years before we met him, in the same ship with Bobus, under a captain whose rule was severity itself, sixteen of the men, amongst whom was Quain, determined to free themselves from the thraldom when they could. They watched the opportunity saved their grog, their biscuits, and their junk, stole other provisions, and managed to secrete enough to victual the long-boat. This boat, after sundry watchings and much trouble, they stole, and dropping over the side, escaped. They were not far from the Polynesian group of islands, when they commenced their voyage, and after severe sufferings for want of water, they reached one of the outlying islets. When they landed they were helpless and almost unarmed, and the inhabitants attacked them, slew two of their number, whom they carried away and ate.

Paddy Quain was then of a very inferior rank amongst the sailors; an Irishman named Connell, a clever but cruel man, planned the expedition and commanded the little party. By forced marches the sailors evaded their foes, marched to the back of the island and in the night surprised a small village, slew the inhabitants and carried away their arms, amongst which were several muskets.

After this they were on a more equal footing, and Connell proved a skilful general. The savages were routed and their chief slain, and Connell avenged the death of his companions by enormous cruelties. The savages had, indeed, put the bodies of the slain into their ovens, and had eaten them, but Connell made no scruple in roasting his foes whilst alive. He spread terror over the whole island. The neighbouring chiefs sent in their submission, and Connell soon reigned supreme.

Cruelty grows by what it feeds on, and Connell grew worse and worse. The white men took to themselves wives, and established themselves around him much as the barons and knights of William the Conqueror did upon this island. Tyranny and excess did not long prosper, disease killed many of Connell's companions; others set sail in canoes to other islands, and in two years after landing Connell and three of his companions were the only English left upon Thikomba.

The savage British seaman lived in the indulgence of his selfish passions two years longer, at the end of which he, weakened by disease, and sick to death, was slain by the club of a young chieftain, whose father he had caused to be slain. But his authority, and the weight of his name lived after him. It is the custom on these islands, upon the death of a king, to strangle several of his wives and his companions, so that he may not go alone to his grave. The death of Connell was avenged by some of his native followers, his murderer was slain and buried with him and two of his wives, and Paddy Quain succeeded to the sovereignty of the island under the title of *Tui Nayau.*

Tui Nayau was to the Fijians a beneficent monarch. Obliged to avenge Connell's death, to lay waste the property of him who slew him, and to destroy his family, he had since that period kept his hands free from the stain of blood. The people over whom he reigned were like most of the Polynesian islanders, thoroughly untrustworthy, cruel, and bloodthirsty. It needed, therefore, no little tact in the Irishman to keep his subjects in order. They were frequently at war. They slew not only strangers, but friends. They would kill their favorite wife, or their friends, upon the slightest pretence, and would feast upon their remains. The two Englishmen who were left were peaceful and loyal to Paddy, but one had died and the other managed to get away in an American ship some little time before we touched at the island, and Paddy Quain was **left alone in his glory.**

He was perfectly satisfied with his condition. He taught the savages obedience, and demanded from them a strict observance of his commands. Traitors he punished with death. An unerring marksman, any one of his declared enemies was certain to perish by his rifle, and Paddy well knew that promptness and decision were his best and only safeguards. His wives, of whom he had three, polygamy being the rule of the island, were faithful and attached to him, and the children of Connell and his companions grown into young men and women, with that rapidity of growth and precocity of mind known in the South Seas, formed his best body guard.

"If it were not for them," said he, "and a few zealous and tried adherents amongst the natives, some of the disaffected chiefs would slay me whilst I slept, and eat my tongue and heart, and offer up my limbs as a *soro* to their gods."

"Are they such terrible cannibals here?" said Flook.

Paddy Quain replied by calling out in the Fijian tongue—for it was in his palace that we sat, a handsome hut some thirty feet long and twenty feet broad, and a native brought him two or three peculiar wooden forks. They were made of hard wood, handsomely carved, cut with four prongs, sharpened and hardened by fire.

"These," said he, "are cannibal forks. They

call the dead body the *bakolo,* and the natives really love the taste of human flesh. The upper arm, the leg, and the heart, are the greatest dainties. Their priests encourage them in the custom, and though I have much authority I cannot cure them of it. Women seldom eat the *bakolo,* but they often form the meal of their husbands or their enemies. It is esteemed a clever, brave, and wise thing to slay the wife of one's enemy, partly because the flesh is tender to eat, and partly because of the pain, rage, and grief it occasions the enemy."

"Are such things possible in this nineteenth century, in this age when we spend so much to spread religion from shore to shore?"

His Fijian majesty, who spoke his native tongue with some stiffness and difficulty shook his head sadly, and the twinkle in his bright eye faded away as he spoke.

"On the big islands out there," he said, pointing over his shoulder with his thumb; "there are missionaries, good men and zealous, but they have little power. They teach and bring up the young, but, amongst so many, what can they do? Cannibalism has existed here for many hundred years. They cannot uproot a foolish, brutal custom. The coming generations may be better. There are something like two hundred and fifty of these islands, and of them about eighty of the largest are inhabited.* Some of these, the missionaries, who now and then visit our distant little island, say contain as many as 30,000, and even 50,000 inhabitants."

"You cannot change the habits of so many people at once. Do what you can, you must have time," said old Flook; "if some of our European conquerors instead of dreaming of, aye, and of attempting to overrun settled kingdoms and governments, and of annexing territory to territory, and province to province, thereby causing, in their mad ambition, the deaths of thousands, and spending millions of money, were to send out two or three small ships of war with a few companies of artillery, and a handful of soldiers, they might overrun the islands, reduce the inhabitants to order, abolish cannibalism, and plant Christianity firmly and for ever. The savage is naturally a coward. He fears and worships the strongest party. He would desert his paltry gods and leave his filthy habits when he found them useless and powerless."

"Bedads," cried his majesty Paddy Quain, " and indeed but you're quite right there, young sir. Might, with these people, means right; and if I had not carried a strong hand over them myself (wake little crature as I am) I should have

* The Fijian group of islands extends over 40,000 square miles of the South Pacific lying between latitudes 15° 30', and 20° 30' S., and longitudes 177° E. and 178° W.

been made bakolo of, and have been eaten clane up, long ago.   There's a signal."

A gun from our ship woke up the echoes of the rocky shore; and, accompanied by the king, we went down to the shore, carrying with us presents of pigs, fowls, yams, and fruit, and promising to visit his kingship again the next day.

# CHAPTER XXXVI.

WE MAKE A SHORT VISIT TO THE FIJIANS—THEIR
APPEARANCE AND CHARACTER.

DURING half that night, as we swung side by
side in our hammocks, nothing would serve old
Flook but to talk of these islands, of spreading
the true religion amongst them, and of making
them into one kingdom, over which an enlightened
monarch might reign. He was so earnest and
hearty about this, that, but for his father and the
dear ones at home, I believe he would have devoted his own life to the attempt.

"Europe ought to do it, Paget," he said. "It
is the bounden duty of one part of God's earth to
teach and civilise the rest. And, oh! what a
field is here. Did you see what glorious vegetation; did you mark the flowers, the fruit, and the
trees? Scratch but the soil with the rude instruments of these men, plant but a few seeds, and
what abundance follows! They might maintain
a thousand times the population they do now;

they might afford a glorious home to thousands of our pent-up town populations, they might become the abodes of happiness and plenty, of law, and religion, instead of crime, cruelty, and murder."

"They might indeed," said I.

"What a life to lead," said he, reverting to our friend Quain. "All alone amongst those savages. He really is an extraordinary man. He, no doubt, might have escaped long ago if he had chosen."

"No doubt, no doubt," said I; "but I presume he likes it."

"And is of use in his generation, too," returned Flook; "perhaps more so than some of us dream of. He told me that since he had been king the population of his island had almost doubled. He has suppressed feuds and wars in which many were slain, and, as he said, has done what he could to uproot cannibalism. Well, I heard, whilst you and I were peeping about the village, that his majesty promised his old ship-mate, Bobus, to pay us a visit on board to-morrow I shall be happy to renew our intimacy with the monarch."

"And I," said I. "Good night, Flook."

"Good night, old boy," said my friend, "I shall dream of being made king of Fiji." So, rocked by the gently rising waves of the bay, we went to sleep.

The next morning his majesty, Tui Nayau, did us the honour to pay us a visit on board our brig. We had made everything taut and ship-shape to see him, and received him with all honours, for he had befriended us, and moreover deserved these honours considerably more than many other potentates, civilised or uncivilised.

Two royal canoes carried the king and his train, followed by many small craft carrying presents to *soro* us, since Paddy had told his subjects that we ourselves were small gods, and could soon make *bakolos*, or dead men of them, if we wished. The remembrance of the tyrant, Connel, and of his doings, taught them sufficiently to respect us, and their king's behests were carried out in perfect faith.

In return for these presents we feasted his majesty on board, gave him a horse-hair mattress for his palace, a hand-basin, glazed inside, some towels, and the best rifle we had. We gave to his subjects some axes, nails, chisels, and plane-irons. We victualled our ship afresh, and filled all our water-casks, and were ready to depart, satisfied with the king, and leaving him satisfied with us.

Our crew had begged, however, three or four days' liberty on shore, and were told out into parties to enjoy themselves. I am not sure but that many besides my friend, old Flook, did not envy Paddy Quain; but a few sights which we saw, and which I will include in this chapter of my adventures, quite cured them of the wish, and they were willing enough to sail with us to old England.

The land itself is a garden, all kinds of flowers make the earth gay, a perpetual summer smiles upon them, the seasons bear a rotation of God's good gifts; the sky is glorious above them, the ocean full of the finest fish, of turtle, and with its very rocks of coral surrounds them, at once their guardian and their benefactor. Fruits of most kinds are to be found—the bread-fruit, cocoa-nut, and yam, the orange, shadock, and the karika, the banana, wis and iri-nut, from which their women make bread; other luxuries, too, they have.

Fine in form, elevated in feature, capable in brain, the inhabitants have yet managed to make this paradise an earthly Hell.

Fraudful, full of deceit and cunning, cowardly, and, like all cowards, cruel, filthy in his habits, with a long memory for wrongs, and a very short one for benefits, the native walks the earth, a curse to himself and to his fellow man. He has some culture, is fond of a kind of system in his war, has a religion, and bows down continually to his false gods, makes poetry, and sings his songs of war, love, and religion, and yet will slay his wife to eat her heart, not in rage, not in revenge, not in drunken excitement, but out of mere petty pride of making himself celebrated as a terrible fellow. With a clean cloth bound about his loins, a bushy head of hair and beard, filled with black powder, and a well-oiled body, the native stalks abroad as proud as Cæsar. Pride, in any, is ignorance. The more any one really knows, the better, the more highly born, the wiser he is, the less will he be proud. I have been out and about a good deal in life, and I have always found that the proudest man in the company had ever the least cause for pride. The proudest man in our ship's company was poor old Stump, whom we were carrying to England to pension and set free.

The Fijian's pride is of the same character. A word, a slight will offend him, and, when offended, he is implacable. An adept at concealing his emotions, no one may know his anger till it suddenly bursts out: then, indeed, it is terrible. The broad brow is wrinkled and puckered, the dull black eye brightens and grows red, the cheeks are distended, the nostrils widen and give out breath like steam, the whole body quivers with rage, and the savage fury stands confessed. If this fury is successful in its object, murder, arson, and all kinds of devilish cruelties follow before it is appeased. The old man and the babe alike suffer, the tender virgin, or the old matron who tends the house.

There were on board our vessel, the " Spread Eagle," one or two old gentlemen professing the then new nonsense, called " Spiritualism," who pretended that they believed that everything was good in this world, that men were not so wicked as it was pretended, and that universal happiness, without any misery or trouble at all, might soon be achieved. I remember that these pious old gentlemen were rather anxious to get rid of any of the observances of religion, and wished to achieve all this universal happiness in a loose, easy, sloppy kind of way, as if no rule, observance, or endeavour, were necessary. Flook and I would argue with them, but to very little purpose. They treated us as boys.

When we came on board, after visiting Thikomba, and told our story about the people being cannibals, Messrs. Silky and Softly must needs deny it. Cannibalism, said they, was extinct. Universal brotherhood about to begin; the savage was a much-maligned creature. Man, who falsely called himself civilised, did not understand the impulses of his more natural brother, and so on. I was glad to be of the party when these American gentlemen went on shore, and, as they professed to love science, examined the scoria on the shore, looked at the sunken reefs of coral which formed the natural breakwater of the island, and pronounced us, perhaps truly, to be standing upon part of a submerged continent abounding in extinct volcanoes. I begged them to travel with us into the interior to study the people.

Our two friends did so, and Paddy Quain having granted us an escort, being well armed also—an unnecessary precaution, said our friends, off we started upon an exploring trip of two days.

We had not gone very far into the interior when our leaders turned aside to a native temple, or bure, to *soro* the gods for our good luck. *Soro* means to propitiate, and certain offerings are there made. Our friends, full of enthusiasm, began to talk about the beauties of natural religion, when one of them, a tall gentleman in blue spectacles, hit his head in passing under a tree against something pendent therefrom. Looking up he saw the limbs of a dead body. The bakolo had been offered to the gods, and after being partly eaten by the priests, was hung up there to dry, and to provide for the after-wants of the professors of Fijian religion.

Bures, or temples, we found in plenty. Never met we such men for praying, propitiating, and sacrificing, as these islanders. They poured libations into the sea when they set out; they *soro'd* the gods when they went to war; they wept plentifully and prayed earnestly when offended; they turned to their deaf-and-dumb idols upon every occasion. It is a land of many gods, from *Ndeugei*, the symbol of eternal existence, to Nangganaugga, the great woman and hater of bachelors, who troubles the spirits of those who die unmarried. The gods are numerous. They are of various rank, and some of them of very little account, so much so that, when angry and disappointed, the Fijian will offer to fight his god, and often thoroughly dethrones him.

Yet, in the offerings made to these fictions, bloody sacrifices are common, and the dead body of a man or child covers the large basket holding the fruit offered to the god. Besides these demons, ghosts and other night-fears, restless souls, little devils, goblins, and wizards, haunt the dark mind of the Fijian. Our learned friends had their eyes soon opened to the native virtues on our journey. We were not very far from a village when we heard sundry cries of triumph. Muskets were fired, conch-shells blown, and a hollow tubular piece of wood, the native drum, beaten continuously. Presently the cause of all this burst on our view, a rabble rout of people, chiefs, priests, and conch-blowers, and girls blowing on a hollow reed, called the nose-flute, came in sight, then a chief, marching proudly with a bleeding tongue, torn from his enemy's mouth, in his hand, and his club over his shoulder.

Next came two women, drawing the *bakolo*— its face to the ground, its hands extended and tied at the wrist. They sang a wild song as they dragged the corpse along — "Come, bakolo, to the oven! You are brave; you have fallen; your heart shall be eaten! The brave to the oven; but the coward runs away!" Such, we were told, was the burden of their song. The crowd passed us, leaving us sick and disgusted, and our friends rather shaken in their admiration of the beauties of natural religion.

In short, we found in our tour all the vices I have mentioned flourishing in great abundance. We were glad to escape from these "purple men." We found them always ready and hot for blood, but cowards at heart. We saw a father slay his favorite son, a husband his dearest wife; not in anger, nor in jealousy, nor because he or she had plotted against him, but because the savage wished to prove himself a very dangerous fellow.

Flook, the philosopher, was quite as much shocked as I was.

"I tell you what," said he, "I tell you what, Paget, if some great European conqueror, instead of spending the lives of thousands, and millions of treasure in invading somebody else's dominions, were just to try the effect of establishing religion in these islands, backed up by actual strength, he might do better. A park of artillery, now, and a regiment of infantry, would make them soon relinquish their foolish bloody gods, and believe also in that God whom our missionaries preach."

"Also can command artillery!" said I; "no, no, Flook, it will not do. The Cross must not be propagated by murder, nor the most gentle faith the world has ever seen, by force. Wait awhile, patience and faith will do wonders, wait till another generation shall have passed. Let us teach these benighted beings better. Let us show them by example that we are not like they are."

As we went on we found their bravery was but a kind of blind and stupid rage. We were present at the ceremony of an old chieftain who was about to be buried alive. We found that it was a common custom there. We begged the old man's life, but he seemed callous to the favour, and the son, who pretended immense love for the parent, replied to our interpreter, " Of what use is life? he is old, let him die, rest is sweet."

Their religion teaches them murder. He who has not slain his foe is subjected to the most degraded punishment after death. He who kills many is blest.

" Let us get back to our ship and set sail at once," said I; " I am tired of these people who have flattering words to the strong, and carry clubs, swords, and arrows for the weak. I will leave this island where everything in nature is beautiful and where only man is vile. I thought, and have read some writers who affirmed, that civilization only brought a curse, and that Europe was more cruel than the East. Henceforward I shall believe otherwise; there are men whose souls dwell in darkness even in this world."

Our philosophers held their peace. The sights around us, the sores, diseases, blindness, both religious and natural of all around, had taught them that man was not blessed because he was ignorant, nor innocent because untaught.

" Henceforward," said old Flook, " I shall add another proverb to that which says, ' Knowledge is power.' "

" What shall it be ?" said I.

" Why, that ' True knowledge is virtue.' ".

" If you mean religious knowledge, that which teaches you your true duty towards God and your neighbour, which after all is the knowledge most worth, I think you are right," said I; " in such a view knowledge is goodness itself."

# CHAPTER XXXVII.



THE next day his majesty, Paddy Quain, came on board, and we made a great feast to receive him. He was so sincerely our friend that we all liked him, although he had adopted not only the morals, but the manners of the natives. He was quite reconciled to his fate, and left us in his regal canoe in great state, obstinately resisting any of our persuasions for him to return to England with us.

We still lay in the bay, our *savant* making various excursions in search of plants, when a canoe came to our side paddled by four young men whose very looks were different from those around them.

In the stern-sheets of the boat lay a poor, young English gentleman, apparently not more than twenty-five, so burnt up with fever that he could not rise. His attendants carried him up the side of the vessel, and explained his story.

He was a Christian missionary from a neighbouring island, who, earnest in his calling, had worked himself to death's door. He was dying when he reached us. His friends knew it, and he better than they.

We had seen enough of the base side of nature. This man showed us what the bright side was.

Reared in luxury, he had yet devoted himself to the good cause, had laboured at it, and had died in harness of his hard and continuous work. Coldness, indifference, persecution, carelessness, cunning, inquisitiveness, which for a time assumed the aspect of devotion and then disappointed the teacher, all these he had to struggle with, and at last overcame. But the effort was too much for him.

He came on board our ship to die, but lingered with us a long time and taught us much.

The Reverend John Fortescue, so he was called, was of a noble nature, noble as his family and name might be. A poet and an enthusiast, he had at college been led away by his companions to ridicule the ignorance and foolishness of the missionaries, and what he then considered the conceit of those who thought to convert whole nations of the heathen. But honest in his antagonism he resolved to go amongst the men he opposed, and happily for him and others he ended, like St. Paul, in propagating that faith which he had formerly bitterly opposed.

He was ordained by one of our bishops, and devoted himself to the task of learning the Tongan and Fijian languages, so that he might preach in their own tongue to those benighted people. When we had the happiness to meet him he had laboured for ten years, and had seen the faith he preached spread widely.

Some of the tales he told us resembled in every circumstance those of the early martyrs, tales of martyrology they were of Apostolic suffering and endurance.

"Do you think," he said to our American *savant*, who, struck with his goodness, reasoned with him upon the folly of having thrown so valuable a life away; "do you think that the Christian Church is less provided with earnest servants than in its first days?" he smiled faintly, "you should have lived with those among whom I have had the honour to exist."

The *savant*, who was one of those too often careless about religion, replied—

"Well, there is no knowing, sir, how far enthusiasm will carry a man, but we live in an age of universalism. Little systems are dwindling away, and the Great God of Nature, of the Hindoo, Turk, Indian, or Tongan alike, known of course under different names, but meaning the same Power, is gaining day by day more devotees."

He smiled, as if he had said something very wise.

Fortescue rose from his chair, and placed his hand upon his heart as if he felt just there a sudden pain.

"As a preacher of Christ's Word, however weak," he said, " I must, dear sir, protest against that false and foolish generation you speak of. Upon the brink of the grave I would not say that I hate any one, but I do say that I hate a system, or abhor a false creed. People veil their apathy by generality, and talk of the God of nature and the Universal Being, and the gods of the Greeks, the Chinese, or the Mogul, as being the same. I tell you He is not. Our God is a jealous God, and admits no other worship. If you wanted your ship to reach Calcutta would you steer to New York? Will the prayer addressed to an idol reach the true God? the sacrifice made to a false system, or an idea, serve also for the altar of Truth?

"Oh, sirs, you should have seen what I have. Of faith, which indeed removed mountains; of the savage turned suddenly and completely to God; of whole villages converted, by poor weak teachers who, in London, would be despised as ignorant. You should have seen the native convert go quietly to certain death to test his faith; you should have watched the gradual growth of faith, breaking over a benighted land, as the sunlight breaks upon the sea.

"In these islands many times our converts are baptised in blood. The missionary and his whole church have been slain, their houses burnt, their place of worship swept away, and yet again their followers preached, and still the pure seed sprang up and flourished. Our own Church has been in the front rank here, good and learned men have been with us, but other Churches have been foremost too; Paul and Barnabas equally have preached, and we have known no difference. Young men, without learning, and with only Christian faith, have come out from home with a simple Christian purpose, and have accomplished their aim. They have sealed their blameless life with a happy death; they have lost wives, children, health, life itself, but they have known such loss was gain."

The *savant* was silent. Here indeed to me was a lesson. I had met in the world with men who told me that only simple people believed in our holy faith. Here I found one of the best and truest and most learned of men throwing away his life and considering the loss gain, as, he said, others had done.

The missionary adventures, related by Mr. Fortescue, were full of interest. We saw religion, faith, gentleness, and love, opposed to cruelty, avarice, pride, and ignorance. We found that on the side of the world, that is, on the side of Power, arrayed in a savage dress, if you like, and holding merely a sceptre of bamboo, but still upon the side of Power, all the vices and ambitions, cruelties and lusts of man were ranged, but that they were yet overthrown, one by one, simply by Religion, without force, without fraud, often without the aid even of eloquence or learning. So strong is Truth—great indeed is she, and will prevail.

The persecutions and the martyrdoms, the hair-breadth 'scapes and adventures of some of the earlier disciples of our preachers were told us in a narrative so affecting and simple that we listened for hours, and often with tears running down our cheeks, to them; but Fortescue's great reward had come. The cause in which he had laboured was successful. Cannibalism and the cruelties of savage life were fading out from the islands, and the dawn of a better era was already seen in the skies.

The full day of civilization, for which he had laboured, he however was never to see.

It seems trying, but it often so happens. The time of harvest arrives, but we live not to reap it; that we have sown should be our sufficient reward.

So it was with Fortescue. He was resigned

and contented, nay, happy, though he was slowly
dying.  He never lost hope or faith as he grew
weaker and weaker, and gradually faded from us.
We sailed as quickly as we could, hoping to reach
England with him, but before we did he died.
The ship lay almost motionless in the calm sea
when he died and gave his pure soul to his
Maker.  He was full of hope, and trust, and
faith, as happy as a soldier marching home.

We buried him the next day in the vast sea.
Wrapped in a hammock, shotted at head and
foot, the body awaited its grave.  As the captain
read, in his rough voice, faltering with emotion,
the words, "We therefore commit this body to
the deep, to be turned into corruption, looking
for the resurrection of the body when the Sea
shall give up her dead," the sailors lowered the
body gently to the sea, and the bosom of the
deep received it gently, and wrapped and hid it in
its waves.

*       *       *       *       *       *

The next day a breeze sprung up, and we sailed
for England.

# CHAPTER XXXVIII.



I WILL not trouble the reader with our return
voyage home. We had no casualties, nor indeed
many adventures after the death of the missionary.
We were shortly afterwards enabled to obtain a
passage in a homeward-bound ship, and, parting
from our American friends, reached London
safely, and then went home.

My first visit was, of course, paid to the doctor
and Mrs. Taw, both of whom I found well, and
indeed the doctor had a piece of news, both sur-
prising and gratifying, to communicate; it was
nothing less than this—he had heard from my
long-lost and mysterious uncle.

"Well, sir," said I, "I am rejoiced to hear it,
although, thanks to you, I do not now want his
help. He is in London, of course."

The doctor shook his head. "If you were to
guess from now till doomsday, you would never

find out where he is. Indeed, he did not tell you, when you saw him in London."

"Saw him in London, doctor?"

"Yes, saw him in London. By the way, Ned, what a fine, big fellow you grow. No wonder Lucy asks after you; as much, indeed, as she does after her brother; but that's neither here nor there, is it?"

I confess that I should have liked to hear more about Lucy, but the doctor did not then gratify my curiosity.

"Miss Lucy is well, I hope, sir," I said; "and my uncle is, where, sir?"

"Now, which is it to be first, Lucy or the uncle? Well, I must begin with your relation I suppose. You see, he left you in such a hurry, or, rather, you left him, when in London, that he could not explain to you his intentions, could he?"

I shook my head, thoroughly puzzled. The doctor continued. "Well," said he, "I will not keep you any longer in suspense. That uncle of yours, I say, you met in London. He was no other than Professor Peter Garle!"

I jumped out of my chair, in astonishment. "An old ras—!" I had forgotten that the doctor had told me somewhat of this when I was last in England.

The doctor held up a finger in admonition. "Never speak against relations, my boy; whatever he has been, he is now reformed. Sit down, and do not open your eyes so widely, and I will tell you all. Men run on, my boy," he continued, after a pause, "in roguery and dishonesty for a long time, but in the end, you may depend upon this, they find out that it is a losing game which they are playing. So it was with your uncle. An educated man, and what the world calls a gentleman, he yet never had, as he confesses, and your poor father experienced, any principle. In consequence, he fell from bad to worse, and at last was known as one thoroughly untrustworthy, so that after the death of your father, he found himself without a friend in the world, and with no one to depend on but himself, and on that person indeed he could not place much reliance. He fell, as I say, step by step, till, after being mixed up in several very dishonest transactions, and finding every day his sphere of action narrowed, he found that he could only depend upon the pitiable trade of a begging-letter writer."

I covered my face with my hands. "My poor uncle," said I.

"Aye, lad," returned the doctor, in a kind voice, "pity him if you will, there is no one so truly deserving pity as he who is guilty; but withhold your sympathy for him, keep it for yourself; he injured you. A dishonest relation, in the world's eye, covers those near him with the reflection of his own guilt. But mind, Ned, in the world's eye only. For myself, I can only say that I honour you more since I have known this, for it appears your own straightforward innocence and honesty wrought, together with other circumstances, a change in the character of your uncle. He is now a changed man."

"Thank Heaven for it!" I ejaculated fervently.

"Amen," returned the doctor, "and for all good things too. But, to return to my narrative. His career, as a begging-letter writer, under a changed name, was getting very perilous, when he bethought him of you. You were young, innocent, and unknown: all this was in his favour, and you, he knew, would be of infinite service to him, and so he wrote to me for you. It does him credit, however, that he wished to conceal from you his own degradation; and he found you so innocent that he had no need to tell you his real name. He purposely let you be, as it were, lost at the inn, assumed intoxication, followed you, and took you home. You know the rest."

"Indeed I do," said I, impatiently.

"Now, pray do wait, and hear the end, Ned," cried the doctor; "it is ever so much better than the beginning. You never discovered what his trade was, but there were others upon the look out; and one fine morning, as you know, the excellent professor was caught. He had been 'wanted,' to use the policeman's phrase, long enough; but his cleverness did not desert him, the proofs were not sufficient, and a clever advocate so puzzled the jury that they would not convict him. Frightened, however, by the trial, and having had time to reflect when in the House of Detention, Mr. Peter Garle, alias Austin Paget —by the way, his real name never came out— shipped himself as a surgeon for Australia, where he now is, a prosperous merchant."

"Indeed," said I.

"Yes, and more than that, he is a reformed man. *Ecce signum!*" The doctor held out a letter. "Fortunes," he continued, "are made rapidly in our colonies, and your uncle was lucky. He is a clever man. He found in Melbourne a young fellow with a capital business, but without a notion of management. He went in, talked as if he were a capitalist, engaged himself for a short time as clerk, mastered his situation, and showed his employer his value. He then bought, by giving bills, a half share in the business, and, throwing his whole energy in it, so improved it in a short time that he is able to send you over, as an earnest of his intentions, five hundred pounds; a sum which, he says, he will make, as an act of just restitution to your father and yourself, five thousand before he dies. Here is his letter."

The doctor was in his element. No one rejoiced over the one sinner who repented more than he. He rubbed his hands, and marched up and down the room in high glee.

"Now, Ned," said he, "what do you think of your uncle now? are you ashamed of him?"

No, I was not. The letter was a simple, plain epistle, full of real feeling, and of sorrow for the past and determination for the future, which, as the reader will afterwards see, Austin Paget did not allow to die away. My heart was full of gratitude, because, by this unexpected stroke of fortune, I was for ever relieved from the idea of being a burden upon the doctor, and at the same time I was enabled to offer him some compensation for the unceasing kindness he had shown me. The offer was made, but, I need scarcely say, rejected by the doctor, who was, however, gratified at the offer.

Besides this good fortune, I and Flook had realised a good round sum of money by our American adventures. Our merchandise had sold well at Santa Fé, and our collection of rare articles, fossils, and precious stones, together with some specimens of rare plants and seeds, were worth something,—this, together with my pay, which I had not drawn on, placed me altogether, and as I then hoped, for ever, out of a state of dependence upon a friend who was, however, the kindest in the world.

After staying some time with the doctor, I made

my way to Yarmouth, and there rejoined the Flook family, who were all very glad to see me; I hope I may add most especially in the instance of Miss Lucy. In my absence she had grown nearly a woman, and her beauty had increased with her growth. It was no wonder that I loved her, for everyone admired her, and I could never forget her kindness to me when a poor, ship-wrecked lad. My good schoolfellow openly told me that he could choose no better brother-in-law than myself, should Lucy love me, and should the proper time come, and I believe that neither Lucy's father or mother were averse to the match. But, meanwhile, my bashfulness held me back, nor could I quite believe, notwithstanding many signs of preference, that Lucy entirely loved me. Besides, I had yet my way to make in life, and it was with feelings of mingled pleasure and regret that I one morning received orders to join my ship at Portsmouth. I was now an officer, and could not think of disobedience; I hastily bade good-bye to my friends, went to London to get ready my uniform and kit, and put myself on the top of the Portsmouth coach to join H.M.S. the 'Thunderer.'

# CHAPTER XXXIX.

### WHEREIN WE SAIL TO BUSHIRE, LAND IN PERSIA, AND JOURNEY TO SHEERAUZ.

I HAD plenty of time to reflect upon life and its ups and downs, outs and ins, overs and unders during my stay at Portsmouth, for the ship had not yet her full complement of men—the captain was particular, and good men were scarce. Captain Becker was rather a martinet, and his character for severity prevented him from filling his ship very readily. Old Bobus, I am delighted to say, was there, a petty officer, and one much esteemed and trusted, for his character was well known in the principal seaport towns. To do him full justice, every one liked him, and he did more towards filling our ship than any amount of bounty, or any promise of prize money, however extravagant, could have done. Prize money the captain was determined to have, not that we were at war with any one, but that he wanted a war, and was therefore certain that we should have one. After we had sailed we opened our sealed orders, and found that we had to proceed to the Persian Gulf, there to aid two ships of the East Indian navy, in obtaining redress for certain wrongs done to our merchants by some of the dependent chiefs of the Shah. Captain Becker was wishing devoutly every day that the Shah would turn sulky or restive, or refuse compensation, "And then," said the Captain, "we will show them what the British sailors can do."

That opportunity—but I am anticipating. I should write that previously to sailing for Persia I received letters from my friend and schoolfellow old Flook, and in one of them he told me how much all of them missed me, and, what pleased me most, wrote that for many days after my departure Lucy was melancholy and very pensive. Indeed, we had rather an affectionate parting, and the recollection of that, with my friend's letter, emboldened me to send her a present, a little *souvenir*, which I hoped she would accept, and which might sometimes bring me to her remembrance. In answer to this I received a very charming letter, which I keep in my desk to this day.

Once more again, then, the reader must follow me on the open sea. All the knowledge I had gained under Bobus, all the lessons which Captain Seth Smith had imparted, I found excessively useful. My fellow midshipmen were younger and less experienced than I, and my former voyages and knowledge of ship life gave me great advantage over them. The captain, who liked smart officers as well as smart men, put me forward where he could, and was very kind to me. All was order and regularity on board his ship, and if discipline was strict I must say that the men were the better for it.

We had no adventures till we reached the Cape. All was smooth sailing, and although in rounding, the ship was nearly thrown on her beam ends, still a storm is hardly an incident worth recording in a sailor's life. At the Mauritius we were joined by two frigates of the East India Company's service, and at once proceeded to Aden. We had certain troops on board and were quite prepared to batter down the walls of Bushire, nay, our captain and several of our crew quite looked forward to the job. As we approached our destination, taking in a pilot to navigate the vessel along a most dangerous coast, we heard rumours of a deadly resistance, and a revenge which the Iman promised to take upon his enemies, which were almost enough to appal any one save an Englishman.

We, I remember, were sailing along in a calm sea, the wind being gentle at the time, and the ocean as quiet as a mill-stream, when Bobus pointed out to me a strange pair of companions in the water. It was nothing less than a shark and a pilot fish. I had often seen the former, but until then had not fully noticed the latter.

It was striped in rings of purple and yellow, and brilliant in colour. It seemed to me no bigger than a mackarel, and was perched on the shoulders or head of the shark.

" Hallo !" cried my old friend, " we will catch him," he pointed as he spoke with his blunt, strong thumb to the shark, " in a few minutes ; now, Ned, watch that 'ere fish, he is the confidential adviser and lawyer of Jack Shark, and a very good one too. Only the old fool does not always take his advice ; now mind."

One of the boys of the ship had run and fetched us a bit of pork of considerable size, and to it we fastened a strong iron hook. The pork was dropped overboard, and the shark soon exhibited a lively interest in it.

" Now," said Bobus, " look at his lawyer."

The legal adviser, *i. e.*, the pilot fish, certainly was not backward in coming forward, he detached himself from Jack Shark, and whilst his client waited in the rear, swam to the pork, looked at it carefully, swam round it, and then back. I cannot pretend to say whether fishes talk. Animals no doubt have a language of their own, and understand each other perfectly, so it seemed to me the shark understood the pilot fish. The latter advised his client not to touch the bait, and perched itself on the top of his shoulders, and away the two swam, leaving us somewhat disappointed.

"Wait a bit," said Bobus, "old Nosey," the bottle-nose of the shark procured him that nick-name, " is far too greedy to leave it at once ; bless you, he will not take the advice of his friends any more than a middy would that of the first-lieutenant ; wait a bit."

The old boatswain was right. Presently, back came the shark, and the pilot fish in a violent agitation again jumped off the shoulders of the larger fish, swam to the pork, hastily round it and again back, taking the same report, no doubt. We could see, through the clear waters, the two fish with their noses together, as if holding a council of war.

" He's a sayin' to him, ' now don't you be such a fool, Jack, don't trust to that deceitful bait,' " said Bobus.

" ' Ille dolis instructus et arte Pelasga,' "

quoted a middy who had been taught Latin, and remembered some of the second Æneid.

" ' For if you does—' " continued the old sea-man,—here the shark made a slight dart forward, and the pilot fish placed himself right before him, " ' you'll be sure to be caught, as sure as my name is Jack Pilot Fish.' "

" ' Timeo Danaos et dona ferentes,' "

concluded the middy.

But it was all to no purpose.   The shark's appetite was too much for him, and with an immense dash he rushed forward to the bait and swallowed it, at the same time that his legal adviser plunged into the waves, with an indignant waive of the tail, as if he had said, "Well, there now, if you will be such a fool, you must be caught; it does not matter to me."

"Off he is, without shaking hands with his patron," said I.

"Aye, and *on* he is," returned Bobus, pointing to the shark, "pay out till he has gorged it, give him rope enough, and let him play with it."

We did so, and the shark fell off a little in our wake. But presently, feeling rather uncomfortable after his meal, he turned round, and wished to swim away. "Now's the time," said one; "we will haul him in." It was no child's play to do so. We bound the rope to a belaying-pin, and then four or five of us, with a heave ho! pulled at Jack Shark, to get him aboard; he was too strong for us, however, and for half an hour we played with him, paying out the line, and then hauling it in, till he was thoroughly tired; then some of our fellows, with a strong pull, a long pull, and a pull all together, hauled him aboard. When out of the water, and coming up the side, he was weak and powerless enough; but when on deck the lashings of his tail were enough to have stove in the sides of a jolly-boat, till Bobus, standing on one side, cut through, with one mighty blow with an axe, the vertebræ of the fish and divided the tail from his body. He lay then quietly enough, only now and then opening his wide jaws and clapping them to again, with force enough, as we well knew, to take off a man's leg. His skin was so tough that none of the youngsters could cut it with their dirks, nor could I with a cutlass. I looked into his cruel, hungry eye, as he lay upon the deck dying, and I fancied that I could recognise hatred, greediness, and terror, even then.

The Jack Tars did not long leave him a whole skin. He was soon cut into slices, and, for a long time after, we could hear the hissing of the frying-pans as the cook dressed cutlets of the fish for the mess of the seamen. Some of the middies, of course, ate some of it; but I was not myself anxious to taste such a delicacy.

It was not many weeks after this incident that our good ship, the "Thunderer," anchored off Bushire, and we there found the commodore of the Indian navy, consisting of three ships, awaiting us. Our arrival was timely, but we were of little actual service, unless we reckon that quiet and, too often, unappreciated use which gains an end without actual violence. In the words of the poet, we might have said—

> "Oh, my lord,
> It needs full oft, the *show* of war to keep,
> The *substance* of sweet peace."

In our case, much to the disgust of the captain, and to that also of several old die-hards amongst the crew, who wished again to smell powder, the show of war procured peace at once. Our consul, who had been insulted, was again received with the most abject courtesy. The Russian agents, who had been, as that power has encouraged them to do for years, spreading money amongst the disaffected, and urging hostile preparations against that power which holds, and, I trust, will for ever hold India, were driven away, at least, apparently so; and, outwardly, the British ensign waved, as it often has done in reality, the sign of peace, power, and of strength.

Bushire was, after all, when I saw it, a miserable place. Our ships were obliged to lie in the road-stead, three miles off, for reefs and sandbanks, which even a small amount of energy could remove, prevented any but small craft entering the harbour. The ruler of the town had revolted against the Shah, and the inhabitants every day expected an army to come and deliver it up to fire and sword. Too weak to repel it, hating alike the emir and the Shah, trembling for their goods and their lives even, the people were full of abjectness and misery. They could not have offered any resistance to an English gun-boat, much less to a ship of our size, had they wished to do so; but so far from resisting us, the head man had cleverly spread the report that we had been sent by the Queen of the Seas to help and aid him. It is curious that, being such universal liars, as they undoubtedly are, in common, I am afraid, with other Eastern nations, it is curious, I repeat, that the people should have believed the report; but I found that liars are also credulous, and this proved it. More respect was shown to the usurper, and, after our approach, the inhabitants became better dressed, and wore more ornaments, they having, under the influence of fear and pillage, buried and concealed their treasures and dressed themselves in old and dirty rags.

After our consul had come on board our ship, and had held a council with the captain and the other commanders, it was determined that a deputation should proceed, not only to the emir but also to the Shah himself, so as to receive from his hand a proper and official corroboration of the concessions granted to us.

I was lucky enough to obtain permission to be one of that party. We therefore dressed in full uniform, with side arms, and as much finery as we could wear, since Easterns think fine dresses a mark, not only of respect on the part of, but of power in, the wearer, went ashore, and visited the house of the *balioos*, or consul, and there met the British resident from the Company's army, a man of great penetration and talent, and an officer of high rank. He was to head our little band, whilst the consul stayed with us.

The Residency, with the British flag flying from the top of the house, was by far the most comfortable and best house in Bushire. Mere hovels, made of mud, leaves, and date-sticks, formed the dwellings of the poorer classes; they called them *kappars,* and so small and low were they, that one could not stand upright in them, even in the centre. The roofs of the houses are flat, on the top of them is a peculiar construction —a square tower, open at the four sides, but covered at the top, and having moreover an opening into the house below. Inside these towers are flat partitions, placed at the different angles, and so managed that, from whatever quarter the wind blows, a draught is received in the wind-tower, and thence sent down through the house below, so that during the heat of summer a constant and very grateful draught is kept up.

The insurgent sheik or emir lived in a mud fort, a little way out of the town, near it was the custom-house, situated on a kind of miserable quay, the sides of which were ruinous and in gaps. The sheik had placed himself near the custom-house, I fancy, for the purpose of laying hands upon everything he could. His exactions, and the duty he had placed upon the articles of daily consumption, from the fruits of the greengrocer, or *bakkaul,* to the grain, milk, cheese, and meat of other dealers had already rendered him odious to the people, who were glad enough to see our little procession start towards his fort, guarded by twenty sepoys, which the consul had spared us out of his guard of thirty-six. In front of the gate of the mud fort a breastwork of earth had been thrown up, and behind it were six large guns, old, honey-combed, and almost useless, but which were kept loaded in readiness for attack, and in which the sheik placed much reliance.

There was some little ceremony at the gate when we entered, a ragged guard of the most villanous ruffians one could see, turned out to meet us, but after a few words, which few of us could understand, we were admitted to the interior of the fort, and our consul had an interview with the insurgent sheik, who was seated on a dais, and who, with the short-sighted pride of eastern insurgents, gave him the airs of the rightful monarch. I was glad to see that the consul, with English straightforwardness told the sheik that he was accredited to a higher court, and that he could not acknowledge his power. The chief was a fat, good-humoured looking individual, and his thick moustache and beard prevented us from seeing any of the workings of his face, or any emotion he might have betrayed. He answered us very graciously that he wished to keep peace with the Chiefs of the Sea, and with several big sounding sentences intimated that he was about to make the Shah eat the dust of the earth, and crawl on his belly before him.

He gave us, however, a pass to set us on the way as far as his authority extended, being afraid of the firm looks of our commanders, and the close array of our little force. He invited us also to a feast of mare's milk and rice boiled up together and rolled into little hard balls, which our men devoured with a great deal of gusto.

After our departure from the sheik we travelled under safe guidance towards Sheerauz, proceeding in a northwesterly direction. We passed now and then through groves of myrtle, which grows wild in Persia, and which fills the air with its perfume. When we were on the plains of Shapoor we found it intersected with water-courses, and thus irrigated the plain produced a plentiful crop of rice. The land was, however, so wet that it was difficult to cross. The Persian ploughs, of which we saw several, were shod with iron; they are heavy implements, drawn by oxen yoked to them by a clumsy piece of wood which lies across their shoulders.

At a distance across the landscape we could see various black tents of the Eeliauts, wandering tribes who lived upon the flesh of their camels, their goats, and the milk of their mares. When they had eaten up all the grass and forage of one place they removed to a distance and again encamped. We passed many of these tribes, and now and then the remains of a recent encampment of the Mamasenni, robbers, of whom solitary travellers and weak caravans are extremely afraid, but the regular march of our men, and firm aspect of our English officers so frightened the spies and scouts sent about us, that we were quite unattacked or unharmed.

In the valley of Shapoor we met with indications of the former greatness of Persia. The hill sides, which are of vast rocks, were here and there sculptured boldly with warriors, and horses, chariots, and captives; a monarch, supposed to be King Shapoor, is triumphing over a fallen foe, who, from the Roman costume which he wears, is thought to be the Emperor Valerian;* the prisoner wears the Roman tunic and short sword of the conquerors of the Old World. The Roman kneels in an abject posture and holds up his hands, which the Persian conqueror looks on with pride and arrogant contempt.

"Ah, ha!" said one of our officers, looking at the rock, "ages have fled and we are a little altered since then. Where is the dust of Shapoor? Where that of Valerian, now?

'Persicos odi, puer.'

so sang old Horace; scarcely three centuries have

---

* This emperor was obliged to yield to Shapoor at Edessa, A.D., 260. In the weakness and decadence of the Eastern Empire relief was hopeless, and the unfortunate successor of the Cæsars, after being treated with ignominy, was flayed alive.

passed when he might have hated them for a better reason. Come on, let us face the modern Shapoor, and see whether he will flay one of us."

On we went, over mountain and plain, over *Kotuli Dokhter*,* or the Simplon of Persia, past the lake and plains of Kangeroon, past *rahdars*, or native policemen, levies of raw troops, dervishes, dancing, praying or begging, priests on donkeys, or with spread out carpets turning and bowing to the East, and worshiping the gorgeous luminary as he rose and set.

Brown hills, dwarf oaks, dates, and palms formed the principal vegetation of the place. I had heard of Persian roses, of wondrous flowers, and I have since read in the pages of Mr. Thomas Moore of nightingales singing all the night long, but I found that the Persia of reality and that of fiction are as essentially different as any two things can be. Bendemere's Stream, whereon in a song which I remembered sung me to sleep as a child, I found had no "bowers of roses" at all, so that the nightingale scarce could sing in them all the night long. But I must hasten to my story. We reached Sheerauz in good time, saw the Shah who received us in a very gracious temper, rati-

---

* My young readers who study the derivation of words, will be amused to find that this word Dokhter (girl) is pronounced as the Scotch would pronounce daughter, and, says Binning, is evidently the same word.—*Binning's 'Persia,'* vol. 1.

fied our privileges, and was extremely pleased
with the account we gave of the weakness of the
insurgent chief. Some troops had already been
despatched, and before we departed we had the
satisfaction of hearing that the rebellious sheik,
terrified at the approach of some regular troops,
had run away in the night, carrying with him
certain pillage, and those of his ragged band of
desperadoes who trusted in him.

# CHAPTER XL.



IN THE PERSIAN GULF—THE PEARL DIVERS AND
THE SHARK.

On our return to Bushire we found things
altered. The true Imann, who was as cowardly
as Lord Mayor Beckford in our riots of '80, had
returned, when the danger was fully over, to his
post, and was blustering and bragging, instituting
searches for the insurgents and despatching
messages to his sovereign full of brag and
bombast.

We ourselves were received with honour, for
by some process of reasoning, which I do not understand, the flight of the sheik was set down to
our valour, or at least to our intervention. The
town, which looked so forlorn and desolate at our
approach, was now full of people and of gaiety.

As we entered it several horsemen rode out to
meet us, shooting off pistols and carbines, throwing up spears while at full gallop and catching
them as they rode, and shouting prodigiously.

Every man was armed to the teeth. Here and there were fellows, whom we saw a few weeks back grovelling in mere terror, swaggering about with huge whiskers and moustache, venting enormous threats against the robbers. Some of these boasters had half a dozen pistols stuck in their belts, and certainly looked big enough to eat the ragged rapscallions of the fort for dinner. But we remembered that those very rapscallions had a few days before terrified these big fellows out of their lives.

"Look! there's a warrior," said I to Bobus one day, when he was ashore with me. I pointed to a fellow with a magnificent sabre, a spear, a kind of tulwar, or curved sword, and four steel-butted pistols in his belt; "there's a desperado."

"A what?" said Bobus.

"A desperate fellow," I returned.

"A desperate coward, you mean," cried the boatswain with a sneer, "bless you, it isn't the looks, its the 'art. Here's one of our Jacks with plenty of pluck, and a little time on his 'ands, 'ud kill ten o' them fellers afore breakfast, ten, aye, twenty." And Bobus puffed a great quantity of smoke into the air and watched it melt away as he turned up his manly upper lip at the manhood of the Persian desperado.

When we had rejoined our ship, we had still to wait about the Gulf and to cruise in a very unhealthy station until the concessions which we had gained for the British residents were practically ratified and enforced. For we well knew that the vice of lying did not apply alone to the people, but to the government of Persia.

During our stay there of several months, I applied myself to my studies very closely, for on my return home I intended to pass my examinasion as lieutenant, and I am happy to say that, what with the habit of studying and the experience I had gained, I stood a very fair chance of passing.

The second lieutenant was very friendly to me, and seeing that I kept the youngsters under me in pretty good order, and set an example of industry and attention, often gave me a good practical lesson in the duties of my profession. I was soon on very friendly terms with him and also with many of the officers in the ship. The crew were kept in health by continual exercise and practice, both at the long guns and the small arms, and H. M. S. "Thunderer," was reckoned, by her officers, at least, the smartest vessel in her majesty's navy.

We were one day on a cruise in the gulf, for the health and recreation of the crew, when we came suddenly upon a fleet of small boats with one sail. This was off the Island of Bahrein, and one of our men told us that the boats were those of the pearl-fishers; the monopoly of this particular fishery, the largest in the Persian Gulf, being in the hands of the sheik of Bushire.

'Ghastly, grim, and poor looked the crews of these boats. On each side sat ten naked divers, and a crew of about eight propelled the boats along. At the rudder was seated the captain of the gang, a wretch with a more cruel face than the rest; at the prow of the boat the medicine-man, or doctor, a kind of priest, who with contortions, prayers, charms, and imprecations, pretended to give prosperity to the voyage, and to keep away the sharks.

"Aye, aye, the sharks are their great dread; look at the shivering wretches! They do not look as if they liked the work, do they, Paget?" said my friend, the lieutenant.

"Carry the ship rather more in shore and let go the anchor, that's what the captain will do; we want to see this," said I.

"I hope so; but there's no breath of wind stirring, not even enough to belly out the latteen sails of those proahs."

It was true enough; but the boats came forwards, at a swift pace, with a monotonous chant. They were rowing from the shore, and, to our great joy, they gathered in a regular array near us, and commenced their operations. We were evidently just over the oyster-ground.

"Look at that humbug," said the lieutenant.

The humbug was no other than the priest of one of the boats, who twisted himself into all kinds of knots, and made contortion after contortion, whilst a gang of pearl-divers watched him very intently.

"Oh, it's all right, old fellow," continued my friend. "I wonder what he's rated at on the ship's books, Paget, eh?"

Rated high or low, he seemed an important personage, for the men kept from the water till he made the propitious sign, and then five of them, each taking a black, heavy stone, to which a leather stirrup and rope were attached, a small iron-pointed stick, and a net over their shoulders, jumped, feet foremost, over the side. Their right hand had a cord round the wrist, a small piece of bent horn fastened down their nostrils, and their ears were stopped with wax.

When they jumped from the boat they went down feet foremost, holding the string in their right hand. "At the bottom," said the lieutenant, "they kick off that stone, pick up the oysters and put them into their net, and, when exhausted, they will pull the string and come up again. The stones, you will see, are pulled up after them, and serves for the next gang."

Surely enough, two minutes hardly had elapsed when first one, and then another, of the panting divers were drawn up, and laid exhausted at the bottom of the boats, whilst the others unloaded their nets, drew up the stones, and placed the oysters in safety in the stern. Then another five jumped overboard, and the same process went on.

This was all around us, and the medicine-men seemed to emulate each other in their prayers and contortions, and tried to excel each other in their prophecies of good luck to their men.

" Does the sheik of Bushire make much by this business !" said I.

" About £250,000 is produced annually, but whether he or others get the best I don't know. This I do know, that the fellows who fish get little or nothing, and, after a life of misery, die of consumption, or ruptured heart, through staying long in the water. And all for what? Vanities ; verily, all is vanity ! A pearl is a handsome thing ; a row of them, with a diamond clasp, looks well round a pretty, fair girl's neck, but they would look worse than sharks' teeth round the neck of a savage, if we thought of the misery by which they were obtained, or the deaths they occasioned. Ha ! what's that ?"

We had been watching the divers now for some time. In the most busy time, when the water is almost tepid, as warm indeed as the air, the divers will go down about fifteen times a-day at the most, on some days they will not go down more than half that number. The day we saw them was propitious, and the divers had been down about six times in various gangs, when an alarm was given of the most dreaded enemy of the diver—the shark !

"Let's bait a hook," said I, "and serve him like we did our old enemy."

"Do you think he will eat pork, when he can get a meal upon that kind of humanity," said the lieutenant, pointing to the divers, who, with frightened looks, came hurriedly up, with their nets half full; "no Jack Shark knows his favorite dinner too well. But they are all up now."

"No," said I, with a wild anxiety at my heart, "there is yet one; the one nearest us is down still."

"Then it's all over with him," said the lieutenant, with a nervous twitching at the corners of his mouth; "I saw the back fin of a big fish stirring just over where he should ascend."

We had not to wait long in suspense. The men in their boat, hoping to rescue their comrade, had rowed a little towards us, and from the violent agitation of the line, which had been made longer and paid out, so as to give the diver space to swim in, his comrades knew that he was aware of his danger.

"Do they ever escape?" said I, in a whisper.

"Sometimes, yes," answered my companion, curtly. "Let us hope this one will."

All this took place in, perhaps, half a minute. The diver had already exceeded his usual stay under the water, but he was known to be an excellent hand. There was, therefore, little fear on that score, providing he was quick enough to "dodge" the shark.

"Hurrah!" shouted the lieutenant, "he has done it."

A black head and shoulders appeared just above the water, about a couple of oars' distance from the boat, and a dozen arms were stretched out towards him. Had he been nearer he would have been saved; but we turned sick as we heard his agonising shriek, and saw the water all round him dyed with his blood, above which, for a moment, flashed the fin of the shark.

The boatmen seemed palsied with horror; but one man caught the dying wretch's hand, and pulled into the boat the half only of his trunk, which had been bitten in two just at the middle, the blood gushing from it like a great flood as he pulled it into the boat.

"Come away, Paget, come away; there will be no more fishing for this week at least, perhaps for months, here. Sharks scent human blood, and a whole school of them will come here. That boat's crew will be so terrified and enraged that, unless he takes care of himself, they will chuck the medicine-man over to feed the sharks, and," he added, "it would almost serve the medicine-man right. Ah," continued my companion, "there is a considerable difference between the pearl wearers and the pearl divers. Death, doubtless, is near us all; not only the soldier and sailor, but the scholar and the clergyman, physician, and tradesman, die at their posts; nevertheless it is something very awful to contemplate lives so completely thrown away as these are in the acquisition of a simple bauble.

"Whether they are eaten by sharks, or die of disease, their lives are equally thrown away, poor wretches. They are the slaves of the speculators and merchants who surround them, and to whom the boats belong. They make fortunes for their masters, but not for themselves. Bees are not the only creatures from which men extract the golden honey and kill the insects in the process."

"That's very true," muttered the classical middy; "but I fancy, old Horace made that observation two thousand years ago; so we are not much changed."

I was glad to find, on our return to Bushire, that our treaty had been ratified, and that we were to return home, they having no further need of H.M.S. "Thunderer," in the Persian Gulf.

# CHAPTER XLI.



WHICH SATISFACTORILY (IT IS TO BE HOPED)
ACCOUNTS FOR OLD STUMP, AND OTHER PER-
SONAGES IN THE STORY.

To a certain extent I have in the last few chapters been anticipating my adventures. I have yet, before I am safely landed for the third time in England, to tell the reader something about my return from Fiji, and to satisfy any curiosity my readers may have in regard to our black friend, old Stump.

Our approach to England, after being so long separated from her, called up, on that occasion, more vivid sensations than at any previous or subsequent time. The British are the most home-loving nation on the face of the earth; the Englishman always returns from India, Australia, Russia, Italy, or France, to his own dear home. Poor Pat, working for gold in California, or adding to the buildings of New York,* turns to

* The poor Irish have remitted to their still poorer country-

his native Irish hills and valleys, or, in the midst of a primæval forest, laying the sleepers of a new railway, or navigating the frail craft which plies in the bay, still remembers home: so doth the rich merchant on the banks of the Hooghly, the far settler in the west, the Anglo-Saxon at the Cape, New Zealand, Natal, the Horn, Spitzbergen, where you will. Struggling with difficulty, or lapped in luxury, we ever love home.

How much we, who had wandered from home for two years, and who had been out and about, longed for the land, I can hardly tell. My countrymen generally will make a fortune anywhere they can, but they look at last to spend it in England. They love not to die away from her shores. They wish to rest with their fathers, and to sleep their last, long sleep, beneath the turf on which at first they trod.

It was such an elation of spirits to all of us that Bobus and Flook were almost for dancing, and old Stump caught the infection. As we passed up the Channel, and saw the white cliffs at a distance, and English ships dotting the offing in every direction, sailing past us, it seemed almost living proof of the majesty and power of our land; our hearts swelled and panted with a

men, in the last few years, no less a sum than seven millions of money! I know of no fact so touching, nor so honorable to the feelings of a nation as this, "verily the poor help the poor."

noble pride. Even the Americans on board felt and shared this, though in a less degree, and in endeavouring to exalt their own country, showed how much they respected ours.

"This land o'yourn," said one, as we were looking out a-head, "is long a comin', and is but a speck arter all. Now, you can sight the shores o' the great U-nited States for days and days, if you choose to sail from north to south. A little speck this mother country, a little speck "——

"But a great heart, sir, I calc'late," said another. "'Tis o'ny fair to the old land to say that she's known every where. There's not a port in the world but what you'll find the English buntin' flyin' in; not a sea but has been crossed by her keels; not a river her boats hav'nt bin up; not a shore on which the feet of her Jack Tars ar'n't set; not a desert which her merchants don't traverse, nor hardly an island, however savage or remote, in which the Englishman doesn't preach his faith, and spread the Bible of the English Church. Yes, she's a little place, a little body like, but with a great heart and uncommon long limbs, is little England!"

"Hallo! there's the Wight," cried the captain.

A little island, a garden isle, in fact, lay before us, and three or four great rocks round which the sea dashed high.

"Them's the Needles, I calc'late," said an American; "bless you, they arn't much."

"No one ever said they were, that I know of," said Flook; "'tisn't the island you must look at, though God has blessed that abundantly, but look at the energy of her people, their constant work, their love of peace, their bravery in battle, in what they call a righteous war, and remember that of late years the nation, as a whole, has acted as one man, has been ever conscientious, and has never done anything which their consciences wholly condemned. Come here, Stump, my man."

"Yes, Massa, here's old Stump."

"When you set foot on that shore, Stump, you're a free man, you can go where you choose, do what you choose, say what you choose, so that it is not flat blasphemy, or that which breaks the peace of your neighbour."

"Oh, golly," cried old Stump, jumping up delighted; "free man at last! you're quite sure you mean true, Massa," he had a lingering suspicion as he spoke, "quite sure, eh? Tank you, Massa."

"Do not thank me," said Flook, "I do not do it, the land does it; no slave can set a foot upon that land. The moment his foot touches her shore he is free."

Old Stump gazed in a wondering admiration

upon Portsmouth Harbour, which we were then entering.

"Wun'ful old land," he murmured, "tell me, Massa Flook, which is the 'zact spot I'm to tread on to gib me liberation."

We were landed at last, and our little party was dissolved. Flook naturally wished at once to hurry home, and I felt most eager to see the dear, good doctor, whom I loved as a father. Bobus would stay for some little time at Portsmouth, he said, to clear our luggage, and old Stump did not know exactly what to do with himself. His liberty rather embarrassed him, as a new coat restrains a boy. He first put it in practice by insisting that Bobus and the waiters should call him "Massa Stump," refused to wait 'upon us, stayed out beyond his dinner time, and came in with a ridiculously important air and with his black nose considerably elevated. Presently the sad reflection beamed upon him that he had no home, and that he must do something for his living. He therefore approached us as we were packing up our trunks without his aid, and very seriously begged to speak with us.

"Fire away, Stump," said old Flook, "go it, my black philosopher."

"Mustn't call me *black*, sar," he said, "me a free man now, not a black man."

"Oh—h," whistled Flook.

"I wants to know what I'm to do."

"Wal'," returned Flook, imitating the Yankee twang, "I calc'late I and Ned will set you up in business, or, look here, they want a waiter here, hire yourself."

"Shan't do no such thing," said the old fellow, ruefully; "I'm a free man now."

"So are the waiters free men. They can go when they like, come when they like, give warning or take it. Sometimes they grow rich and take hotels themselves."

"Oh golly," said Stump, as if the prospect was too much for him; "tell ye what I'll do, Massa Ned," said he, looking to me, "I'll come and live with you, if you'll let me."

"So you shall, Stump, my boy," said I; "I'll take you to the doctor's, and hear what he says."

"But mind, Massa Ned, I can go when I like, come when I like, and gib you warning,—when, sir?" he asked suddenly.

"When you like," said I, "every month if you wish it."

Stump made a mental note of that circumstance, and forthwith installed himself as my free "help." Every month since that time he has, however, made use of his privilege, and gravely gives me warning, which I take as gravely, knowing that he regards that privilege as the palladium of his liberty.

Flook soon departed to his home, Bobus was busy and promised to rejoin me quickly, and I, with a dozen or so of curious little presents, with cowries and nuggets of gold, Spanish dollars, and sprays of coral, soon found myself and Stump at the gates of the old school. I had written to the doctor as soon as I touched land, and was delighted to see him toddle out, rather feebly, for he had had a touch of the gout, to look at me and embrace me. Mrs. Taw, still active and as upright as a dart, came out too. The delight of the doctor was unbounded, he shook hands heartily with old Stump, and was amazingly tickled with that black gentleman's honest grin.

"So," said he, "this is our Charleston friend, I suppose he is a fixture."

"Massa, the Doctor," said Stump, "I ain't no fixtur', I am Massa Ned's free servant, no black-a-man now."

"Well, well, you have been a good friend to our Ned, here, and so welcome."

Old Taw carried away Stump, and the doctor and I were alone.

After supper we kelt down and gave thanks that we were again brought together, never more, we hoped, to be long parted again, and that God had kept me safely in all my wanderings.

The next morning, and indeed, for fully a week afterwards, I had to give an account to old Taw of my travels. She wondered and listened, and listened and wondered in a most amusing way; and old Stump, who in going out and coming in occasionally helped me in my narrative, came in for his full share of praise. Indeed he wanted more than his share, and was continually re-counting his own exploits.

"Dar's dem sarpints, Massa Ned, did you tell Missis Daw of dem won'rous sarpints. How dey crawl in, and crawl out, and pison each oder and demselves, and tie dem tails up in mighty big knots, de beasties. Yah!" He shuddered as he spoke. "Den who kill de berry big biggest o'em? Dat was Stump! Brave old niggar dat. Who kill great grizzly bahr? Why Stump, any-how! wid his gun. Show you de 'dentical, gun wid de 'dentical flint-lock. Save Massa Bobus life, Stump did! Lucking ting, purchase Stump at Charleston. Val'able niggar dat; but not a black now: oh no, him free, coloured genl'm, him is." And having poured all this out with a splash, as one would water out of a wide-mouthed jug, away the coloured gentleman would run.

# CHAPTER XLII.



TAKING up the thread where I previously left it, I must explain to my readers that, in my Persian voyage, I was benefited thus far; my Arctic expedition being kindly counted as time served, I was enabled to pass my examination and to be placed on the list of lieutenants R.N., shortly after my return to England. The liberality of my uncle and my own good fortune had placed me in an independent position, and it was with feelings of a hopeful certainty, that I, after having passed, hastened to Yarmouth on a visit to my friends.

I found Flook and his family in excellent health and spirits. They were delighted to see me, and Bobus, who had been there for some time, was absolutely getting tired of shore life, and talked of taking another voyage. He was the warmest of all, except one, to congratulate me on my new rank. The parents of my school-fellow seemed as delighted to see me as if I were their son, and I could not but feel grateful for the kindness shown to one who had first visited them as a poor, shipwrecked boy.

Flook was not present when I mentioned my gratitude to them, and thanked them from my heart. But there was one whose welcome I had not received, and whom I said I wanted to thank for nursing me, when I lay sick to death.

"I can never forget it," said I, "I must thank her, sir, myself."

"She will be very willing to receive those thanks, Ned," said her father, with a smile, and a peculiar and not displeased glance at his wife.

I divined the meaning of that look, and turning the conversation upon Doctor Leatherby's goodness, told them how he had welcomed me, how the poor neglected boy might now be reckoned almost a rich man. Their praises of his liberality were as warm as my own.

"And now, sir," said I, again interrupting myself, and turning full towards him, "have I your full permission to thank Miss Lucy myself; to thank her with my life?"

"Well," he said, smiling "I think you may, but you will not find her very cruel; I don't think she will want your life, Edward. But you are eager to find her;" he looked at his watch, " it is Wednesday, she has gone to evening prayers, you will meet her now returning across the fields."

Eager-hearted, and full of hope, I thanked Lucy's father, and then set off across the fields to meet her.

COMING HOME.

CHAP. 47.

I saw her at a distance, and stood still and blessed her as she walked demurely and with downcast eyes.

Then I bounded forward.

"Miss Lucy," said I, meeting her.

She stood still, the colour coming and going upon her fair face, as she looked up at me. The evening breeze stirred her clustering hair, which played round her pure white neck, and mingled with the brown ribbons of the country-hat she wore. Her eyes, clear, large, and lustrous, met mine, shot out a stream of kindliness and recognition, and fell beneath my glance. She was silent.

I held out my hand, and took hers and pressed it warmly. She returned the pressure for a moment, then relinquished the hand and walked by my side.

The summer sun had just set behind a hill, but the sky was still bright, and the air pure and balmy; beyond the shadow of the hill, the sunlight still threw long shadows on the grass, the cattle browsed calmly on the dewy grass, and the tinkling sheep-bells in the distance only broke the silence.

We walked towards home.

"I will not," said I, speaking with an effort, and yet upon so simple a subject; "I will not ask you whether you are well, Miss Lucy; I never saw you look so well, so—" I hesitated a moment, "so charming."

Lucy looked up and smiled.

"Have you learned compliments at Astrakan, or *politesse* from the Fijians, Mr. Paget, that you compliment me?"

"'Tis no compliment, Miss Lucy," said I, gazing earnestly at her; "I remember the face so well, oh, so well, and every feature is improved by time, every—" here I stopped and 'brought to,' as Bobus would have said, rather abruptly.

"Did you really think of me, then," she said, with a a soft inflection in her voice.

I drew her arm through mine, and answered—

"Think of you! In the long, dark nights in the Atlantic sea; in the calm, weary days, crossing those vast grassy plains; in the bare mountains, in the arid desert, and in the wild and far off island, I still thought on you. There was not a night, but that when lying on my pillow and praying for safety and for aid, but that I thought of, aye, and prayed for you."

I pressed her arm closely to me as I spoke,— after a pause she answered me.

"And I of you, dear Ned."

"Thank God for that, dear Lucy."

"For what, dear Ned?"

"Why that one true heart did think of me, and, and—love me."

Her arm pressed mine at the word.

"Others love you too," she said, "my brother loves you well, there's not a letter that he has written in which he does not speak of dangers overcome or braved, of kindnesses done by you, of noble deeds and words of yours. But more than this, he spoke of one great crowning virtue, Ned, of an English virtue, which long has made, and I pray long will make the glory of this land, of modest worth which did much and said nothing; which spoke of others, but forgot itself."

"Oh, Lucy, Lucy," said I, my heart beating with an almost painful pleasure to hear her speak so; "what can I answer to all this?"

"I thought, Ned, as I read those letters that I would some day humbly thank my brother's friend, and tell him how highly I must honour him. He told me that when others lost heart you did not, that you went on firmly and cheerfully, that you practised faith, hope and charity, and these by deeds, not words."

"Dear Lucy," said I, suddenly stopping, and catching her hands; "spare me. I do not deserve this praise. You have made a fond ideal of your brother's friend. You know me from his letters; not through myself. But oh, dear Lucy, were I all you say, aye, and ten times more, I could not equal you, nor half deserve you; but yet I trust that you will pity me, and look on me kindly when I offer you my love."

She looked half startled, half rejoicingly, in my face, and drew back a moment, as she murmured, "But my father"—

"He knows it all," I answered, quickly, "deeply as I love you, Lucy, fondly as I have ever prized your love, and wished the day to come when I could ask it, I would not speak to you, or seek to influence your heart, until I knew my love was sanctioned by him who has chief claim upon his daughter's heart."

She suddenly drew her hands away from me, looking up with such a sweet smile that I see it now, and cried, "So like you, Edward, so like you to the last. And so it all depends on me; well, well—" she beat with her little foot upon the grass, and then suddenly looked up. "You have won me fairly, Edward; take me now." Both hands were placed trustingly in mine. I took them with a sacred joy; her face looked up to me, her eyes beamed on me, as if all her hope now lay in me; her face was raised to mine, and I bent down and kissed her lips.

The evening closed in very rapidly that night. I remember that it was nearly dark when we reached home, and that they had been waiting tea, they said, for some time. It was not far from church either, said my fellow-traveller. "You and Lucy must have missed your way."

"Pardon me," said I; "I have found it."

Lucy ran to her mother, and bent down over her dear, fond face, and kissed her. She then ran to her father, whom I had thanked in a low and earnest voice.

" 'Tis all settled, sir," said I.

He smiled, and answered, archly, "Ah, that accounts for the distance, I suppose."

In the mean time having found a mother, I had had a father in the doctor long ago, I took the privilege of taking her kind hand and kissing her forehead.

" Hallo !" cried my schoolfellow ; " I shall be jealous, soon, Ned."

" Yes," returned his mother, " I have two sons now."

" And pray, mamma, then," replied Flook, " give your family some tea."

Happy, happy evening ! The time to part came. Bobus, who had been to see a friend, came in to say good night, before going to his hotel, and soon made out the signals, he said, which were run up. Both Lucy and I did put such signals out, I fancy : I, in my confusion ; she, in some of the sweetest, brightest, and most charming blushes in the world.

" And, Mas'r Ned," said Bobus, " I've seen our first officer of the old " Lively Bessy," and he says that, when he commands his new ship— he is post-captain now—you shall be installed as second lieutenant.  Here's an opportunity.  Two more years spent in the Arctic regions, in finding out the old doctor's iceless sea, would—"

" I am afraid, Bobus, I cannot do it," said I ;

"the doctor cannot spare me; and there is some one else to consult now."

Bobus grinned like a good-natured dolphin. "Ah," said he, "I see it all. Safe in port, safe in port. I shall go into the coast-guard service, for, I suppose, that here's an end to OUT AND ABOUT."

Not quite an end; a few more words before we take leave of our readers.

The doctor retired from his school, and settled with me and my wife, when after due time we had married, in a little sea-port town, quiet and retired, the front of which looked on the sea, and the clean streets of which led up to the loveliest county in all England. Bobus kept his word. He was good-fellow of the sea, sea-y; of the brine, briny. He was appointed superintendent of the coast-guard, and the service had no better officer. He wanted a housekeeper, and took old Mrs. Taw to preside at his table, and talked gaily of settling in life with her. She, good soul, glad of being near us, spent half her time with us, and looked upon us as her children still.

The doctor, who had brought up so many good boys, and had instilled into so many young hearts the principles which ensure true wisdom and happiness, in the evening of his honoured life, now amused himself by some work of use. He is working at a Latin dictionary, and has got as far as the letter B.

Sitting one day in our parlour and study, we were surprised by Stump, who is our major domo, announcing a gentleman, who walked in just as his name was pronounced as " Mr. Badgeit."

" Paget," said the gentleman, softly bowing his white head, and looking at us all with a countenance half full of humour and half of shame; " Edward, I am your uncle."

" Professor Garle!" cried I, in astonishment.

" Professor no longer," he said, sadly. " I hope that now, I shall profess nothing but simple honesty.  Young lady," said he, turning to Lucy, " you must have heard the beginning of my story ; hear the end.  Too indolent to work, and without principle at all, I sank, step by step, till I did that which now I cannot even mention.  I looked upon all men as dishonest, as thieves, for I was unsuccessful ; I thought it no sin to cajole and cheat them.

" The sequel is soon told," he said.  "I was punished ; I determined to reform, and, in our new world, Australia, did so.  I was successful, and am come to place my fortune in my nephew's hands, to make amends for the wrong I have done him."

" You have done so, sir," said I, taking his hand, and touched by his tone; " I have found indeed a friend—a father."

The doctor's spectacles were dimmed as he in his turn spoke.

"Mr. Paget," said he, "a man who lives a pure life is a noble spectacle, but he who recovers from a vicious course is, perhaps, a stronger and more instructive one. It is easier to step aside and fall than to climb. You have shown us all, poor sinners as we are, that it is never too late in life to commence doing good. Sir, I thank you for the example."

We spent the happiest evening, since I had been married, upon the day when my uncle returned. And he was as good as his word. He lived very simply and quietly, and spent his money in doing good, and the doctor and he were firm friends and aided each other in their works.

My schoolfellow, Flook, who was heir to a competent fortune, still thought it the duty of a young Englishman to be up and doing, and went a voyage to the East Indies, where he engaged in some of his engineering propensities, and spent some few years in planning roads and in carrying civilisation forward in that vast country. When the insurrection came he was far up the country, and was one of those noble Englishmen who, by their constancy and bravery, kept down the flame of rebellion, and helped to win back that great empire to the English crown. His deeds were rewarded, and he has lately returned to England, full of honour and renown, preserving still the same honest simplicity which distinguished him at school, and which made him first my friend.

Old Bobus has grown quite grey in the peaceful service of his country. He is as stalwart as ever. Whenever a storm sweeps the coasts where he dwells, Bobus is first with the life-boat, and is as ready, as if he were but twenty years of age, to peril his own life to help others. Need I say that he is as much loved as such a man should be. The world, after all, honours a brave persistence in good deeds, and Jack Bobus has many, very many, admirers.

Old Stump and old Taw are still alive and merry. The white head of the former looks as if it had been powdered. Liberty agrees with him, and a more portly or respectable major domo than ours does not exist. Taw has been much interested in him, and having taken it into her head that he must be a poor heathen, endeavoured to convert him. This kindness was answered by Stump proposing to her, which proposition she answered by boxing his ears for him, and being indignant for some few days.

So the river of Time flows on. I am a boy no longer, and school and early life and travel too seem distant now. Bless all true boys, all bold, brave boys, who will carry out our English name and nature into strange lands, who yet will preach our faith and spread our tongue still more, who will do their work manfully, and God's work nobly in seas of ice, or in tropic climes, in the heart of continents, or in the far-off isles,—there is and there will be for years to come room and work enough for them. Let them be up and doing, the field is white for harvest; may they grow quickly to strong and earnest men, to sow Truth, and Faith, and Charity abroad—to scatter noble deeds as a sower his seed upon the broad plains all ABOUT AND OUT.

THE END.

PRINTED BY J. E. ADLARD, BARTHOLOMEW CLOSE.